Jane's Suitcase

A NOVELLA JOURNALLA

A story…a journal…a novella…sprinkled with
fictional and non-fictional stories, hopes, fears,
dreams, opportunity, a loss, a new chapter in life,
changes and chances of a life-time…

JANEAN J PHILLIPS

First Printing: 2016

ISBN 978-0-9971375-2-1

Cover Illustration by Craig V. Thomas

Typefaces:
Adobe Garamond Pro, 1989 by Robert Slimbach
Great Vibes, 2012 by Rob Leuschke

Printed and Published by Braughler Books
www.braughlerbooks.com

Thank you so much to my beautiful children,
Craig and Claire and Marta and Josh
and their families, and to my grandchildren,
to my brother John and my dad Charles, and my family.

Thank you to all of my dear friends. You know who you are…

Thank you to June for proofreading and advice,
to Kathy, Diana, Christina, Chris D., Amy H., Lorraine, Amy
and Tom, for giving constructive criticism.

Thank you for all of your support and your words of wisdom.
Thank you for accepting my late night calls…
Thank you for putting up with my woes and sticking by me
through all of the good and the bad times.

My life has been truly blessed by knowing you.

The trip to Europe was not the beginning or the end of her journey...

*L*oss. Jane knew that it would happen one day. After her son, Sawyer, had left for college, it was just a matter of time that some handsome young man would sweep her daughter, Megan, off of her feet. It was just the natural cycle of life.

Megan's marriage occurred and soon after, Jane's granddaughters arrived and life continued.

It started months ago when her son-in-law made the life-altering decision to join the military. With that decision, Jane knew that he was hoping to secure some future for his family. She could not find fault in that decision. However, when her daughter, Megan, called her to tell her that news, Jane experienced something for the first time in her adult life: Selfishness.

Her first thoughts went to her young grandchildren:
"If they leave, when will I see them again?"
"Where were they going to be stationed?"
"Was I going to survive this emotional alteration?"
Well, that last question was a bit ridiculous, but it occurred in her head all the same.

Months later, after her son-in-law went through boot camp and AIT schooling, he left for Germany. Then Megan, and Jane's two granddaughters (ages 2 and 3) plus their cat, moved in with Jane and her brother Ed. The small house in which they lived, immediately became smaller. Jane had moved in with her brother for financial reasons. *"Thank you, again, Ed,"* she had said many times.

Despite her fears of flying, Jane agreed to travel with Megan and the girls to Germany, to reunite them with her son-in-law when the time came. Jane continued to worry about whenever the trip was to occur.

Once they moved in, they shared doing the laundry, they took walks for fun and for exercise and took turns on the treadmill. They went grocery shopping together and separately, watched movies and TV, played games with the girls on the inside, played outside with the sprinkler and with sidewalk chalk. They washed their vehicles, gathered the mail at the curb (that was a big deal for the girls), they walked up to *'the giant rock'* which was in the yard next door, climbed up and jumped off, almost daily.

Anytime they could, they included the kids with chores of cleaning, sweeping, laundry, putting away items, etc., and of course, there was reading books, using scissors under supervision, coloring, writing and painting (sometimes). And all the while, her brother's home became somewhat trashed with stains on the carpet and on his leather couch, marks on the walls (*"How did that get there?"*) and chalk on his motorcycle in the attached garage. He did not seem to mind. Jane knew better, but what else was one to do?

Ed took it in stride, with the expectations that they would leave someday. However, Jane knew better still. Her brother enjoyed playing with her granddaughters on a regular basis and he was good at it. So Jane sometimes wondered why he never had children of his own, for he would make a great dad.

He tossed them around, they played with him on the couch, played Hide-and-Seek, he lifted them up high on his shoulders, up high to play on their cat's scratching tower and perch, and he even let them play with his extensive and prized hat collection. That was fun to
watch and she was sure that it was fun for him. They adored him and vice versa and they would miss each other. Of that, Jane was certain.

During their time of living together, her oldest granddaughter turned 4 and they celebrated her birthday by going out to breakfast. There were other parties to attend, like birthdays of some of the family and ones that her daughter attended that were on her in-laws' side of the family.

Together and separate, they went to lunch dates with their friends, gatherings, outings, dance clubs, festivals, concerts, etc. Sometimes, Jane would watch the girls when her daughter was out and about, for hours at a time. And (*"Shhh!"*) she would spoil them, which was her 'grandmotherly right'…with hugs and kisses, popsicles and chocolate. Not a lot, mind you, for she would also have to attend to their needs as they *"came down"* from any sugar highs! She would let them play on her tall bed, take more walks with them, let them play in the back yard, digging in the dirt and examining bugs, etc.

It was the *"etc"* which Jane would miss the most...

In addition to all of that; there was a funeral of a dear friend and a trip for Jane with friends and strangers to Put-In-Bay. That was a blast, especially when she kayaked across Lake Erie for the first time in her inexperienced, naive life.

There was a falling out, over words that could never be taken back and where no apology would be accepted, with some family members regarding their dad's will (with whom Jane was close and who was not deceased!). There was another falling out with a friend, which caused a major parting of ways. A sad and pathetic situation all the same, but *"for the best,"* Jane told herself.

During that time, there was also a break-up for Jane, in which she had dated a man for under 4 months. She felt somewhere in her mind that perhaps it could have lasted, if only he had tried harder and was less selfish. It was quite hurtful and oddly devastating, for being such a brief union. The break-up caused her to be understandably unsocial, uncommunicative, sad and distant, and not tolerated by all. But not with her household family, who loved her very much and understood her pain.

That break-up was hurtful because she was feeling unrealistically hopeful and then very rejected (again). When her boyfriend told Jane, *"You should be thin by now. You had your daughter 20 plus years ago"*...Jane was done with another shallow, selfish and narrow-minded man, who decided to reveal his true colors in short order. To add insult to injury, he had commented that she had no real friends, because she was too outspoken and somewhat irritating. *"Ouch…and how untrue!"*

Deep down, she had finally admitted that she knew it would not last and that he was not a real man for her, but it hurt all the same. Rejection can be hard on a sensitive soul like hers, but once he threw insults on top of being a ass, she made up her mind that she had had enough of a man like him. He did not seem to appreciate the look of a real woman's body, naked or otherwise.

Her daughter and brother were very supportive of her moping. *"Thank you for putting up with me,"* she would tell them, whenever she could remember to be grateful. She reassured them that she was not going to be sad for much longer.

When she was feeling a bit back to normal, his insult seemed to force her to do a daily workout and to do what she called *"Cussing Sit-ups,"* whereas she got rid of ten pounds in one week. She told herself to never forget what he had said, no matter what else life would dish out. Mind you, she was not that big to begin with, a simple 130 pounds,
but when she did her sit-ups, she would yell out *"F*ck You!"* upon sitting up and then yell *"That's what I said!"* when in a reclining position.

Some days, she would change the cuss words, but altogether, it made her feel quite bold. She did that workout out of the earshot of her young granddaughters.

Jane, Megan, the girls and Ed stayed busy with hectic and wonderful things to do. There were also meetings with new people and getting to know acquaintances better and a major surgery for a friend, in which she knew he would be fine. Then a chance meeting for Jane, on a wonderful, balmy, summer Saturday night, with a tall, dark and handsome man. Pascal.

That is another story, but here goes some of it:

Pascal's family was from Europe and the U.S. From the very beginning, he was excited and very supportive of her, with many words of encouragement regarding her pending trip to Europe. *"Thank you, again, ever so much, Pascal, for being you,"* she would tell him. He had faith in her (along with the faith she had in herself) that she would be fine on her solo travels.

Jane had said for some time, that *"If I can survive the death of my mother, then I can survive anything."* She was very thankful that he was there for her.

For a few months in which she had just met him, they became fast friends and lovers, spending lots of time together, eating out, meeting and visiting with their friends, watching movies, vegging in front of the TV, talking a lot and learning all about each other. He made love to her like no man had before and she felt as if she could become obsessive, possessive, and even fall in love. And knowing that she was going to leave months later and perhaps never come back, they cherished every moment that they could together (or at least she did). She had no regrets on that. Nor would she.

And like everything else in Jane's life so far, all good things had to come to an end, but how was she to know that she was going to suffer so much again and so quickly?

From time to time, throughout her adult life, Jane would say to herself, *"Life is not just short, but it is a running joke…and I feel like the punch line."*

Since Jane and Megan did not know how much time they had to prepare for their trip, they took their time with details. Jane and Ed moved Megan's family in, with the physical labor of moving her furniture and putting most of it into Ed's garage. Then they helped set up the spare bedroom, where Megan and the girls would sleep. They ate together, prepared meals together and they did their best not to kill each other, when they disagreed.

Jane and Megan got into a huge argument one day. Sadly, they did not speak for a while. Jane's belly was sent into a knot making her so ill, that she could not sleep, could not and did not eat, making her sick with worry, which was what she did best.

If there was an Olympic event for worry, Jane would have the Gold! This was one of the many things that Jane wished she could change about herself, but so far she had no luck on that.

Megan did what she was supposed to do, with (military) phone calls and paperwork. Jane made a list of things that she needed for her journey, not knowing exactly the rules of air travel. She kept up with laundry, thinking that that was a good thing. She had last minute lunch dates with girlfriends, especially her friend Toni, who was super excited for her. Jane got hugs and words of encouragement from all of her friends and even words of envy from some.

She searched flights from Dayton to Frankfurt Airport, train travel info to Vienna or Graz, Austria and bus travel, hotels and hostels in Frankfurt. She kept up with text messages and emails with friends. Jane also contacted her Austrian friend Joseph, whom she knew from high school, to let him know that she was coming to visit him. But even with all of that, she was not prepared for what happened next.

After months of living together and months of preparation and with just one day's notice, the military called Megan and told her to drop her car off at a port in Illinois. Megan left with her kids and her mother-in-law, and did just that. Then on her way back from that 10-plus hour round trip, Megan texted her mother to let her know that they were to leave for Nuremberg the very next day! Not to Frankfurt, in which they were preparing.

Jane called Megan, who was still on the drive coming home, to get more details about the trip and to have this very important conversation:

"Are we okay?"

"Yeah, Mom, why?"

"Because we were fighting… Are you asking me to go with you…not

knowing how you felt since we weren't talking?"
"YES! I'm asking you. I need your help."
"Okay. Are we going to discuss our problem, our disagreement or are we sweeping it under the rug?"
And like the quick-witted child that she was, her mother's daughter, she said, *"Let's use the rug this time."*
"Okay…"
And that was what they did.

So, like a chicken with its head cut off, Megan and Jane texted, called and emailed friends and family about the news of their immediate departure. Ed and Jane scrambled to search new information on the internet, regarding her travels, all the while Jane worried about some major things: She needed to do laundry, she needed to buy a carry-on suitcase, she needed to get money from the bank and some transferred into another account…and…

"Did I need to get traveler's checks?" She needed to say Goodbye to Pascal properly, and she needed to calm the hell down!

Her daughter's and granddaughters' flight arrangements were already made by the military. After much time on the phone and surfing the internet, Jane was able to secure a seat on the three flights that they would take to Nuremberg. They were to travel from Dayton to Atlanta, Atlanta into Amsterdam, then into Germany. She got her confirmation number from the airline, made phone calls, then eventually got her head on straight and drove confidently to a nearby department store for a suitcase.

Jane had been at one of the malls and was looking for a nice carry-on piece of luggage. She was convinced that she could find one that was made into a back pack. While in one of the stores, she became very openly elated that she had found what she was looking for, so she grabbed it up, unzipped this part and that part and pulled on the telescoping handle. There was a cute older lady being helped at the counter and she must have turned around when she heard Jane's many *"whoop-de-do's."*

She asked Jane if she had ever wished to have been the inventor of the luggage on wheels. Jane smiled and told her that she did. As Jane brought the luggage up to the counter and asked the clerk to hold it for her (for 24 hours), she struck up a conversation with the older woman, who had inquired where Jane was going.

Her name was Lorraine and she was as cute as a button. *"Just like my mother,"* Jane thought. Lorraine had told Jane that when she was much younger, she had traveled to Europe several times and those trips were some of the best times of her life. She told Jane that she traveled a lot with her husband and that she was still mad at him for dying years earlier. Jane thought that statement was very sad, but she understood how that would feel.

When Jane told Lorraine of the reasons for her travels, Lorraine wished her luck but was worried about Jane traveling alone, saying, *"At least when you travel with someone, you can recap your adventures when your heads hit the hotel pillows."*

That was the sweetest thing that Jane had ever heard, especially from a stranger. Jane agreed, but told Lorraine why she was eventually traveling alone, with the hopes to journal and taking lots of photographs and then meeting up with a friend in Austria later. *"Good,"* Lorraine said.

She was genuinely concerned for Jane and asked if it was okay to give Jane a goodbye hug and Jane readily accepted. They hugged each other, repeated their names and Lorraine wished her luck again. She told her that she was looking forward to seeing Jane's published photographs some day. Jane thanked her and went on her hectic way.

"Now that was a great reason to visit the mall," Jane thought. She did not think that she would ever make it back there, for she could never afford to purchase that expensive piece of luggage anyway.

After leaving the mall, she went inside a local department store and went directly to the luggage section. She was disappointed that she could not find what she was looking for, so she went to the information counter. The young clerk offered to call another store for her, but Jane asked for the number so she could call it herself.

She did just that and her jaw hit the ground when the other store clerk quoted her the price, which had gone from $90 dollars months earlier to $240 dollars for one simple bag! She told her *"Thanks, but No"* and drove like a bat out of hell to a nearby superstore. Jane bought a carry-on piece of luggage, which came with two other smaller bags, all for the wonderful,

"I-am-so-poor-I-could-just-scream" price of $40 bucks! *Whew!* It

was not a backpack, but Jane would take what she could get.

From there, Jane ran to the bank, then to see her dad at his work. He handed her his credit card. *"Thank you so much for all of your help!"* with hugs and kisses. She high-tailed it back home, where she proceeded to do laundry and pack, call the airline and pay for her ticket and make more calls that took up much of her time.

Jane could feel the anxiety building up. She could feel the nervousness swelling in her belly and in her already aching head. She could feel the possibility of a nervous breakdown coming on, but was not too sure of that, for she had never had one before. But she knew that she had no time for that, so she soldiered onward.

She called her son, Sawyer and he told her that he was coming into town from Columbus, to go with them to the airport the next day, to say goodbye and give out hugs. *"Okay and that would be very nice, indeed."* She emailed Joseph and he eventually responded. He told her that he would be out of town until Tuesday and could pick her up in Vienna on that day.

"Oh my God." Jane's flight was leaving on a Friday, she would get into Europe on Saturday! What in the world was she going to do with that extra time? A hotel, of course! So, she searched with no success, not knowing exactly where she was going to wind up. *"Can I afford it?"* She was very poor after all. Her nervousness went into overdrive at that point.

Jane had no clue on how to make hotel arrangements online, especially since she was not that computer savvy. *"But I will learn to be,"* she thought. She had faith that she was going to be able to do whatever it took. Besides, she wanted and needed to help Megan and her two beautiful granddaughters make their way to their new home. *"It may not be a good way to travel, especially for the first time abroad,"* she thought, *"And when you don't know where you are going."*

From time to time, Jane referred to herself as *"The List-Maker"* and *"The Double-Checker."* She was also *"The Spontaneous Planner."* Jane had planned spontaneity! Not knowing the details of something, just may not be a good way to live, for someone like her. Jane thrived and survived on details and lists. She also called herself *"The Nervous-Nelly-Who-Gets-Her-Belly-Tied-Up-In-Knots-When-She-Feels-Out-Of-Control."*

When Jane knew that people were mean to her and that they were lying to her, she would get flustered. As long as she could remember, she knew that she took everything very personally, especially when she knew that she deserved better. She wanted to be more self-sufficient, and to not make a big deal of not feeling like she had control of things. Not having details and plans was not the way she wanted to live her life, but for now, she was willing to try. She was going to venture into the unknown. And she was scared.

But Jane was a former Girl Scout. No one is actually ever a former one. Once you are accepted into that wonderful club, you are always a member for life. She was good with maps and directions and was good at finding her way around. She was determined to prove to herself that *"I can do this!"*

Jane was going to find her way to Europe and around Europe, come hell or high water, and she was going to find a way to suppress her fears and have fun, dammit.

Jane did not want to live her life in fear for the rest of it, no matter how long or short it may be.

She wanted to be courageous, to continue to be hopeful and to continue to have faith that she was going to survive. She felt that most people in that part of the world would be kind to her when she got there.

She was naive, yes, but she was also a realist, and cautious, friendly and gullible. No matter what challenges had been dished out to her, Jane had always known that she would be okay. Jane not only had faith in it, but she just knew it and she thanked God for every ounce of time that she had had on this Earth. She lived with no regrets.

That was one of many things that she did love about herself, although she felt that no one else did. Her list of things that she did not like about herself, and the list of what she would love to change about herself was much, much longer.

Megan and the girls eventually came home from the trip to Illinois and they did what they could to prepare for their immediate journey. They did their best to finish up at a decent hour, but failed at that. Around 10:00 p.m., Jane ran to Pascal's house, where they sat and talked and hugged and kissed.

She told him that she needed to leave to go to see her father. He was genuinely disappointed. He actually made an *'Aww-aw'* sound, so she offered to come back to see him, which she did.

Why was she needing to say goodbye to him, to let him know that she was going to miss him? She was coming back, safely, she hoped. *Hmmm...* She ran to her dad's house, gave back his credit card, thanked him profusely and hugged and kissed him on the cheek. He wished her luck and a safe journey, telling her that he was very proud of her. They said their goodbyes with heavy hearts.

Jane drove back to say goodbye to Pascal and he greeted her at the door. *"He is a wonderful kisser,"* she thought as they proceeded quickly with saying their goodbyes. They cuddled and kissed and hugged and made wonderful noises in his bedroom, for quite a while. She did what she could to burn that night's memory of him into her brain, for she knew that she would miss him.

She did what she could to concentrate on everything that he was saying and doing, to memorize his face and his expressions and to focus, focus, focus on his eyes. *"He has beautiful eyes,"* she thought.

When they were done and he was not paying attention to what she was doing, she stole one of his expensive, gray long-sleeved shirts and sprayed his cologne all over it. She stuffed it into her purse. She was amazed that he did not smell the wafting aroma or comment on it.

They kissed and hugged goodbye and he told her to be safe and have fun, then he reminded her not to be one of those *"Arrogant Americans,"* but added that he knew that she would not be. He said, *"The Europeans will love you, as I have come to love you."* And then he added, *"But you know what I mean?"*

Jane smirked and thought, *"Yes, Pascal, I knew what you meant."* He meant that he had come to love her as a very good friend but by far was not in love with her. She knew it, she felt it, especially with how he looked at her and she secretly wished that that would change some day.

She closed the front door behind her and meandered to her car. She was feeling as if she had been awarded a lightness of her spirit and an awakening of her heart. She thought, *"Man, oh man that was fantastic, and boy oh, boy he was so wonderfully thorough. Thank you!"* She wondered if the neighbors had heard them.

Jane went back home, with a smile on her face. Her daughter was still up, they finished laundry and then they went to bed around 1:00 a.m. Jane could not sleep because she had Pascal on her brain all night, plus the thoughts of the trip.

Jane and Megan were up before sunrise and they packed the rest of their luggage.

Then, as Ed watched the girls as they still slept, Jane and Megan ran many errands. They took the cat to the vet to get a shot to knock him out and to finalize some paperwork. That took some time. As her daughter went inside the vet clinic, Jane sat in the car and called

16

her friend Toni.

They talked about her trip, her nervousness, and they also laughed about the strange things that could go wrong. Jane told her that she loved her, they said their goodbyes and Toni wished her luck, to be safe and for Jane to have fun.

Megan and Jane ran to four different banks to close accounts, make withdrawals and deposits, then to a superstore for a few last minute items. They went to an electronics store, where she bought a small video game for her oldest granddaughter to occupy her on the flight. When they were there, Jane somehow forgot to buy an electronic power adapter for her computer, for use in a foreign country. *"What was I thinking?"* Jane was not thinking clearly and she was surprised that at least she remembered to shower and get dressed that morning.

In between all of that, Ed and Sawyer, who had arrived at the house, helped with hauling the luggage to the garage and helped feed the kids and so on. When they got back from running their errands, Megan bathed and dressed the girls, while Jane ran to another bank to deposit money. She was aware that she was doing shallow breathing, and as it got closer and closer to the time that they were to leave for the airport, she was certain that her breathing would eventually stop.

Once Jane got back home, the three adults told her that it was eerie to watch the medicine kick in for the cat. They told her that he stumbled and became limp as they put him in the animal carrier. *"Awww."* Jane took a moment and hugged her son. She was so happy to see him.

They loaded up the cars with kids and luggage and then stood around for a minute to take a deep breath and double-check everything. Megan thanked Ed and told him that she was sorry for leaving such a huge mess behind. He told her not to worry about it. She thanked him again for taking care of the rest of her belongings and that the shipping company would contact him soon.

Jane handed Ed the keys to her car, so he could drive, because she was too nervous, and then they were off.

Jane traveled in Sawyer's car with him and the other four were in her car, as they caravanned to the Dayton International Airport. She and Sawyer talked during the entire drive, as he could tell that she was nervous and anxiety-ridden. They talked about his fiancee, Maria, and their upcoming wedding in April of the following year. Jane told him that she was very proud of him for securing a better job that took him to New York and back to Columbus. She told him that she was excited about their wedding, expected it to be perfect and she told him that she loved them.

Jane did so, without hesitation, but with a slight heavy heart, for she was fearful that anything could happen on her travels. She wanted to make sure that he knew that she loved him and she knew that he knew, but she needed to say so, just in case.

They got to their destination in short order. They unloaded the vehicles, let a skycap haul their luggage into the airport and Ed tipped him. They gave hugs and kisses and well wishes, then

Jane, Megan and the girls went inside. Jane wondered what the conversation would have been like, between her son and her brother, on their drive back home. She never knew. Jane was not breathing by the time they got dropped off.

The skycap helped them get their boarding passes from an automated machine. They checked in and checked some of her daughter's luggage at the counter. They got their seat assignments. Jane fed the girls some snacks, while they waited in the main lobby for her daughter to finish declaring her cat. The girls made a mess all over the floor, which Jane picked up and threw away.

Jane wondered if they would even remember her when they saw her next; in three or more years. She wondered if they would remember the next several hours. She was feeling the pangs of something more than mellowness coming on quickly, but she did not want them to see her cry. She did not want them to see her being sad. *"Makes me want to bawl,"* she thought.

After thanking the skycap for his help, they made their way to the departure gate and waited…and waited. Jane got snacks from Megan's backpack and her own computer bag and they eagerly ate. Jane read somewhere that when one was angry or agitated, one should munch on crunchy items and she did just that. She acknowledged her nervousness.

Jane went to a cafe and bought two very expensive bottles of water for all of them to share. *"I'm sorry. It is just a crime to charge that much. Really? No airport should charge so much for food. In addition, no movie theaters either, dammit!"* she thought.

The announcement was made for their flight, they boarded the plane along with many other passengers. After a bit of a delay, they were off to Atlanta, settled into their seats. Her oldest grandchild sat next to her, and Megan and her two year old grandchild were in one row back and across the aisle. They could see each other and that was a great comfort.

Jane was a white-knuckle flier and that day was no exception. She was worried that most of her flight was going to be a blur. She had heightened anxiety and was scared, but she was determined to do it all the same, no matter what. Jane had adopted her own mantra and repeated it to herself, in times of trouble, stress and anxiety. She repeated that mantra in her head, on that particular day:

"YOU ARE STRONGER THAN YOUR BIGGEST WEAKNESS."

Jane was going to miss her family, as they settled into their new life in Germany, but she also had faith that they were going to be fine. She repeated to herself that all of them were going to be okay, on that flight and the next two flights as well. They were going to be fine in their new home, experiencing new things and foods and smells and people. Jane was determined to stay focused and not become scatter-brained.

She knew her grandchildren would possibly be able to pick up new languages and meet new people and be changed for the good, forever. Her daughter and son-in-law would meet new friends, with open arms and an open mind and they, too, would learn new things that would enrich their lives.

"Why wouldn't anyone want that for another human being, for themselves, for their own children?" But Jane was feeling a bit selfish and she knew it, and she did not like being that way. That situation was new to her, too. She was going to do her best to let them go… literally and figuratively, spiritually and selflessly…and start her own new adventures, her own new chapters in her life. Which she did.

Jane was starting a new chapter in life anyway, without her children being nearby, with being a far away grandmother and with having a new love. That was always scary within itself, for one never knew what was around the corner with that kind of situation. She was dealing with death and loss again and again, and starting a new life when she would return to Dayton. That was sort of forcing her to make new friends, too.

She would have to find a new job, after losing the job she was so good at, and saying goodbye to old friends and co-workers. She was losing her home. She was working on continuously exercising and successfully losing weight, for her own health, not for any man. Most of all, she was becoming a better, stronger person, in spite of herself.

Jane felt stressed out and horribly confused lately with being in between jobs, in between homes, in between dress sizes, families, religions and relationships. *Hmmm…*

Any person would be apprehensive, scared and hopeful about any of it, or about all of it and about starting anew. Jane was no different. It made her feel quite normal at times, venturing out into the unknown, as most mothers do, when her kids are growing up and going away.

She thought that she had to find a way to a new identity and not as a mother, sister, friend or lover, but as something more than just *"Plain Jane."* It was good to feel normal, whenever she could feel that way, she thought. Because for most days, Jane felt odd and non-typical, for she knew that she was strange or at least quite different.

Jane knew that she didn't have a filter and she knew that she was *'stand-up comedian'* funny. She knew that she had compulsive issues, as she would speak before thinking, and she felt that she was an undiagnosed adult.

Jane had a tendency to diagnose herself, mentally, physically, medically…and she meant to keep it that way. She learned of things about herself and about her ex-boyfriends, while surfing the internet and reading books. She learned about general behaviors, insecurities, about drinking and driving, and smoking addictions. She learned about fatherless men (which, ironically, were all of her exes) and their adult behaviors, about compulsions, why men cheat, how to sleep better, how to exercise more efficiently, how to cook better meals for low blood pressure and low iron, etc.

She wanted to learn and experience everything that she could and she wanted to learn more about herself, in order to find a way to be peaceful and content about her life.

Jane knew that others knew that she was weird and also quite funny. But it was her strong, compassionate and patient friends who stuck around and wanted to be there for her, in her times of need. They would be the ones to listen when they could, who wanted to spend genuine time with her, because they loved her. She knew that it was invaluable to have such friends in one's life.

She would never want it any other way. Jane loved herself most days, for she had faith in herself, in her family and in her future. She knew that she could wane, from time to time, in her faith in herself, but she was determined to keep that at bay for now.

She had faith that she was going to be okay. She had to be strong, level-headed and cautious, with eyes wide open. She had to push fear aside, in order to survive, to function, to see her new life unfold in front of her. There was no time for her to be selfish. She also knew that during her trip, there was no time to be her regular, neurotic self.

On that flight, Jane had a snack of peanuts and pretzels, water and a diet Coke. Her granddaughter's excitement was amusing to her. The little one was happy to experience the take-off and landing, seeing the sky and the clouds, and was having fun playing with her toys and her coloring books. She was happy and excited to know that she was going to see her dad some time soon, but she was also oblivious of the possible dangers of air travel. Jane knew that, and did her best not to let the little one sense or see her anxiety. She thought that she had succeeded on that. They ate their food, they played, they rested. Then they were off like crazy onto the next flight.

Atlanta was huge! They got some advice..."*Thank you, sir*"...to take the tram to their next destination, as they waited for the one elevator that was working. They were crammed into a small area with other patrons to get on the elevator, and they were too near the escalators. They felt as if they were in the way of other patrons, which was aggravating to everyone. Jane thought that was a horribly, non-strategically placed elevator. *"A man must have designed it!"* she sarcastically thought.

They made their way onto the elevator, after many attempts, then down one story and ran to the tram. They ran from the tram to their next flight, which was the one to Amsterdam. They jumped on it and it seemed that everyone was waiting just for them to arrive. The entire flight staff were very patient and kind, which made their travels bearable.

The day before they had left, Ed had stated to Jane that *"Everyone on the plane is going to hate you"*...when he was verbalizing about how much her youngest granddaughter seemed to like to scream. She would do that from time to time, with being two years old, and when not getting her way, when tired and/or when she was trying to communicate something. Jane knew what he had said would be true, but she responded to him with a *"screw 'em"* attitude.

"Too bad and too-too late." Jane would not want her youngest

granddaughter to be any other way. She was a typical two year old and Jane loved her as is. She was perfect!

That flight went as smoothly as the first, with help from the staff and their surrounding passengers. She was a bit miffed with one small detail: She could not sit with her family and they were many rows back from her. But she sat next to a man who was slightly talkative, and just as interested in watching movies and the TV. So that was what they did.

They watched, ate, slept. They used the bathroom, slept, watched and waited...for that eight hour flight to be over. She heard her granddaughter scream only once and it was a short tantrum. *"Way to go, sweetie. Great recovery,"* she thought.

As she thought about it, sitting away from them was a small price to pay to be on that long flight, in the big scope of things. She could not get comfortable, could not sleep peacefully, could not digest her food well. She could not sit and cuddle with her granddaughters, but overall they made it. They lived through it and it was not that bad.

If Jane were to die that day, she would have done so by being happy and content, peaceful and having faith, that she was a kind and decent and funny and giving person. She was the best friend that she could be, a sweet woman, a good mother and a patient grandmother. Jane had faith that she knew where her soul would go.

She was very happy that she did not die that day, for it was not in her original plan anyway. It was not on her list of things to do!

Besides, she knew that she had many more adventures and challenges awaiting her:

She had heartaches and heartbreaks to go through, but she hoped not many...

She had new foods to taste, at many new restaurants...

She had shopping to do, for others' birthdays, holidays, etc...

She had massive love-making to do, and she hoped with a man who would love her unconditionally and who would be strong enough to love her for the rest of her life...

She had a new job to find, to enjoy and with which to be productive and appreciated...

She had many more potential friends to meet and to love and with whom to spend time...

She had future parties to attend...

She had much dancing to do (especially partially naked in the privacy of her own bathroom, listening to her favorite radio station, Mix1077, with blasting wonderful music. Jane did that often, and before her family came to live with her and obviously when her brother was at work)...

Jane had more traveling and sightseeing ahead of her, with travels to more foreign lands, to see historical places, the Seven Wonders of the World, including many places in America that were on her list...

She had schooling ahead of her, to learn new things and she had a degree waiting for her some day...

She needed a new home to find her....

She had a need to learn new languages, to learn to play the piano and guitar, to start a band, to sing on stage, to dance on stage, to watch her children and grandchildren grow…

She had her son's wedding to attend…and she had lots more crying to do…plus journaling, dreaming, texting and great foreign movies to watch.

And she had laundry to do. There was always laundry.

Jane, Megan and the girls went onto the next flight, in which they had a long layover. They got a few doughnuts and juice in the airport. *"Again, robbery!"* Then they boarded a bus to another plane that was waiting on the tarmac, which required them to climb stairs. *"Great!"* Somehow the cat got heavier and heavier.

Days earlier, Ed and Jane tried to convince her daughter to get rid of the cat and to get another 'German-speaking' cat once she got to her new home, but *"No way,"* was the response.

That third flight offered more drinks, and being a stress-eater and stress-drinker, Jane partook, but only had water and chocolate cookies. Actually she saved most of the cookies for another day. Before they knew it, the flight from Amsterdam to Nuremberg was over. It was a perfect Saturday in August, to be exact. But it could have been any day of the week and it would not have mattered, as far as Jane was concerned.

They exited the plane as fast as they could, gathering their bags and getting the stroller from inside the gateway, making sure that they stayed out of the way of all of the other busy-body passengers. Jane wanted to kiss the ground, but she did not have time.

They loaded their things onto a waiting tram and walked away from that flight, feeling free from being so cramped up for the past twelve or more hours. She could smell the crisp free air and she could feel more anxiety building up. Jane wanted her *'movie-type airport goodbye,'* but she did not get that at all.

Jane was pushing the heavy stroller, with the cat in his carrier on one of the girls' laps. Plus she was hauling her heavy computer bag. Megan was lugging the rest of the luggage. Once they got towards the front entrance, they saw her son-in-law, who had picked up the rest of the checked baggage. Jane smiled at him and her daughter ran out the front door. Jane was stopped by security because of the cat, so she missed their hugging and kissing reunion. She felt that it was not any of her business anyway, but it would have been nice to witness it all the same.

She called to her daughter to show the security guards the paperwork for the cat. Megan came back inside and did just that, and then they were free to go.

Once they got outside of the airport, Jane hugged her son-in-law. He mentioned that they needed to leave right then and there, because one of his friends was waiting on them in his car. Jane started crying, then turned to Megan and hugged her goodbye. They didn't want to let go. Jane knew that it was going to be the last time that she would see her, for a long time…and possibly forever.

Jane's hands and eyes and thoughts were all a-flutter, for she wanted to take the girls out of the stroller and hug on them and love on them, and kiss them all over. She wanted to have them look at her in the face one last time. Jane was prevented from that and all she could do was lean down and kiss them on the forehead. They were oblivious to what was about to happen and she knew it.

Jane was so heartsick, so heartbroken from that moment, that she did not think she would ever recover from it. Moments later, she was bawling.

She felt as if she looked like she was about to die, or like a deer caught in headlights, and she was forever deeply saddened that she did not get that anticipated moment with them.

She wondered if they would remember her. Jane had read somewhere, that when a child under the age of eight years old experiences a grand loss of some kind, they may have trust issues in adulthood. The loss of a loved one could be either by moving, divorce or death and if not treated properly, with therapy, they may have some issues. She was a big part of their lives since birth and all of a sudden she would be gone.

She thought about the fact that they were not prepared for their travels, not prepared for their move, not prepared for the knowledge that they were leaving behind everyone that they knew and loved. That included many aunts and uncles, cousins, grandparents and great grandparents. Jane assumed that they were not properly prepared and so, she assumed that they, too, would be dealing with anxiety of some kind. That did not make her feel any better.

Megan continued to hug her mother. She asked again if Jane was going to be okay. And Jane did the best that she could to tell her that she was going to be fine, when in actuality, Jane did not know. After one last long hug and a kiss on the cheek, Jane went back inside the airport and stood in the middle of the lobby area. Within the eyes and ears and cameras of the airport staff and other patrons, Jane bawled her ass off.

She recovered in a short order and looked quite pathetic. She approached a counter and asked for help to get to the main train station into Vienna. The cute female clerk wrote down some words and *dammit!*, it was so foreign to Jane, literally. The clerk gestured for her to go outside and get a ticket. Jane also asked about exchanging money, so the clerk gestured for Jane to locate the booth for that transaction. *"Okay."* Jane decided to do that first before going back outside. She did not know how much to exchange, so she exchanged $200 dollars, per Pascal's advice, which turned out to be sound advice, indeed. *"Thanks, Pascal!"*

From there, she went back to the area of the counter and out of the blue, like the Hollywood moment that Jane did not expect, Megan came back for her mother, to see her…to check on her… to let her know that she loved her. Megan was worried about her mother and offered for her to stay with them until Jane knew where she was going.

That was one of the most selfless acts and one of the single most wonderful things that Megan had ever done for Jane. And no matter how hard life got for her, that was the one thing that Jane would always remember. Megan held her mother's face for several minutes, having her look her straight in the eyes as she repeatedly asked her mother to stay with them.

Jane closed her eyes for a moment and sarcastically wondered aloud, *"Perhaps I could stay…and meet several cute military men, stay with them, bouncing back and forth from one barracks to another, undetected by security. I could stay with you and them on base…having them fall in love with me and having me break all of their hearts."*
"Mom, I'm serious"…

Jane told her daughter that she was kidding. She looked Megan in the eyes, then wrapped her arms around her and told her that she so appreciated her offer and it was the best thing that she could have ever offered to her. Jane wanted to take her up on it, but she told her, *"I am going to have to politely decline…for I need to let you go…and let you start your own life and adventure. I know that I can do this… and start one of my own."*

Her daughter hugged Jane so tight, telling her that she did not want to let go, but then, she did let go… Jane watched Megan walk away from her and out of the doors of the airport…for the last time. Jane was bawling, again.

Jane turned around, walked in circles for a moment then back to the counter, then changed her mind. Then she walked over to a gift shop, then changed her mind. Then she went out of the front doors of the airport, which was making her feel trapped, but somehow secure. It was a place that she knew that she was going to have to leave, and then face the wide world that awaited her.

If, for one more moment Jane had hesitated and talked to her daughter and held onto her for one more hug, she would have missed one of the most wonderful strangers that she was to meet on her adventures: Maury, from Australia.

Jane went outside and walked up to what she assumed was the subway ticket booth, which had too many buttons for her to decipher, especially under so much stress. She heard someone speaking English and she quickly approached a cute, tall man. He was helping another female stranger, but Jane rudely and purposefully interrupted their conversation. *"Sorry about that."* The woman looked as flustered as Jane did.

Jane asked for help and he immediately acknowledged her, stating that he would show them both how to get a ticket, and he did. The woman had more luggage than Jane did, but she was also traveling with another person. *"Lucky dog,"* Jane thought, for she felt so all alone. He gave them instructions on how to take the subway into the train station, then to follow the signs to where they wanted to go from there. Jane must have looked more confused, but then he offered to walk them to the subway. They followed him, on faith, that he was leading them to their correct destination, and he was.

The others left as they were armed with accurate information. Maury stayed with Jane the whole time and she could not have been more grateful. He offered to go with her on the subway because he was going that same direction to go shopping for himself and his family. He helped with her luggage as they got onto the subway car and introduced themselves. They sat down across from each other, talked the entire time regarding their adventures and the reasons why they were in Europe.

Maury worked for a medical company, he traveled back and forth to Europe a lot for business and he had a family. Jane told him about herself, of course, and why she was there and with whom she was going to visit. When she told him of her trip from Atlanta to Amsterdam, he used the phrase *"cattle class"* and each day that she thought about it, that phrase still cracked her up. It was an accurate way to describe just how packed they were inside that large plane.

He gave her advice on how to ask for help and he also reassured her that almost everyone that she would run into, would be helpful and kind. She wanted so much to believe him and everyone else who had told her that same thing, including Pascal. It turned out that all of them were right.

They made it to the train station and she eagerly followed him… upstairs, down stairs, and to the information booth. The information booth clerk sent them to the ticket depot, where they had to take a number and wait. She closely followed the signs, in which she was having trouble because she was so overwhelmed. Maury seemed to know it. She wondered how her face looked that day.

While they stood there, he told her that it would be in her best interest to ask some questions (Of course! But how would she know what to ask?). By then, she was still wondering about the cost of a one-way ticket. He told her to ask the difference in prices between a direct express train and a train that would make either some or many stops, or a train that would make transfers.

Her number was called and they approached the very helpful and cute, middle-aged woman, and Jane made her inquiries. It was 79 Euros for a train that would make five stops, but it was 99 Euros for a non-stop train to Vienna. *"I will take the non-stop train!"* Jane exclaimed. She paid the fee and got her information and her ticket. Maury walked with her to the train terminal. He placed his hands on her shoulders and sat her down on a bench... literally, and told her to wait for the next train, which was arriving in 15 minutes. Jane stood up, hugged him so tightly, and profusely thanked him. She got his permission to take his picture and thanked him again, and then he was gone.

Jane would never forget the kind, gentle spirit of Maury and the hope that she had that day, that she was going to meet more strangers like him. She loved to listen to him talk. And for that matter, Maury, Jane did not consider you a stranger any more. She wished that she had gotten his email address that day, in order to let him know of her continued, safe adventures and vice versa.

With his help, Jane made it to Vienna and meeting him was well worth her trip, indeed. Maury gave Jane hope and continued faith in mankind. He made her feel less scared and she would always remember him. Also, she would have liked to have known what he had bought that day when he went shopping for his family. Jane was always just curious like that.

Soon the train came and she got on it, not realizing the enormity of it all. That express train was packed to the gills and all of the individual cars were not connected by doors. The interior of that train car was narrow, with many seats and areas for dining, which Jane thought was odd, but okay. She made her way through the sea of people, through a galley, and then spoke to a woman who had reassured her that she was going in the right direction.

It was after many moments of maneuvering, leaning and scooting and walking through - with many comments of *"Pardon me"* and *"Excuse me"* and *"I am sorry that I just hit you with my bag, again"* - that she had gotten to the end of one train. She had to exit that train, flag down a conductor and be directed to another train car to locate her seat. *"Really?"* How was she to know that?

Jane finally got settled into her seat and was ready for her five hour ride. She was tired, flustered, anxious and sort of hungry, but she was also bloated, dizzy, light-headed and headachey. A typical reaction for her, when she was under lots of stress. She wanted to sleep but she also worried that if she did, she would not wake up and she would somehow miss her destination.

An elderly woman sat next to her, at the window, and they were able to strike up a conversation or two, without really completely understanding each other. The woman told her about her hometown of Vienna, about her kids, her deceased husband and her grandkids. Jane also chimed in about her granddaughters. Although each of them could only understand every other word that the other was saying, they seemed to do pretty well for a couple of strangers. Jane watched the mouth of the woman with such intent, making sure to try to understand what she was saying.

Jane was fascinated with the elderly woman. She thought that it was great that she was still traveling about the countryside, visiting relatives, going shopping and so on...all by train, which Jane guessed was quite expensive. Jane had to remind herself that that mode of travel was probably typical for everyone who lived there, but she was not sure of that. She was glad and comfortable that she was able to sit next to the kind woman. She was cute and patient, and somehow reminded Jane of her own mother.

Jane quickly rushed the thoughts of her mother from her mind, for she knew if she spent any time thinking of her, she would begin to cry. She was aware that the thought of her mother popped into her head more frequently, especially when she was under stress. She wanted to keep her memory at bay, for the moment. Many times she had wished that her mother had lived to see another day, another year, and to see the birth of her own great granddaughters, for she loved babies and she would have loved them.

Jane also thought that perhaps it would have been okay for her mother to have met her ex-boyfriends. That way, she would have been there for Jane, during those times of grief and sorrow. And perhaps if she had been, Jane would have been able to recover from those heartbreaks a little more quickly. Jane knew that it was not possible, but she could wish.

Jane watched the landscape go by, mesmerized and still feeling surreal about where she was and what she was doing. It was dizzying and strikingly beautiful, with many homes and businesses, retaining walls and open land. There were pastures and hills, farms and fields, clouds galore and at one time, the threat of bad weather. During that long ride, Jane was able to sleep some. She was sure that for some of it, she had had her head cocked back and her drooling mouth open…snoring, perhaps, but she did not care. She was mentally and physically exhausted, but spiritually and faithfully enriched all the same.

During her ride, Jane befriended an Italian family of three: A mom, a dad and an adorable two year old girl, named Julietta. That little beauty had auburn hair and was as cute as a button. Her mom was petite and beautiful; thin and fit, and ate more food than anyone Jane had ever seen lately. She had brought out many foods from her backpack, including sandwiches and snacks throughout the entire ride. Jane could not see how she was able to eat so much. *Where was the fairness in that?* Jane could eat one pecan and bloat up like a damn balloon! *"Not fair!"*

The mom was about Jane's age, with more hair than she knew

what do with. She had some of it piled on top of her head with a clip and some was swept down against her neck. She was a very attentive mom. Although Jane could not understand exactly what she was saying, Julietta knew her mother's tone. Jane knew all along that no matter where one had gone in their travels and no matter what one did, that the word *'No'* was universal. Julietta got a lot of *"No's"* from her parents and from Jane, too, as Jane prevented Julietta from escaping and running down the aisle of the train. For some reason, that was fun for Jane and for Julietta.

Julietta's dad was very tall, very thin, very handsome and reminded her a bit of her son-in-law. She wondered about him, how he was faring in the military and she wondered about her family throughout her entire journey. Julietta's parents played with their little girl, they laughed at her, then they fed her and all the while, Jane was able to witness that wonderful family dynamic. That dynamic made Jane quite mellow, quite melancholy.

Jane thought, *"Where did the time go?"* Her family was moving away, her family was moving on, her kids were grown and her grandchildren may not even remember her. *Wow…was that a pathetic, sad thought, again?* Jane had hope that she would have more grandchildren some day.

And soon, *"I will be all alone."* That thought made her not only sad, but it also made her hopeful. Jane believed that some day, she was going to be able to travel more, possibly alone, throughout the world, meet new people and get re-acquainted with old friends. Would she possibly allow herself to fall in love again…or maybe get married again some day? *"Is it in the cards for me to be in love again in this lifetime?"* she wondered. *"Will I be able to experience all there is to see in the world…good and bad…to write about it and photograph it?"*

Jane wanted to leave her worries and woes behind, but somehow, they followed her to Europe. *"Did my woes sneak inside my suitcase somehow?"* she jokingly thought. She was hopeful, but apprehensive about Pascal. She was rightfully worried *(Olympian!)* that he, too, would cheat on her and lie to her, because so far, they all did. *"What's a girl to do?"* she wondered. She was worried about making a fool out of herself, with falling in love again. She was concerned about crying a lot out of fear, feeling silly and childish and giddy, expecting and hoping for him to love and cherish her, like she knew that she needed and quite deserved.

She was worried about letting her guard down and pouring out her heart and soul to him, like she had done so many times (to boyfriends and friends, alike) and having him not feel the same way. She even thought about him being able to find a way to use her words against her, like it had been done so many times before.

Jane worried about how much she had felt free enough to share herself with him physically. And somehow, that was going to come back and bite her on the ass. She jokingly thought, *"If only ass-biting would happen more often with him, then that would be quite okay…"*

Strangely, she was also concerned that he would fall in love with her and she would let him down, by not being able to live up to whatever expectations that he might have of her or that she would disappoint him somehow. She was also very concerned that he would feel free to tell her about his disappointments in her, to feel free to criticize her...like the others had done, too. She genuinely worried about him, and his drinking and smoking habits.

Jane was worried about being insulted by him and she worried about herself and why she stuck around just to take one more insult from the others. *"I was just joking"*...was a quote she had heard many, many tiresome times in the past. And, mostly, the criticisms came along very subtly and without warning. She dismissed them for the most part, until she could not dismiss them any longer.

Jane could never understand all of the comments and jabs regarding her height, weight and looks. They felt free to criticize or negatively comment about the color of her hair, about her job or lack thereof, her ongoing struggle to find another good job, although Jane almost always worked two to three jobs at a time. They commented on her income or lack thereof and about her car, her furnishings, her clothes. They commented about her being too sensitive, too intimidating, too accommodating and they made comments about her home going into foreclosure. They commented about the color of her children, about their friends not liking her, and their friends being tired of pretending to like her.

They made false and unrealistic comments about how she did not have any real friends of her own. She did have friends, but only ones that mattered. They talked about her large, estranged family, etc. Their comments and insults did not happen all at once, but they felt free to say what they wanted all the same.

Jane rightfully worried about those things, for it was those things, those comments, that she felt defined her, for the moment. It was those terrible insults and comments that she took for a long time, from each of her ex-boyfriends, her ex-husband, some male and female co-workers, all ex-friends, some family members and even strangers from around town.

Jane was justly tired and did not want to spend much more time worrying about those things that she could not change in others. She wanted to spend the rest of her life as someone else, not the sort of neurotic person that she thought she was born to be, and that she had self-diagnosed.

Jane wanted to be loved *"as is,"* because she loved others, as is. She could never understand that since she could do that naturally, then why could not others be like that towards her, too. She was a puzzle to figure out and she knew it. But she wanted to be the puzzle that some man was *"man enough"* to solve.

Jane wanted to journal her thoughts and woes, get them off of her mind, get them off of her chest, and tuck her journal away, into her suitcase...and leave it there for all time.

As she watched that family in awe, she thought about her own life and how blessed she was for doing what she was doing. She was blessed for what she had done in the past, by raising two beautiful, responsible, productive and healthy kids, mostly on her own and doing a good job. She loved her children, she missed her children, *"But it was now Me time,"* she thought, and everything was as it should be.

Julietta's presence forced her to miss her own granddaughters. Julietta let Jane play with her and her toy cars. Jane showed her mirror to Julietta and she was fascinated by her own reflection. Julietta broke Jane's mirror stand and the mom apologized, but Jane let her know that it was quite okay...and it was. Time was rapidly going by and wonderfully so. Playing with Julietta, conversing with her parents and her neighboring passenger, made the time fly and she was quite okay with that. Jane took note of the time, which was displayed in digital red numbers at the top of the front-facing doorway. She tried not to concentrate on that too much.

Although it was an Express, they made at least one stop and a group of seven guys boarded the train. They had been smoking and donned several beaded necklaces apiece and sombreros with hand-written name tags on them. They had been partying, she guessed, and continued their festivities in the car in front of them. She hated to admit it, but that was where Jane wanted to be. She wanted to be at a party, to get drunk and pass out, among the safety and security of her friends. However, this group of people were not her friends, but she had a wonderful time watching their antics, their laughter, their continuous drinking and singing.

She thought about how great it would be, to be at a party with Jimmy Buffett and Kenny Chesney, Rascal Flatts, Jason Aldean and Dierks Bently. *"Sigh."* That would be fun, too! These guys were in their twenties and having fun. *"What is wrong with that? Nothing,"* she thought, as she watched in envy of their youth and carefree spirit. She guessed that no matter where one goes, *'twenty-somethings'* drink and have fun almost all over the world. *"Way to go, guys. It was fun watching you,"* she thought.

About three hours in, Jane guessed that she must have been relaxed enough, to realize that she had to use the bathroom. Around that time, for the second time, the conductors had come around to check and validate everyone's tickets. For both times, she had eagerly awaited and anticipated their presence and handed them her ticket with enthusiasm.

On the second time around, she had tugged on the shirt sleeve of the cute and tall conductor and asked one word: *"Toilet?"* (She needed to know where the closest one was). His response was not only quick, but instantaneously not humorous to her, but moments later, it was funny. He stated, *"I'm sorry. There are no toilets on these German trains."* She was puzzled and responded with a disappointed *"Okay."*

There was a split second of silence, then out and out laughter from all who were within ear shot of his comment and there were plenty of patrons, including her elderly neighbor. It took Jane a minute, but she nervously burst out laughing, too, as she grabbed his hand, looked him in the eyes and said to him, *"Oh, you are one of those European comedians!"* (Stressing the word...*Eur-o-peeee-an*). He laughed even harder and so did Jane. He patted her on the shoulder, as he directed her to the back of the car.

She got up, still laughing and shaking her head. She took her computer with her and went to the toilet. As she did her business, she was tossed around a bit inside that tiny space. The bathroom was about the same size as the airplane bathrooms. She laughed the whole time, because of the jerking motion of the train and also because she was impressed with the conductor's humor, even though she was the brief brunt of his joke. Very funny, indeed.

When she was done, she sat back down in her seat, feeling some relief. At one point, Julietta got away from her parents and headed in the direction of the party-goers. Her dad jumped up and scooted her around, but let her take a much needed walk, for she had been fussy. Upon her return with him, from the front of the car ahead, Julietta stopped and stared at the young guys. They put a sombrero on her head and took her picture. She seemed to love the attention. All the while, the landscape was flying by, and the time was flying by for Jane.

Then, after five hours or so, the train was at its final destination at Vienna's Main Train Station. A new set of challenges were to begin for Jane. That new set of challenges would make or break her, for she was scared, but determined to not let her fears and insecurities win over her. She was very scared, indeed, but she did not realize how much, until it came closer to nightfall.

Everyone exited the train. That was the last stop. Jane got her bags and said goodbye to her elderly passenger, who quickly disappeared. As she got off the train and walked toward the Main Terminal, the Italian family asked her if she needed help. She told them she was going to try to get information at a booth and get a hotel until her friend from another part of Austria was able to pick her up. They made their way inside, they asked Jane again, but she thanked them and reassured them that she would be fine (But would she?). Then they were gone.

Jane stood there for a moment and wondered how her life would have been different if she had let them help her. She did not realize until much later that she should have let them help her. She wondered how Julietta was faring for the rest of her trip.

The train station was huge and crowded with people from all over Europe and from all over the world. It reminded her of a mall, with several levels of subway tunnels underneath. It had many restaurants and food options which smelled so good to her. It had escalators, a non-working elevator, areas roped off and under construction, ticket booths, a grocery store, cigarette machines, accessory stores and an upper outdoor level, which at that point in time, faced the setting sun. There was a lower street level, with many taxis, buses and cars, with people walking about and some were smoking cigarettes. There were 'Help' phones, many bathrooms, and so on.

She found a large booth, with a large lady inside and asked about a map and about hotel info. The clerk quickly handed her a brochure and Jane looked at it and tried to understand it. She purchased an international phone card for 10 Euros. For the next two hours, she would walk down stairs several times, upstairs several times and she tried to use the phone, but could not understand German. *"What in the hell is the operator saying?"* she thought.

Jane cried a lot as she paced around. She went outside to get a feel for the receptiveness of her new surroundings and was not feeling good about it. She sat for a spell on the ground near the entrance, then she eventually went back inside to feel safe. Jane took note that the scenery was breathtaking with many buildings of various sizes, street signs, traffic and noises galore, with people of many shapes and sizes, coming and going, with bags and without.

Before she went inside, a cabby called to her and she waved, indicating that she did not need his help. Then a woman approached her for some money and she turned her down, but Jane felt so bad for doing that. Jane saw what she assumed were hotels across the street, but she wanted to know if she could afford them first, before leaving the safety of the station. There were lots of smokers in the front of the terminal, which made her think of Pascal. She wondered what he was doing at that moment and she briefly got a smile on her tired face.

When Jane went back inside, she sat down on the floor near the center of the station, with her back against a railing. She tried to understand the map and hotel brochure. She stopped a lady, who looked Italian, and asked her if she could translate the symbols on the brochure, which she happily did. The woman showed her what most of the symbols meant and after she left, Jane managed to map out where she was. She was able to understand what hotels were where and the cost of each type of hotel. But none of that gave her any reassurances on whether or not they were available.

Since she could not use the phone, she did not want to walk around Vienna, with heavy luggage in tow, without knowing where she was going or if it was safe. She did not know if she could find her way back. She did not know if she should take a cab and have the cab driver act as if he did not understand her, driving her around in circles and charging her an arm and a leg.

She had no idea about the time or if the station was closing down or if it stayed open all night. She asked several people for help, but they, too, seemed lost and in a hurry to get on another train or subway to their destinations. Jane felt stuck.

As soon as Jane saw them, she grabbed up two female security guards who spoke some English and they finally directed her to Ibis Hotel (pronounced Ee-bees), which was *"across the street."* They told her that it was moderately priced and she should be okay just walking there.

So, Jane took it on faith that they were right and with luggage in tow, she headed out the front door. She knew full well that it was quite possible to get lost, even though she was a Girl Scout. She knew that she could get mugged or hit by a bus. She could fall down and break a limb or she could get swallowed up in a sewer grate or she could be swept away by a large, freakish wind and never be seen again. Despite the uncertainties, she left the confines of her safe spot, not knowing what was ahead of her.

She walked tall and straight and with confidence and a *"DON'T BLEEP WITH ME"* attitude and headed south and east toward the hotel. The streets of that area were not straight, so when she rounded a curve, she literally ran into many people and kept walking. She followed the rules of traffic, including the street signs that she could not read but could guess what was being communicated to her. She had a *'look both ways before crossing the street'* mantra, that she had recited many times from childhood and to her children. She finally saw the hotel and high-tailed it across the street and into the lobby. She was able to do this all without being swept away by anything, other than pride.

Jane met a wonderful, very receptive and communicative clerk at the desk and inquired about staying there. He told her that the hotel was all sold out. *"What the hell?"* she thought. It was quite a busy Saturday, indeed. The hotel was huge and it was hard for her to understand that it could be sold out, but she had to believe that she was being told the truth. He told her of another Ibis Hotel and she asked if he could check to see if they had availability. *"Oh, yessss, indeed,"* he said.

He called the hotel and they did have a room. He reserved a room for her and he offered to show her how to get there on her map. He told her that she would have to walk a few blocks and then get on two subways and walk again for another few blocks to get to the hotel. *Hmmm…*

Looking at his sweet eyes, she could tell that he knew that she was flustered and had been crying. Her voice got a bit low and quivery as she asked him one, very important question: *"Can I get there before dark?"* He reassured her that he knew that she could. She was so glad that he had faith in her, for at that moment, she was not feeling so confident in herself. Speaking slowly, he precisely showed her on the map, where to walk from the hotel, then indicated which subway to take (the Red line) and which place to transfer to (the Orange line). He told her to exit on a specific street and walk about two blocks to the other hotel. *Sigh and huff and puff.* She took a deep breath and profusely thanked him for his help and took off bounding for the subway.

Jane was able to get help from a very tall security officer, who directed her to the automated ticket machine. She got a ticket and went down a few flights of stairs to get to the subway train that she needed. She was very proud of herself for not panicking so far, but she knew that at any moment she could have a panic attack. She stood there, with many patrons, some of whom looked questionable.

Once the train came, she jumped on and got a seat right away. The subway was crowded. She looked around and made herself very alert to her surroundings, as they traveled a short distance. She heard the announcement for the stop that she needed, but she could read each name of the marked stops prior to that one, indicated on the subway walls.

She got off of the train and onto the next train with minimal waiting and was on her way towards hotel bliss. Again, after a small amount of distance traveled, she got off the second train, where she became instantly aware that she was a bit disoriented.

On the last part of her journey, she was not too clear on the directions that she was given from the hotel clerk. As she ascended some stairs and came out of the subway station and onto a surface street, she must have looked confused. She was quickly approached by two men. They somehow seemed to be aware that she was in the wrong place, as she had looked at street signs and looked frequently down at her map.

One of the men spoke English, but with another type of accent other than German. The other one did not speak to her at all. They were disheveled and perhaps a bit tipsy. The two of them spoke frequently to each other in another language and she assumed it was about her. As one of them took Jane's map right from her hands, he had told her that he was willing to help her, because he knew what it was like to be lost in a foreign country. He asked her where she needed to go.

She told him that she was trying to find Ibis Hotel on LaSalle Street and he told her that it was in the other direction. She was immediately cautious and nervous, but the hair on the back of her neck was not raised just yet. That was good enough of a signal to her to trust those men. *"Have faith, Jane"*...was being whispered in her ear by some angel or by some disembodied spirit. So she did.

Again, Jane took it on faith that she was going to be okay following them, and as she followed them, she kept asking one of the men if he was taking her to the surface street that she needed. He repeatedly told her that he was. They went upstairs and they went downstairs and they even got on a small elevator. Inside the elevator, she was uncomfortably close to them.

Jane was okay with him taking her map, but she thought that if they offered to take her bags, she was going to scream and run. Once they surfaced on the street, he pointed to the direction that she needed to walk to get to the hotel.

Now, bear in mind, it was dusk and still too dark for her. She was on the right track. She saw the street sign with big lettering and a big label on the subway entryway which indicated to her that she was on LaSalle Street. She profusely thanked them, as he handed back her map.

She could see in their faces that they knew that she did not completely trust them, which later on she felt bad about. Jane just could not help it and *screw that!* She was a single woman, alone with perfect strangers…or maybe not so perfect. She thanked them again as they began to walk in the opposite direction, which made her think of a few things to ask herself:

"Why were they there…on that wrong street…in the first place?
Were they placed there on purpose, to do a good deed?
Were they angels of some sort?
Why was I so quick to judge, and why didn't my neck hair raise up? Now that they know where I will be staying, will they show up

sometime later and attempt to converse with me?..."

Makes one wonder about the world and one's surroundings, now doesn't it? She was grateful that they were not out to mug her or worse. For that, too, had crossed her mind.

Jane hurriedly walked towards the hotel, as she was able to see it down the road. She was feeling elated as it got closer. Feeling as if she did not want to press her luck any longer, she rushed inside the front door. She felt as if she was afraid to be hit by the last remnants of the sunlight, which was dancing in the distance and fading quickly beyond the horizon, among the surrounding trees.

Dealing with exhaustion, Jane approached the front desk and was immediately greeted by a very tall and cute young man. *"There seems to be a lot of tall and cute in Europe,"* she sarcastically thought. She gave him her name and a bit of a story of how nice the clerk was at the other hotel. He found her reservation and she asked if she could possibly stay for three nights. He checked and he said that she could. *"Yes!"* she exclaimed, embarrassingly.

He gave her some information regarding checkout, the hours of the restaurant and they exchanged pleasantries and her credit card. He gave her the room key and directed her toward the elevators. She thanked him, got on the elevator, found her room on the 6th floor, went inside, turned on the light and locked the door behind her. She put her bags down on one of the two twin beds and plopped right next to them, curled up in a ball...and bawled her ass off.

After a while of crying and feeling silly, Jane rolled over onto her back and just lay there for a moment and listened to the sounds of the silence that surrounded her. Other than the occasional sob that came from her throat, she could hear and feel her heart beating heavily in her chest. She could hear the distant traffic on the street below. She felt as if that room was going to be her home away from home, at least for a while and she had just better get used to it, starting right then and there.

A little bit later, she got up, went to the bathroom looked at her fatigued reflection. She smirked at herself after realizing that all of her mascara was gone. She brushed and flossed, then lay back down on the bed and napped for quite a while. *"What time is it?"* she wondered, as she drifted off to sleep, wondering about her family and wondering about Pascal.

She wondered if she was going to be able to communicate with someone that she knew, regarding her whereabouts. She wondered about what she was going to do next, as she was to wait for what seemed like an eternity to talk to Joseph, her dear Austrian friend from high school.

Jane eventually got up, tired but a bit rested. She looked around her room. It had two single beds with high wooden headboards, a small table and a light on each side of the beds. It had a built-in bench along the back wall, which she used to place her luggage, and a built-in long desk with two chairs that spanned the width of the room near the very large window. On the right side of the desk was a phone, the hotel restaurant menu and a hotel brochure. On the left side was a TV and its remote control.

It had wooden floors, an open closet with extra bedding and hangers near the door, a long mirror across from the closet and a very small bathroom with only a shower. *"Damn!...I wanted to soak in a bathtub."* There was an odd plunger for flushing the toilet, a narrow vanity for her toiletries and a hairdryer on the wall. *"Awesome!"* She approached the long mirror to check to see if it was a 2-way mirror and it was not. She always had to check that at every hotel. It all was nice, indeed.

She walked over to the window, opened the curtains with a pull handle and looked outside. The window faced the street and there were cars and cyclists coming and going. Off in the distance, in the western sky, was an amusement park, where she could see a Ferris wheel with many lights and a tower of some kind. The setting sun's dim rays were like strobe lights within the spokes of the carnival wheel as it slowly turned. It was very pretty, very mesmerizing. She could not hear it, but she could imagine the screeching sounds of the happy kids and adults, alike, who would be having fun at that park. She felt alone.

Jane picked up the phone and took a chance that she could get a hold of Joseph. She remembered to dial *'0'* for outgoing calls and dialed his number. *"Success!"* She got his voicemail and left a message of what time it was, what day it was, where she was, the phone number of the hotel, and that she was glad to be in his country of many hospitable people.

She was elated to hear his voice, if only on his answering machine. She felt a huge smile appear on her face, as she hung up the phone, having hope for another day. His voice gave her comfort and she somehow knew that she was going to be okay.

Jane realized that she was hungry, since she had not eaten anything since breakfast into Amsterdam and now she needed real food. So, requiring to be presentable, she stripped and took her time in the shower. She washed away the dirt and grime, and worry and stress from her body and from the very long day, along with shaving away a day's worth of unwanted hair. She felt so much better.

She donned blue and white striped lounging pants, a white tank top and a grey T-shirt, which read, *"I Only Date Athletes."* She looked at herself in the mirror and for some reason, she jokingly thought that she would have welcomed a buff football player to cuddle with that night, with his large, strong arms to wrap around her and make her feel safe. And yet, he never showed up!

She put on a red casual jacket, put a light coating of makeup on her nose, combed out her hair, topped it off with a brown headband, and grabbed her purse and room key. With a notebook in hand, she went down to the lobby and restaurant to feed her body and to feed her senses.

By then, it was 9:30 p.m. and it was still Saturday.

She entered the restaurant, which was decorated with tan, light green and deep orange-colored furniture. There were table settings of greenery, candles and condiments. The overhead light fixtures were silver and multi-colored spheres with many mirrored trinkets, to bring out the brightness of the bulbs. The restaurant had large, wide and tall windows, that faced the street.

It was quite modern, with many standard-sized tables and chairs and a section of high tables, high chairs and a long padded bench. That was where Jane opted to sit, since that section gave her the best vantage point for people-watching. There were outdoor seats along the sidewalk, with three couples there and two families inside at the tables across from her. There was an upper section, too, which had the same type of furniture, along with orange and green sofas, surrounded by railings of glass and orange painted metal bars.

Jane had a smile on her face and her head was bee-bopping uncontrollably, as she listened to American music on the PA system, which included Katy Perry's *"Last Friday Night,"* some music from The Cure and REO Speedwagon's *"Gonna Keep On Lovin' You."* She was happy at that point and she was singing inside her head.

The cute, chubby and balding waiter came over to her table and handed her a menu. She told him that she wanted water and that she needed another moment before ordering. He attended to all of the patrons, with a smile on his face. He came back to her table and gave her some water, then she asked about the food. She put in her order and she was served promptly.

She had potato soup with parsley and finely chopped mushrooms, a huge salad with mixed leafy greens, Roma tomatoes, red bell peppers and thin strips of sliced ham, with a mixture of balsamic vinegar and light ranch dressing. It was very good. However, Jane had to admit that if she was served an old gym shoe on a platter with parsley, she probably would have eaten that, too, especially if it had gravy on it.

She eagerly ate it all, even though she should not have. She was not going to waste it, plus she had nowhere to store any leftovers. She should have just ordered the soup. She took her time eating, watching and listening, jotting down notes from time to time. By the end of her meal, she did not feel as bad as she had earlier. She finished, paid the tab with a nice tip, which was around 11 Euros (She rarely paid that much at home for herself because she was poor and she was frugal). She thanked the waiter and went back to her room.

She brushed and flossed, kicked off her sandals, fluffed up the pillows, laid her back against the headboard of one of the beds, turned on the TV and channel surfed. Just like home, there was nothing on of much interest. She could only get one channel with international news, whereby she could understand what was being said.

Jane decided to watch a comedy that, despite the language barrier, had her cracking up with their slapstick antics and strange humor. She opened up her computer and journaled some, but eventually pushed that aside. Moments later, she was leaning. She curled up in a ball under the covers, slowly closed her eyes and was out like a light. She was sure that she was safe and that she was going to have pleasant dreams or no dreams at all. She was drained of energy, but satiated, exhausted but content and she was hopeful. She had faith that she was going to have another day of positive encounters, despite her self-induced, and not so self-induced, stress.

As she drifted off to sleep, she said, *"Thank You for letting me be here. Thank You for keeping me safe and warm. Thank You for another day on this great Earth. Amen."*

The next day...

Jane woke up from a deep, sound sleep, with the phone ringing at 9:30 a.m. It was Joseph! She was thrilled to hear his voice. They spoke for an hour. She told him that she was having trouble getting ahold of her family. He told her that she needed the USA country code of *'001'* when dialing out. She did not know that. He was surprised that the hotel clerks did not tell her that when she checked in. They talked about being divorced and she did not know that he had been divorced for quite some time.

"How did I miss that bit of info?" she wondered. Would that fact have changed her mind about staying with him, with this single man? No, probably not, but she was not sure how she had missed that one. He told Jane that his daughters were both over 18 years of age, with one living nearby and the other in another country.

She told him that her flights were good, and cried like a baby when she parted ways with her family. She told him that she did not get the sendoff and goodbyes like she had wanted at the Nuremberg airport. He told her that he would pick her up around 5:00 p.m. at the hotel on Monday. She knew that he could hear the anxiety in her voice about being alone.

She was thankful that he was available for her and that he made the exception to pick her up early. *"Thank you, oh so much,"* she told him. He told her to go sightseeing at Stephansplatz, that same day or the next day, by taking the subway and his directions for her were very thorough. He mentioned that Monday was a holiday, so some of the stores may be closed. *"Okay. I will go."* She thanked him again and they hung up. She was very excited about her day.

Armed with accurate and helpful phone-calling information and using her new phone card, Jane called Ed and left him a voicemail message with hotel info and phone numbers. Then she called her dad and was able to speak to him, although it was super early in the morning. Or was it late? They cried. He was thrilled to hear from her and told her that he was very proud of her and of her accomplishments. She decided not to tell him too much, especially about how much she cried and of how scared she was. He told her that he would call her son-in-law's parents and give them the info, so they could get a hold of him and pass on the info to her daughter. They exchanged *"I love you's"* and she thanked him and then they hung up. *Sigh.*

By then, it was 10:50 a.m. She turned on the TV and watched commercials and trailers for upcoming movies, including something with Jackie Chan. She watched *"Lost in Space"* for a moment and some other odd programs. She flipped the channels from soccer, to a local talent show, plus another comedy and back and forth. It was difficult to stick with something that she could not understand, but it was exciting all the same.

Around 11:30 a.m., she ate a granola pretzel snack and a leftover banana, which she thought she would regret later, because she was allergic to bananas. *"Does one's body still get the nutritious benefits from bananas or other food items, even though one's body is allergic to it?"* she asked herself. *"Hmmm. I am still so curious about that question,"* she thought.

Since she could remember, Jane had always had many sporadic and disconnected thoughts and questions in her head, something of which she was made fun of, by all ex-beaus. One beau in particular would state that Jane was distracted by shiny objects. Jane would be slightly insulted by that comment, and also questioned herself, *"So what? Now what?"* Being easily distracted did not make her any less of a wonderful and creative human being. He was quite the ass, for cheating on her and letting her go, after all.

Jane made the bed, took photos of the room, balanced her money, organized her purse and got dressed in shorts, a dressy T-shirt and sandals. She put on some makeup and styled her hair, then around 12:00 p.m. she grabbed her things and went to the bar in the lobby. She bought a bottled orange juice for 1.60 Euros. She exited the hotel and turned to the right, per Joseph's instructions and headed out for her first, deliberate European adventure.

It was a beautiful summer's day. The sun felt wonderful on her skin and she was so happy to be out in it. She walked north, past many closed businesses, including a bank, a couple of diners and pubs. She walked across a couple of side streets and parking lots and to the subway on Praterstern at LaSallestraBe Streets. She waited patiently as several people were trying to use the automated ticket machine.

There was a small gathering of young people, who were leaning up against the wall of the stairwell, who didn't seem to want for anything. They were just hanging out, Jane concluded. There was also a family, who had one young woman asking questions as they were trying to use the subway ticket machine. She told Jane that they were from Romania. Jane had approached the family and inquired about going onto the subway to Stephansplatz. The chilled out youngsters were of no help to the Romanian family, which Jane decided was deliberate. There might have been a communication barrier, but Jane thought that they were just choosing not to assist the family on purpose.

One woman from the family spoke some English, so she told Jane that the rest of her family did not speak English at all. Jane did not speak Romanian, but somehow, they were able to communicate a bit. There was a mother and four young kids and two teenagers. Perhaps the woman who spoke with Jane was a sister or an aunt.

It was fun and funny for Jane, to try to read their faces and for them to read Jane's face. Everyone started laughing at each other as they tried to communicate their questions and stories about themselves, to their interpreter to translate to Jane. Jane was not suspicious that they actually knew what she was saying.

Between all of them, there were a lot of shoulder shrugs, hand gestures and head shaking, but it was comical all the same. As Jane spoke, they indicated that they understood *'mother'* and *'mom,'* *'children,'* *'grandchildren'* and *'kids.'* They also understood *'money,'* *'Romania,'* *'America,'* *'subway'* and *'visit,'* *'travel,'* and *'touring.'* Overall, Jane thought they did pretty well. Jane helped as best she could. They got their tickets and seemed very happy.

Finally, it was Jane's turn to use the machine and she got a ticket. The ride cost 1.80 Euros one way. She said goodbye to the family and wished them luck. She went down the stairs and waited, then got on the right car, which was crowded full of excited patrons or at least they seemed excited. She was thrilled to be there among other people, wondering where they were going and why. Even though she was cramped, she was happy to be moving. She finally got to her destination and successfully followed the signs to the plaza.

As she walked with everyone, up the stairs from the subway into the sunlight, she took her first photo at KartnerstraBe station. She could not believe she was in Stephansplatz, Austria and at the main plaza shops. The sounds and smells were incredible, with people buzzing about, left and right. For a brief moment it was a bit overwhelming, breathtaking and over stimulating. *"Could it be possible? Do I hear "Good Golly, Miss Molly?" Really?"* Jane wondered where the music was coming from.

She walked a few feet forward, then put her back up against a 'closed-for-the-day' business and took photos. She panned from the left and then to the right, as she snapped away. She saw hundreds of people, strolling about the many cafes, jewelry and dishware shops. There were knick-knack shops, clothing, accessories and purse shops. She saw a Forever 21 store, a McDonald's sign, signs for money exchanges and banks. Joseph told her that most of the shops would be closed due to the holiday and he was right, but that did not stop the slew of visitors that decided to frequent that exciting place.

She walked down the main street, taking her time and taking photographs, but took the same route when she headed back to the center of the plaza. She decided that if she got lost, she could just refer to her photos to find her way back to the subway. On her way back, she saw a street performer with a monkey puppet playing a small fake piano with Elvis music playing in the background. *"This is originally where the music was coming from,"* she thought.

Many patrons were gathered around the performer and tossed coins into his strategically placed traveling trunk. He was very entertaining and he animated the puppet to react to the different types of donors. He would have the eyes pop out of the monkey's head when pretty girls and women tossed their money. It was quite funny. But Jane was leery of most street performers, so much so, that she sometimes shivered. *"Creepy,"* she would say to herself. That performer did not give her the creeps that time.

She took photos of the various, beautiful and historic architecture. She took photos of families, singles and couples. She watched how most of the women carried themselves and carried their purses. The women were very casual, with a lighthearted attitude and almost carefree gait. In Jane's eyes, everyone was beautiful.

Jane felt as she had gotten older and perhaps a bit more cautious with each passing year, that she held onto her purse with a tighter grip. Perhaps it was because she felt frail and small on some days. But that day, she felt very safe at that moment. She began to travel west. She followed the sun and yes, she knew which way was west. She took her time, as she walked away from the main plaza.

She saw hot dog and sausage vendors. It smelled so delicious, but she could not partake, for her belly would not appreciate it. She saw a Starbucks. *"You can't get away from those guys."* There were also many assorted types of bars. She wished that she could go into one, but she would never enter a bar alone, she had told herself many times. There were more cafes as she passed several more side streets, then she walked to the end of plaza and headed south.

She came upon a small shop that was open and she entered for two reasons: She needed some immediate shade and she wanted to inquire if the clerk knew if any of the other shops were open. She walked around the tiny shop, looked at the many trinkets and knick-knacks, as she waited her turn in line. The customer in front of her was purchasing containers of assorted coffees. Even though Jane didn't drink coffee, because it was too acidic for her belly, she was sure that she loved coffee in another lifetime, for it always smelled so good.

She finally got to speak to the clerk named Sebastian. After exchanging pleasantries, they talked about why she was in Europe. He was cute and very personable. He did not seem to mind that Jane was able to share small talk with strangers. Jane asked if she could take his photo and he agreed. He stood next to her and she snapped the picture. The photo turned out to be kind of funny, with the two of them not completely in focus. They laughed about it. She took another photo of him behind the counter and continued to converse with him until the next customer came in. She thanked him for his time and his hospitality and then left. She felt good for having met another nice person.

Jane continued walking down the street and then she rounded a corner. As soon as she saw the spectacular domed church, her jaw hit the ground. She gasped. It was so beautiful and quite massive. She took more pictures of the shops and other outdoor decor as she walked down the street to the church.

On her way, she saw horse-drawn carriages, chocolate shops, pastry shops, with many window boxes and planters full of bright and beautiful greenery and flowers. She also saw many unique eclectic signs and shop shingles.

She approached a circular grassy area that was surrounded by crescent shaped buildings. There were more travelers of varying nationalities, who were also snapping photographs. She went past the many carriages, into the open-aired body of the church, which was having a Spanish exhibit. After taking photos of the sculptures and exquisite ceiling carvings, she walked through and out to other side. Then there was more gasping.

One building was as beautiful as the next. The area was filled with more people. There was a spacious park, buildings in the background, with statues of men on horses, and statues and carvings on the facades of the buildings. There also were statues on top of some of the buildings. She could see that that area went on and on, and it would have taken her many more hours to see it all. She wished at that moment that she was younger or at least had more energy to keep on going.

Jane thought that Lorraine, from the mall, was right. It would have been nice to have someone come along with her, to encourage her to keep on going. It would have been nice to have the strength to go one more mile and have someone with her, with whom she could share the gasping. It would have been great to be with someone who would have appreciated it as much as she did.

But, No. There was no football player or cowboy to cuddle with and smile at, at nightfall, as they talked about the sights and sounds that they had enjoyed that day. Jane was so happy to be there and could not have wished for a more beautiful day.

Jane was sweating and loving that feeling, for sweating made her feel quite alive. She was also feeling light-headed and overwhelmed, for she realized that she was on the constant verge of crying. It was sunny and it was hard for her to see if her photos turned out okay or if they were just too blurry.

She realized that she was hungry, so she went back inside the church for shade and to inquire with someone of the time. On her way back in, she met John and Dianne of Texas. *"Big-hearted people must live in Texas!"*

They told her that it was 2:00 p.m. They talked for 30 minutes or so, as they told each other why they were traveling. They told her that they had a blended family with all adult children and some grand kids and that they just came from Venice. They were missionaries. Dianne told Jane that meeting them afforded her to *"Experience a God moment."* They were just about to go the other direction, but somehow they and she bumped into each other out of sheer fate or out of an intervention. They were kind and sweet and wished her luck on her travels. They could not believe that Jane was traveling alone and that she was old enough to be a grandmother. Jane could tell that they were worried for her, as they reassured her that God was with her and would keep her and her family safe in His embrace. They wished each other well as they parted ways. She was happy that she had taken their photograph. A nice and much-needed encounter, indeed.

Somehow, Jane got lost upon her return from the church to the main plaza, but she had fun finding her way back. She took more photos of practically everything and anyone, then eventually, *"Viola,"* she found the main street that she needed. By then it was 3:00 p.m.

She took video and audio of her overwhelming experience at

the plaza, holding back tears as she spoke of what she was seeing. Then she walked east and found the subway, which confirmed that she was back from where she had started. She sat in a bit of shade, on a narrow ledge in front of a closed watch shop, and continued to people-watch. It had been about three hours since she had left the hotel and she was now very hungry and headachey. She had a bellyache and was also very thirsty. She took a moment to drink some water.

Many patrons had stopped near her. With cupped hands at their temples, they peered into the shop that was behind her. They looked inside the dimmed store, at the many pretty and expensive watches on display in the window. It certainly was a colorful display and way out of Jane's price range. Besides, she did not need a watch. She had a cell phone and she had the sun to guide her.

As she rested, she watched lots of families strolling by, with small ones in strollers, along with toddlers and preschoolers. There were teenagers with moms and dads, grandparents and friends. *"Sigh... Families."* Jane asked herself, *"Am I going to meet Pascal's kids? Am I going to have a lasting relationship with him? Or is fate going to be cruel to me again?"* She missed her kids the most at those moments when she saw happy families. She also missed her kids when she saw arguing families.

"Arguing and disagreeing was just a part of being in any kind of relationship," she thought. But she knew that there has to be a way to disagree without being hurtful. She never argued too much with Pascal, although he wanted to argue or debate...anything. But Jane

68

knew that she feared getting into arguments of any kind. She feared confrontation.

Arguments were very unpleasant when she was married, because her ex would call her names. Jane never got into arguments with boyfriend number one. Even though he was not always right, she dismissed most of his negative comments. He was negative about himself and about his job, among other things. She had to admit that she never agreed with his negativity about himself, because she had loved him so. She missed him even still and once had hoped to be a part of his family some day. Although he had cheated on her, she secretly wished him the best of luck. She was convinced that fate can sometimes be cruel.

As Jane continued to watch the families pass by, some of them were eating ice cream and it looked so good and refreshing. *"It certainly is not a good time to be lactose intolerant,"* she thought, but somehow she knew that was not going to stop her that day, if she chose to have ice cream. But she knew once she partook of the stuff made of dairy, she was certainly going to regret it somehow.

Jane wished that she was not lactose intolerant. But, there were many things that Jane would like to change about herself. She convinced herself that she can and will. There were many things that she would like to change and cannot, at least not on her own.

She sometimes believed that making necessary and unnecessary, permanent changes about herself would require a surgeon's knife and an orthopedist. It would require a full-time chiropractor and a hairdresser. It would require a digestive specialist, a trainer and lots of money. Or her life would require a super, fantastic, understanding man, who would give her faith in the world, that he would love her just the way she was.

But fear was also in Jane's head. She felt that she wanted a man in her life who would have to be *"man enough"* to do more than just tolerate her. He would have to *not* want to cheat. He would have to be the kind of man who would *not mind* the occasional weight gain and the occasional change of hair color. He would have to love her for her body, heart, mind and soul. He would have to love her for all of her oddities, strange and creative thoughts, and for her bizarre dreams and ideas.

Jane felt that if she found that man, then, *"I would have faith that I could have it all in this lifetime."* There were no assurances in her relationships with men. She was convinced that was just a part of life. There were no assurances and there never will be...

Jane knew that she was blessed to be there, right at that moment. Never in her life would she have thought it were possible, even on her own. Jane felt that she was blessed for being alive every day of her life.

Jane wanted to continue to believe that she was on some path, but she did not know where it was leading her. She had become accustomed to being poor, having limited resources and experiences, and she had accepted all of that. She had lived her life around that thought and realization.

She was quite aware that everything in her life had had a purpose.

Even though she may not have liked it or understood it, she had accepted it, knowing full well that she would understand it some day, as forever became apparent to her.

Jane felt that she had been blessed to have had many things in her life that brought her joy. She had been blessed to have had the many challenges that she had faced, in order to become the person that she was today. She had been blessed (and cursed) in knowing the many people in her past and in her present and will know in her future. At that very moment, she felt that she would not want to change her life in any way.

So far, she did not live her life with regrets. Maybe there were some things that she wished she could forget, especially her very bad decisions. But it was her troubles and her challenges...and...it was her grief and losses and blessings and faith that had brought her there to that very moment. She would not want it any other way, for it was those things and those experiences and more, that had given her inner strength.

She did not *need* a man in her life to make her feel fulfilled. But it would be nice to share those experiences with someone. It would be nice to hold his hand, as they lay down together at night, facing each other and talking about their day. Seeing his face, seeing his eyes and having that be the last thing that she saw as she drifted off to sleep, perhaps forever. She knew deep down that that was the stuff of fairy tales and fantasies, but she was a hopeless romantic at heart, who wore her heart on her sleeve...and on her shoulder...and on her back…and everywhere else.

Jane thought a lot about her life, as she sat there. She was aware that her thoughts were slightly disconnected. *"I can dream, I can hope. I can plan. I am very tired of crying myself to sleep a lot. There are many challenges that I have faced and will face, in my physical life. There are many challenges in my spiritual life and in my family life. There are many challenges in my financial life, in my home life and in my romantic life. I am also tired of being not just alone, but very lonely. I have faith that in the end, all will be okay. I not just believe it, I know it."* Jane was exhausted from thinking so much. Pascal popped into her head and she quickly got rid of him.

Jane also realized that days like that one were best experienced by her… alone. Her traveling experience had changed her, making her realize that she was capable and that she was strong. It made her realize that she was determined not to let anything break her or kill her.

"I am alone in this crowded, foreign place, but I am truly never alone. If it was meant to be, then it was meant to be." As she had stated before, she just better get used to it. *Whew!* What a lot to digest in such a short order. She had thought about all of that and more, as she sat and watched.

Jane began to hear church bells, which made her perk up. *"Where was that coming from?"* she wondered. As she sat there, she took more photos of the many surrounding shops and signs, like Rolex, Coca-cola, Konditorei *(What does that mean?)*. There were signs for Bipi (which she believed was a chain of cafes) and Salamander Firenze Restaurant. She wondered what they served or what foods they featured there. *"I must come back and partake some day,"* she thought.

She realized that she needed to get up and find food soon, but she needed to do more resting, especially for her lower back. Jane sort of regretted wearing her sandals, but her ensemble looked totally cute. She smiled as she thought of that.

Jane opted to go to McDonald's, which by doing so, made her break a promise to her friend's son-in-law. A month earlier, she had met him at a funeral and she had promised him that she would not eat there, while visiting Europe. As they conversed during the wake about her plans for the summer, he told her, *"You mustn't eat there!"* He told her to eat at the local diners and cafes, to experience the whole of European culture. Jane promised him and agreed with him at that moment in time. As a matter of fact, Jane was basically excited to experience new foods, but was also aware of her temperamental tummy. But for the moment, Jane went where she needed to go, based on three main things: *Affordability, Convenience and Familiarity…and that was that.*

As she walked into that small, narrow restaurant, that was packed with customers from all over the world, she could hear American music, playing on the PA system: *"Never Gonna Leave This Bed"* by Train, was the first song. Jane had no trouble bee-bopping her head to it and singing along, while standing in line, which she was sure irritated the other patrons. She eventually heard The Plain White T's, Coldplay, some Country music, some music that she did not recognize and some other music from the 80's.

She stood in line, waited and listened to the many accents of the workers and customers, as she figured out what she wanted to eat and the cost. *"Do I see beer for sale at McDonald's? Man, oh, man, that sounds so good at this moment!"* she thought.

She asked the young cashier if she spoke English and the cashier responded with the hand gesture of *'a little'* by holding up her hand and indicated *'a small portion'* with her thumb and forefinger. By then, everyone had responded that same way to Jane. Jane ordered a hamburger sans onions and cheese, an ice water, a diet Coke without ice and some fries. She had cut fried foods out of her diet, but somehow forgot that day. It cost 7.30 Euros, plus a bit extra for ketchup. *"Ouch. Some things should just be for free, dammit!"* Jane thought.

With her tray in hand, Jane headed upstairs and found a small table in a corner with her back to the wall so she can observe the crowd. She sat down and realized that she was badly shaking. She took a deep breath, prayed that she would not pass out and that someone would not steal her purse, if she did. She said Grace and began to eat. *"Damn! They put onions and cheese on my hamburger, plus it has 2 patties, not one,"* she thought. On any other day, she would have made a small fuss, but she opted not to, at that time.

Jane was weak and tired. She did not want to think that someone would spit on her food if she complained, but that thought had popped into her head all the same. It was just easier to try to scrape off the onions and cheese, so that was what she did. She downed her drink too fast and had to stop to breathe.

Her head was pounding, but slowly began to feel much better as she took her time eating. She ate only a few fries and was proud of herself for that. She briefly spoke to the family sitting next to her, who spoke with an Italian accent. There was a mom, a dad and a daughter, who looked to be about 8 years old. They commented on the food being very good and the music, too, as they all observed the daughter singing along. She was so cute. For some reason, Jane thought for a moment that she would not ever change the fact that she could talk to perfect strangers at any given moment... anywhere...any time. That was one thing that she liked about herself. And that was one of the things about herself that most of her ex-beaus disliked. She never understood that.

Jane eventually finished her meal, threw away her trash, went downstairs and out of the building, walking west, then turned south to visit the rest of the main street. As she walked, she saw a different fast food restaurant three blocks away. She listened to the buzzing sounds of multiple conversations that she could not understand. She also saw a clown, piddling about, making balloon sculptures. *"F*ck! I hate clowns! No offense to those who need to make a living, while covering up their faces with makeup to hide their true* *expressions. Sorry."*

Jane took more pictures along the way. She heard someone laughing, who sounded like one of her previous co-workers. She was still a bit headachey and she made a mental note that she was squinting a bit. On her stroll, she saw a variety of people who were normal, average, typical and not so typical-looking. She saw that all young children behave the same, when fussy and agitated and tired. Some people were large and some were small. Some people were particularly scary-looking and some not so scary. Some people were gorgeous and some were not so easy on the eyes. She thought that life would be boring, if everyone was the same.

She saw another Starbucks *(Damn!)*, more jewelry stores, money exchanges, accessories and more watch shops, more cafes and some hotels. She stopped for a moment or two at an outdoor flower shop and took many photos of the various, colorful plants and arrangements. The bright display was invigorating. She thought that it would be nice to get some flowers, but then, where would she put them? Jane loved many varieties of flowers. She loved picking them, growing them, smelling them, having them and she felt as if everyone should have flowers in their lives…daily. She leaned down, smelled them and took in their pleasant aromas. She felt better having stopped there. *"Since I took some photos, I can have flowers on my desktop everyday, if I so choose."*

Jane finally stopped at a large intersection, realizing that that, too, went on forever. She wished at that moment that she had the stamina to continue, but, alas, she did not. She took a deep breath, a deep sigh and turned around, and she was sure glad that she did. She approached two young and attractive men, who were patiently waiting for customers to need their services as rickshaw drivers. They were sitting still in their flowery-decorated vehicles, taking a break in the shade of their canopies. She immediately struck up a conversation with them.

She met Shayne from Spain, who was twenty-two years of age and Ben, who was twenty-seven years old and from Nuremberg. They were University students and had answered an ad in a local paper, in order to get their jobs.

She told them that she was touring. She got their permission to take their photos and to talk about them in her journal. Ben asked if she was married and after much laughing, Jane told him that she was old enough to be his mother. Jane felt that he was flirting and she thought it was quite cute of him to do that. He guessed that she was thirty-two years old. *"Bless your heart!"* she exclaimed, and again, she laughed. She had guessed their ages and she was exactly right. She told Ben that he was the same age as her son and she told him that she was also a grandmother.

Jane thought that tidbit of information had intrigued Ben all the more, as she saw a glimpse of a spark in his eyes and as one of his eyebrows was raised. She took a moment to tell them about her grandchildren. At that moment, she jokingly wished that she had stamina, indeed, as she thought that it would have been wonderful to take a ride on Ben's rickshaw.

She thanked them for talking with her, then she left. As she continued to walk back towards the subway, she caught a glimpse of them in the reflection of a nearby store, as she saw that they had looked back at her. *"What were they looking at or looking for?"* she wondered. At that moment, she was thankful of how diligent she had been with all those leg lifts that she had done lately, as she was almost sure that they were looking at...and thinking about...her cute butt.

On her way back, Jane walked past a small church entrance, that was narrow and almost hidden among the other shops. She smelled the distinct aroma of incense and the smell stopped her in her tracks. She took a deep breath and actually closed her eyes for a brief moment. She was instantly taken back to her childhood of many visits to her family's church for mass, school and other fond playful activities.

Jane had heard or read a long time ago, that the sense of smell was one of the strongest senses that humans have. It can take one back to good and bad memories from childhood, and so on. She smelled the incense and she could recall good memories of singing along with the choir at church. As a youngster, she was told on many occasions that she sang too loudly, but although the comment was meant to embarrass her, she did not care. She loved to sing, whether or not others thought that she could sing well.

Jane thought for a moment about when she smelled oranges, tangelos and walnuts, she was taken back to Christmas, when she and all of her siblings got those items put in their stockings. That was always a good memory. Any time she smelled homemade green beans with ham hocks, she was taken back to the memory of her grandmother, who seemed to make the best green beans on the planet.

When she smelled snow, she was whisked away to childhood memories of being on a sled and flying down the *'suicide hills'* of Sandalwood Park and on the property up the street from her childhood home in Dayton. When Jane tasted and smelled licorice jelly beans, she thought of her family's Easter gatherings. She could recall herself and her sisters wearing white cotton and silk dresses and her brothers wearing black suits. She recalled a photograph of them, posing in front of their garage, from back in the mid-1960s. Some Easters were warm and some Easter days were very cold. Either way, those memories were always good, too. It was always a joy to look for pastel-colored eggs in their backyard.

Wax candy, hot dogs, white-powdered doughnuts and apple cider brought up wonderful memories of trick-or-treating on Halloween. Almond-scented and cherry-scented lotions reminded her of her mother. Vapor rub reminded her of her mother, too, for it was her mother who took care of her, when Jane was sick.

Of course, there was also the bad or unpleasant memories from the past, too. Once Jane smelled the cooking combinations of sizzling onions, green peppers and mushrooms, she sometimes wanted to regurgitate. She had had that concoction around the time of having the flu. It was very unpleasant. When Jane smelled root beer, she thought of being around ten years old and throwing up at Kings Island Amusement Park, after getting off of one of the roller coasters. It had taken her years before she was able to drink that beverage again. To say the least, the smell of that incense was an enjoyable one.

Jane heard some music and walked a few steps back to see two musicians rehearsing on their guitar and saxophone. They were playing *"The Pink Panther"* theme, which for some reason, made her laugh. She smiled and took their picture. She needed a short break, so she sat next to a tired woman, on a square bench that was attached to a very low and wide planter. Jane had realized that her left leg was fatigued and started shaking. *"What is that all about?"* she thought. It was time to go back to the hotel and rest up for the night.

Jane's back was hurting and all she could think about was how much she regretted not bringing her back-support belt with her on the trip. She was looking forward to resting on the bed at the hotel. She got back to the subway in a short period of time, got a ticket, got on the subway and was back to LaSalle Street around 5:00 p.m.

She was exhausted and still overwhelmed for some reason, as she was aware of a pending surge of emotions that were beginning to well up inside of her. She wanted to bawl and she was not sure why. However, she held it together as she walked down the street back to the hotel.

Once inside her room, she plopped down on the bed on her belly, lay there for a minute and just closed her eyes and rested. She knew that if she stayed in that position for too long, her lower back would be killing her that much more. She eventually rolled over onto her side and curled her back, with her knees up to her chin and just lay there and smiled, thinking about the day's events.

A bit later, she got up, turned on the TV and sat on the edge of the bed and watched in amazement of all the silly things that were on the tube. There was a comedy show, with actors dressed as Roman gladiators. They were behaving very effeminately and she could not understand a word that they were saying, but it was hilarious anyway.

She watched quite a bit of *"Flubber"* with Robin Williams. Since she had seen it before, she could follow a bit of the plot even though it was in German. As always, he was hilarious. For some reason, she thought of Mr. Williams and how fun it would have been to meet him and how fun it would be to be stranded on a tropical island with him. He would have been able to find humor in anything. She thought that she would love to be in love with a man who had a natural, great sense of humor. She thought of Pascal and again, she quickly rushed him out of her mind.

She turned the channel for a little bit and listened to a music station that was playing 80's tunes. When she got tired of that, she watched some weird commercials and could not figure out what was being said or what was being sold. She left the TV on for the noise, then got out her camera and took pictures of the scenery outside. After that, she sat at the table and ate the rest of her hamburger from lunch. It was something that she was sure to regret later.

While sitting there, she zoned out for a bit, just thinking of her wonderful son and his beautiful fiance. She thought of her beautiful daughter and her handsome, brave husband who may get deployed to dangerous lands. She thought of her beautiful, beautiful young granddaughters, then from out of nowhere, her subconscious mind made a statement: *"Let them go"*…

That snapped her to attention. She bawled for quite some time, feeling sorry for herself, thinking about all of her compiled sadness about her home, about her past loves and her need for employment. She regrettably thought of her estrangement from most of her family members and of some friends and for what she felt was the largest loss of all in her life: *Her kids.*

She felt sorry for herself, as she thought of her son getting married and moving farther away, possibly to New York, with his wonderful, intelligent and beautiful new wife. She felt sorry for herself, for she knew things with Pascal were not going to last. She just did not know how she knew that, but she felt as if she did.

She asked herself these questions:
"What signs were there to let me know this?…
What things had he said or did not say, that make me know this?…
What things have I said or did not say that make me know this?…
What same behaviors and mistakes was I making to ensure this?"
And the most baffling question of all was, *"If my mother was still alive, would I still be behaving like this?"* Jane was willing to tackle the answer to that question, most of all.

She felt sorry for herself for a bit longer, as she wondered what direction her life was going to take. Was she going to successfully go back to school and find another rewarding job? Was she going to find true happiness with a nice man some day? Was she going to find a true best friend, who was her age and knew what it was like to be *'this old,'* who would treat her like she deserved to be treated? And would that best friend be able to travel with her, go camping with her, as they journeyed together into the last days of their lives?

She realized that it was the exhaustion from her outing, which was contributing to her feeling a bit blue. She also realized that those were only some of the many thoughts that loomed over her head on a daily basis lately. She realized that it would be up to her to deal with them, to process them and to realize that was just a part of life in general and for her to *"just get the hell over it."* *"Someday, I will die"*...she thought... *"and in the long and short run of life... none of this will matter in the end."*

Once she was done feeling sorry for herself, she tuned back into the shows on the TV and there was a program that was similar to Guy Fieri's *"Diners, Drive-Ins and Dives."* The host was a very large man, who really loved to eat. For some reason, she found the show to be hilarious. She thought that it was too bad that she could not see Guy. She really loved that gorgeous hunk of a man!

Around 7:30 p.m, she took a moment and dialed her friend, Toni, and got through. It was so good to hear her voice. They talked for about 20 minutes, as Jane hurriedly tried to update her on what she had been doing.

Jane asked Toni to call and leave a message with her dad and with Pascal, not knowing if giving her Pascal's phone number would be well received. She took a chance and she was glad that she did. She hung up with Toni, then stripped off most of her clothes, then downloaded the 139 photos from her camera onto her computer. She labeled some pictures and enjoyed recapping the moments from earlier in the day. She watched soccer for a while, then she decided to do some yoga and sit-ups on the floor.

Recently, whenever Jane was getting ready to do yoga or a workout, her thoughts would unfortunately drift to her one of her ex-beaus. She would look down at her chubby belly and frown. He had called her fat and made fun of her for not being able to do sit-ups. Ever since they had broken up, she had made it a loose habit to try to work on that task. She had convinced herself that she was doing it for *Jane,* not for him. By the time she was able to take her trip, she was able to do sit-ups with success, but when she did, she had mastered her strange mantra. And that day was no different.

While her back was on the floor, she said: *"You can, you can, you can"*...then she would sit up and say: *"...do this, you mother-f*cker."* Then she repeated that with each motion. When she was done, she yelled out, *"Tell me that I can't do that, you stupid mother-freaker"* She finished her cussing sit-ups, then she took a shower, brushed and flossed and put on some lounging clothes.

Jane felt so much better, at least for a while. She sat in bed and journaled about the day, then she started to get a bit of a bellyache in her upper belly. *"I knew it!"* Jane came to regret the banana, fries, cheese, hamburger and pop that she had had at lunch. She had not been eating well or making sound food choices and she knew it had something to do with her anxiety. She needed more fiber and some over-the-counter fiber meds now. *"But where can I find some?"* she wondered.

Jane continued to let the TV run, occasionally flipping channels, as she loosely watched some of *"NCIS," "Two and a Half Men," "The Bourne Identity," "Nickelodeon," "Crocodile Dundee," "Hawaii 5-0"* and *"La Chocolat."* That movie was so good. She had seen it at least two dozen times. She was happy that she owned the DVD and she could watch it any time she desired.

She bawled at the scene where the mom thought that her daughter was dead. She bawled like a baby. Jane tried to turn away from it, but somehow she just could not. As she watched the TV mindlessly, she realized a lot of those shows were repeating again and again, over a period of several times and in several days. That happened at home, too. How boring.

She wrote down some words, from commercials and such, to show Joseph and ask him what they meant. She learned some small words and words for days of the week and of the month. She was slowly making progress, but she was not expecting to learn the entire German language in 10 days! She envied her granddaughters, for they would be able to pick up that new language in no time.

"Sigh...grandchildren." Jane knew that she would miss them a lot.

Throughout the course of the night, she heard many emergency vehicle sirens and wondered what that was all about. Sometime later, she turned off the computer, did some more yoga stretches, opened her luggage and got out the stolen shirt with Pascal's cologne all over it. She had secured it in a plastic baggie. She turned off the lights, left the TV on low volume, plopped back into bed and opened up the baggie. Jane took a deep breath, closed her eyes and drifted off to sleep. She was snug under the covers, on her left side, with a pillow between her knees.

Jane thought of Pascal's strong arms wrapped around her. She thought of his warm steady breath on the back of her neck. She truly loved the fact that he genuinely loved to cuddle. In her thoughts, he kissed her cheek then she turned to kiss him. He wrapped his fingers in hers, holding hands, like they had done so many times before, with their hands resting against her face. Jane missed him to her very core and she wondered if he missed her, but somehow deep down, she knew better. *Sigh...*

"Despite that last thought, Thank You for another great day. I am so thankful for my many blessings. Please keep me and my family in Your prayers. Amen."

Monday...

At 1:30 a.m., Jane awoke with dull pains in her lower belly. What specifically was causing her ongoing bellyache? Could it be the caffeine, too, that just woke her up? She wasn't sleeping well anyway. As she was waking, she had a thought of her granddaughters and she wanted to cry, but she was happy that she did not. Jane was bloated and belching. *"Nice going there, lady! Is it my food from lunch or was it the diet Coke or could it just be all of the above, plus stress?"* she wondered. She turned on the TV. *"City Slickers 2"* was on and she watched that for a moment, then turned to other channels.

Jane accidentally found a channel with some kind of porn, with five half-naked girls in a kitchen. So being the curious woman that she was, she watched for a split minute, but then she remembered that that stuff gave her headaches. She always thought that it was possibly due to being formerly Catholic, so she quickly turned the channel to find something else.

"NCIS" was on again, plus *"La Chocolat," "Funny Girl," "The Fresh Prince of Bel-Air"* and *"The Mentalist."* As she had said before, *"All and nothing is on."* Although she thought the lead on *"The Mentalist"* was downright hot, she turned off the TV and made herself fall back asleep. His image was the last thing that she saw, so she was okay with falling asleep with him on her mind.

Around 10:00 a.m., Jane woke up, turned the TV back on and watched soccer. *"I can always watch that and never get tired of it,"* she thought. She used the bathroom, then lounged around for a bit, happy that her bellyache was gone. She still felt very exhausted, then she eventually showered to feel refreshed. She got dressed in plaid shorts, a white tank and an orange top, plus sandals. She put on some makeup and blow-dried her hair. As she saw her reflection, she thought that she looked pretty good for an haggard, tired and scared Daytonian grandmother.

She was done by 11:30 a.m., so she went downstairs, stopped at the lobby bar and bought a beverage. She went out the front door, sat at the outdoor cafe and ate a fiber bar and drank her orange juice. Once she was done, she took a deep breath and walked south and into a run-down looking neighborhood.

Jane was not sure if it was truly safe or not, but for some reason, she did not care as much as perhaps she should have. She wanted to go a different direction, instead of the same way every day. It was another beautiful, sunny day and she needed the fresh air. She wanted the brisk walk and to be just out and about among some people, taking photos and sight-seeing.

Within minutes of her walk, it was quite clear that she was in a bad part of town, with its broken down and boarded up buildings. There was trash on the sidewalks and in the streets, with trash cans and recyclable receptacles overflowing at the curbs. She noticed that there was lots of graffiti and broken glass scattered about and that the bus stops were not pristine, like she had anticipated. Why did she think that all parts of Vienna were going to be well groomed? Why did she assume that to be true of any city? For some reason, Jane expected more when she walked that alternate route.

Within minutes, she had realized her possible mistake, but kept on walking anyway. She did not feel in danger quite yet and had faith that she was going to be okay. She took photos, here and there, keeping aware of her surroundings.

As she continued her walk, a car pulled up to the curb in front of her and a man exited the driver's side, then came around and opened the passenger door to remove a box from the front seat. Once he did that and then turned around, he shot a sort of look at her, that made her instantly uncomfortable. It was a backhanded compliment, so to speak, of admiration, but of disgust all the same. He winked at her and whistled a quick note, indicating *"Ooo-laa-laa."* She was slightly insulted. *"Oh, please, and shut the hell up,"* she thought. She could do nothing but smile a fake smile and went on her way.

At that moment, she guessed that everyone in the neighborhood must have known everyone else. There was lots of talking going on, all of which she did not understand. Somehow, it was quite evident that she was a stranger. She was basically well dressed, but not too childish-looking. She felt okay to keep walking, but kept her peripherals in check. The man entered the building that he had parked in front of, and she wondered if she was going to be safe upon her return.

Jane continued to photograph the old buildings, the hotels, the dilapidated doors and windows, and the closed store fronts and cafes. She photographed the busy street and the bus stops filled with many people and the beaten down pauper strips, filled with weeds and wildflowers. She even took pictures of the pigeons that were pecking the ground. They didn't seem to mind the attention.

As she crossed the two intersections that she approached on her little tour, she got whistled at and gawked at and even got yelled at, from some people in the moving vehicles. She had no clue what was being said, but she was sure that it had to be along the same dialogue as what that earlier man was thinking.

What was Jane thinking? She was not, which was good for the moment. What was she doing or wearing to provoke that immature, sophomoric behavior from those adult men? It did not matter. Men are pigs. Why didn't she turn back? *Curiosity.* Jane was not sure why, but she just felt compelled to keep walking.

At a corner, she passed a cafe that had many patrons. There were families, singles and couples and waiters of various sizes. Jane could smell the aroma of pizza and pasta and it was a wonderful, welcoming smell. She was now near a highway, with one huge overpass ahead of her. There was a bike path in front of her and as she rounded the corner, there was another vacant outdoor cafe. It had many tables, chairs and large, red umbrellas. She guessed that the cafe was closed for the day.

Jane kept walking and watching many people. There were many families on bikes, behind the sparse trees and bushes that lined the bike path. She was near a park and she could hear the laughter of children and hear music. That section of town was unlike the area where she had just rounded the corner. There was more cafes and stores, but the ethnicity was somehow different.

The people there were possibly of middle-Eastern decent. The restaurants were serving a different kind of fare, for the smells were different, but good. She chose not to walk any slower and she also opted not to take any more photos at that time. Along the sidewalk were park benches and more cafe tables and chairs, all occupied by many men. She did not see any women near the stores at all. *"How odd,"* she thought.

Jane met eyes with all of them and smiled and they all smiled back. Again, she was not feeling threatened, but she was aware that the hair on the back of her neck was slightly raised. She did not feel in complete danger, but she also felt that that feeling could change at any moment, at any time…without her being too aware of what was happening.

She did not consider herself stupid, but she was very cautious. She turned to the left and walked along a tree-lined, park bench-lined, paved path which led to a courtyard and to the steps of a beautiful, huge church. She took photos of the church and of that path, for it was a bit run-down, but still pretty. *"Like I am,"* she sarcastically thought.

She convinced herself to take a more brisk walk home and then rest and wait for Joseph. No one knew that she was there and for some reason, a thought hit her brain, that if something happened to her, no one would know. Why did she think that? *"What provoked my brain to have that thought?"* she wondered.

With that, she turned and headed home, without taking her time to take more photos. She did not want to waste any time to figure out why that popped into her head. *"Just go,"* she thought, *"and you just better listen to whatever or whomever is telling you to do that."* And she did.

Jane was fine, upon her return. She was fine, even during the walk, but anything can happen...any time...any where...and she was aware of that. She wanted to feel alive, and yet she did. She was not going to let too much fear rule her world, although she lived with some kind of fear of something, every day. She had tried to keep that battle of fear in her life under control and so far overall, she had achieved some degree of success.

As long as she could remember, Jane suffered from unfounded and genuine fear and physical pain, much like her mother did. Jane even had some of her fears provoke her headaches, her ongoing sadness, her upper belly bloating and bellyaches and her many heartaches. She did not like it and had always wanted to change it and she knew that mostly it was out of her (immediate) control. Especially when she was not immediately aware that it was fear that she was facing.

She had always said about herself that *"The light bulb goes on so late for me, most days."* But in Jane's opinion, her mother did not do much to alleviate her own fears. Her mother did not face them head on. She did not try to understand them, Jane thought. Her mother stayed at home and suffered in silence.

In regards to her mother, Jane believed that all of her siblings knew what their mother's fears were. One of her fears was going out in public. Jane believed that even her mother did not understand them. Jane knew that when her mother had some fears over something, her mother had belly issues, too. And when things changed around her, that she could not control, her mother would get very upset and sometimes inconsolable.

One particular incident from her childhood that stood out in Jane's mind, was the time when her mother went grocery shopping on a Saturday, which she almost always did. When her mother had entered the store, most or all of the displays and aisles had been changed since the last weekend she had been there. Her mother had always made her grocery list based on what was in each aisle, which Jane had always thought was very strange. On that day, her mother was all a-fluster. Her mother could not concentrate, she could not think and she could not shop.

So she immediately left the store and got back in the car. Jane's dad, who always drove and who was sitting in the front seat waiting for them to finish shopping, had to go into the store and shop for his hungry family.

Even currently, Jane had thought that it was that incident from her youth that made her subconsciously make the decision to *NOT* be like her mother.

So, as Jane had gotten older, she took chances, like speaking to anyone and speaking to strangers. She rode her bike as far as her little legs could drive her, all around her own neighborhood. Jane went into unknown stores, taking her time and buying new and different foods to eat. Since she had to walk to and from grade school, which was a mile one way from her home, Jane took her time doing that, without fear.

Since she had to walk to and from high school, which was two miles one way, she also took her time doing that. But sometimes that was sort of scary, but she did it anyway. Once Jane was able to afford a car, she drove wherever she wanted, all around Dayton, Cincinnati and Columbus. And once she had gotten married and had children and had a great job at the airport, her family took vacations together to New York, Florida, California, Texas, Chicago, Boston and Colorado. They even went camping in the Grand Canyon.

As Jane had gotten much older, ironically she had to admit to herself that she was more like her mother, than she wanted to be. Her mother was not all that bad, Jane thought.

When she was in grade school, Jane wanted to have a mother like most of the other kids in school. She wanted her mother to go shopping with her at the mall, go trick-or-treating and go to King's Island and ride the roller coasters. She wanted her mother to be a volunteer Girl Scout leader, to be involved in band and in choir and to take Jane to ballet lessons, soccer practice and games and softball games. She wanted her mother to let her go to cheerleading camp or even horseback riding.

When Jane had her own children, she wanted her mother to travel with them, to stay in hotels and visit far away states. She wanted her mother to hike with them in Yellow Springs and drive with them to visit her sister in Tennessee. Jane encouraged her mother to get on an airplane, but her mother never could muster up the courage. Jane felt that her mother was paralyzed by her fears.

With her own kids, Jane made a grand effort to be the mother that she always wanted her mother to be. Jane feared those three flights to Europe, but she got on them anyway and she was proud of herself for doing so.

Her fears were not limited to travel or strangers or eating strange foods, because as she had gotten older, she had fears of abandonment of some kind as well. Jane never knew where that fear had come from.

After her divorce, Jane had waited many years before she knew that she was strong enough and therefore, capable enough, to date. So, she agreed to go out on a blind date. But Jane was the one who was blind...

When she was involved with boyfriend number one for about three years, she was happy and quite content for a while. Later in the relationship, she had suspicions that were ultimately right. Her very first boyfriend after her divorce, which was three boyfriends ago, had been cheating on her. Because of his cheating and her suspicion of it, she had massive headaches and her belly had been horribly distended. She was a *stress mess*.

She had many visits to her digestive specialist and was scheduled to have her gall bladder removed. When she was able to confront her suspicions and admit to herself that she was right, it was too late. He admitted that his cheating had been going on for ten months! He broke up with her on a holiday, via texts and during one dreaded phone call initiated by Jane. Jane's life was forever changed.

Jane let her anxieties and fears of his cheating rule her gut. She let it rule her belly, her digestion, her health and her physiology. It ruled her world. Therefore, she believed that it caused her to have physical *'inner'* pain and suffering, which can be deadly. It caused her to be bloated and it caused her to not eat and sleep. She also missed several days of work because of it.

In the long run, her instincts about him were right. Jane had feared being cheated on and she had told him as much, when they had first met, because of being cheated on in her marriage. To add insult to injury, he backed out of helping her, in her time of need, during and after her gall bladder surgery.

From that day forward, Jane wanted to be able to speak out when she felt that she was right about her intuitions regarding her relationships. She was never able to accomplish that. She wanted to be wrong, but she was rarely wrong. She was just making mistakes and staying blind. She wanted to remain happy and she wanted to be loved.

Even to this day, Jane had always felt as if she had never recovered from that heartbreak. Oh yes, she was over him, but she was never over *what* he had done to her. She had feared that so much. She had even asked him not to lie and cheat on her, but inevitably, he did. It was hard to admit that she had met another liar and cheater.

Jane's sadness lasted a very long time, even though she knew that their breakup was inevitable. She had to admit that the worrying and the ruminating that she did over many things that she feared and could not control, were some of her many shortcomings. It was up to her to handle that stress and move on from it.

"I am still a work of art in progress." she would tell herself.

Jane feared getting divorced, even though she was the one who initiated it and moved out with her two kids. She feared being on her own financially and did not know if she was able to support her kids. But she did it, by working three jobs and going back to school full-time. She was very proud of herself for that. She knew that getting divorced was one of the best things that she did for herself and for her kids and they are better because of it.

Once back in the hotel, Jane went straight to the restaurant and motioned to a young waitress. She came over and gave Jane a menu. She sat in the far corner, at a booth, with her back to the wall and a good view of the rest of the restaurant and of the street. She took some photos from her vantage point, then looked at the menu, happy that everything was in dual languages.

The waitress came back to the table, Jane ordered dinner, then she helped herself to some prepackaged breadsticks that were on the table centerpiece. Jane wrote about her day on a small notepad and listened to the music in the background. She bee-bopped to *"Sharp Dressed Man," "Last Friday Night,"* and *"I've Gotta Feeling,"* among others. Her food was served quickly and she enjoyed it all.

She had grilled chicken, with rice and a light gravy, along with broccoli and water. She took her time, feeling as if she needed to eat and prayed that as soon as she would get back upstairs to her room, she would have some lower belly relief. When she was done, she paid 17.00 Euros for her meal, gathered her things and went to her room.

She took a quick shower, then got dressed in casual shorts, a pink top, white undershirt and sandals. She blow-dried her hair, put on some makeup, then packed up her belongings. She checked and re-checked the bathroom, the bed and the table for misplaced items.

The room was not that big, so she was not sure why she thought she would have lost anything. She made the bed, turned on the TV, sat on the bed with her back against the headboard and watched, mindlessly. She was so happy to be resting.

A bit later, it started raining and the sound was very welcoming. The phone rang and it was Joseph. He was running late due to the storm and the heavy traffic, but he would be at the hotel in about 30 minutes. *"Cool,"* she thought. She told him to be careful and as she hung up, she had a smile on her face. *"Finally,"* she thought, *"a real friend to talk to, to have dinner with, with whom I can share my experiences."*

She watched the rain come down with force, against the glass barrier that was attached to the fire escape near her windows. She hoped that the rain would let up for their hour drive back to Joseph's home. She gathered her things and *'blew a kiss goodbye'* to her room. She was happy to leave, for the most part.

Jane went to the front reception and two clerks greeted her. The cute male clerk, who had originally checked her in, helped with the check-out procedures. *"Thanks."* She turned in the key and gave him a credit card. She paid the bill, then she thanked them for their hospitality and walked away. Jane was thrilled that that was over. She walked outside and stood under the overhang and waited. By then, the rain was down to a heavy drizzle.

Just a few minutes later, a silver car pulled up, parked and out from the vehicle emerged Joseph. As soon as he saw her, they smiled and she was immediately taken back to high school. He looked exactly the same, but older, because they were both older. His smile was just as beautiful as the last time that she had seen him some 25 years ago. He was just the welcoming sight that Jane needed. It was as if time had stood still. She approached him, they greeted each other, they hugged and he helped put her stuff into the open trunk of his car.

Now, Jane had to be honest with herself. She sort of perceived a bit of disappointment from him. Was she mistaken? She thought, *"I am not the cute, bubbly, thin cheerleader that he had known and liked and remembered many years earlier."* So, for some reason, she sensed a small regret, but not by anything more than a feeling that she had gotten, when their eyes had met. Damn, she hated to be right…as she hoped that she was not.

She thought, *"I am not shorter, just older. I am not ugly, but I am not a "10." My hair is not as super-long and thick as it once was, but I do have thick, healthy short auburn hair, thanks to hair care products."*

"I am not fat, but I am not thin. I am not a trendsetter, but a thrifty, single, divorced mother of two. I am a cute, perky grandmother,

at that…and I am SIMPLY COMPLICATED."

Jane was still not so sure why she had sensed that in him, but it did not matter. He welcomed her all the same and she felt welcomed. She was not sure that she was expecting anything more than true friendship and hospitality and that was what she got from her wonderful friend. *"Thank you, Joseph, for being you."*

As they drove, the rain held out a bit, then returned with some force. They talked about her three flights, her hotel stay, the trip into Stephansplatz and her ex-husband. She knew that Joseph was still friends with him since high school, too. She told him that her talented son was getting married to a wonderful girl, whom she adored and had come to love as her own daughter. She told him that they were working together for the same company and sometimes traveled to New York for work.

They talked about her granddaughters and she boasted how beautiful they were. They talked about her beautiful daughter and her sweet husband, who was in the military. They talked about his daughters, his ex, his work, his parents and his siblings.

They had a lot to recap, but they were able to stay focused, even with the storm and the traffic. He drove fast, when he could, in his super-hot Alfa Romero. A sleek silver car with fine lines, gray leather interior, deep red dash lighting, with all the extras that a car could offer. It was very cool, indeed.

Jane just relied on a car that worked and didn't care whether or not she owned a vehicle with all the bells and whistles that Joseph's car had. She wouldn't have cared if her car had rust, if it would be a disgusting mustard color or if it even had doors, but just as long as it got her from *"A to B."* Her car was simple and old and reliable, just like she was, and she was quite comfortable with that.

He drove around parts of Vienna, pointing out historical places, churches, buildings that diplomats and even our President had visited. He showed her the farmer's market, The Opera House, places where he previously lived and many restaurants. It was nice, but hard to see because of the rain. She promised him that she would come back and visit.

A bit later, they hit the highway and were on their way to his village. The highway was smooth sailing, with minimal stops. The city, and then, eventually the countryside, was swooshing by and she was a bit disappointed that she could not see much of anything for quite some time. They went through a village called Pinkafeld *(the pink river)* and by then the rain had virtually stopped. That was one of the cutest places that she had ever seen. It was small, quaint, with many of its buildings and homes close to the street, with narrow roads and narrow sidewalks. She saw window boxes and planters full of flowers, placed outside of homes and businesses, making that place all the more sweet. The colors were soft and deep, light and pale. She could imagine herself staying there and getting to know its people.

They drove through and outside of the village, traveling along rural streets, going through a circular intersection, then into Oberwart. He asked if they could stop at his work so he could feed his fish and she agreed. They did just that, passing by the hospital where he used to work and where he did his clinical studies. Right next door was his office. They parked and went inside. By then, the rain was done for the night. His building was made up of other doctors' offices and was very typical looking. He turned on some lights and showed her around, after he fed the fish.

Joseph was a medical doctor, a psychologist and a neurologist. He gave Jane one of his business cards. He showed her his specific office where his desk was, the exam rooms and the reception area, too. She was happy that he showed her this aspect of his life. It was clean, bright and welcoming. What a major accomplishment to have had schooling for three major careers!

From there, they drove to his home, past other businesses, through the downtown area, past pastures and fields, then into the driveway of his row house (condo). He activated the garage door opener and they drove inside, exited the vehicle, gathered her things and went inside his home. His home had a narrow porch and a doorway to the garage off of the porch. It had a foyer where he kept his coats and jackets on a long rack and also a place for his boots and shoes, including an umbrella stand.

There was a set of steps to the right that led upstairs and a set of stairs to the left that led downstairs to the main part of his home. They went upstairs first, where he showed her the spare bedroom and they put her stuff there. It had wooden floors, a futon and two large windows that overlooked the backyard, plus a small piano and a large plant. He showed her how to operate the blinds, which were attached to the outside of the windows. *"How odd,"* she thought. Then he showed her his daughter's room, that had bunk beds, a desk and a dresser. He showed her where the toilet was, which was in a its own individual, narrow room separate from the bathroom. *"How odd, too."*

Next to that was the bathroom, which was huge, with a very large tub and a telescopic shower head at the base of the edge of the tub. The main hallway was vaulted to the ceiling with two skylights. They went up another set of steps and around to another small hallway, which led to his study and to his bedroom. There were wood floors galore, the bathroom had off-white ceramic tile, the walls were bright white. It was a very nice place indeed.

His study faced the driveway, which originally faced a short cement wall and an open lot. Currently, there was a building being constructed there, which was being turned into an apartment. He told her that that would be finished in a couple of months. *"How sad,"* she thought. His view was going to be obstructed from the street above, from which he would not be able to see the foliage and cornfields above that and the fields and pastures to the north.

After touring that part of the house, they went back down the steps to the ceramic-tiled hallway that led to the living room. They passed another bathroom, a very large closet, a built-in cabinet and drawers, a full wine rack, his telescope and the door that led to the basement. They went through the open double glass and wood doors and into the wood-floored living room, which included the dining area.

"What a bachelor pad," she thought. He had cream-colored leather furniture, with a couch and two over-stuffed chairs. There was a wood coffee table, a large screen TV, a dresser with a stereo, plants, a fireplace, a large dining table with two chairs and a long matching bench. There were double glass doors that led to the outside patio, which had a picnic bench and chairs, several potted plants, including two tomato plants, a large section of black-eyed Susan flowers and other unnamed plants and many bushes and trees that lined his small backyard. Very quaint.

Off the dining area was the kitchen, which was very modern, with stainless steel appliances, which were very small, compact, space-saving and convenient. It reminded Jane of the items at the Ikea store near Dayton. It had an ample pantry and one window, but plenty of light. Again, very quaint, indeed.

After a quick tour of his home, they went back upstairs and he got out some linens for her sleeping quarters. He flattened the futon and they put the sheets on the bed. He put a slip cover on a comforter and on a huge pillow, then they went back downstairs, where they sat for a bit and talked a bit more, then he offered to make some dinner.

They washed their hands and while he cooked homemade pasta, that he bought during his recent backpacking tour of Italy, she helped put together a salad made up of greens and tomatoes, olive oil and balsamic vinegar, dashed with sea salt and pepper. Everything smelled and looked so delicious. She felt warm and domesticated.

Jane helped set the table with place mats, water glasses, salad bowls and utensils. He got out two beers and they sat across from each other and ate their supper. He offered up two different types of pasta toppings, which included the best-ever tasting pesto that Jane had ever had. As a matter of fact, it was the first time that she had tasted pesto and it was quite delicious.

As they ate and talked, she realized that her eyes were bigger than her stomach. She had a great time talking with him, catching up and she came to understand that she was a very lucky woman to have this man as her new-found friend. But, damn. Jane had to admit that a girl could get used to the company of a nice man, who not only loved to cook, but was actually breathing and was employed!

After dinner, they cleared the table and she washed the dishes and cleaned off the countertop. He loaded the dishwasher, then he brought his laptop computer to the table. They sat next to each other and looked at several photos from his many trips to other parts of Europe, including his trip to Italy and photos from back in the 1980's, when he was part of an exchange student program. That was when he came to America and how they had met in high school.

Jane busted out laughing at the fashions from way back when. *"Time can be cruel for some,"* she thought. Sometimes she felt that that did include her, but somehow, time for Joseph had not been cruel.

He was the same handsome and dashing, sweet person with a great smile, that she had known from many years earlier. He had been brought up well, with manners and taste, intelligence and wonderful humor, a giving and worldly and tactful attitude. He had an open mind and an open heart. Not to mention that when he sat next to her, he smelled so good. Jane sat there, just lingering in his manly scent, hoping that he would not notice her leaning into him. Her thoughts drifted to Pascal, who also smelled so wonderful. She immediately got mellow as she missed Pascal.

"Is this time in Europe, visiting with Joseph, going to be difficult for me?" she asked herself. "Am I going to miss Pascal so much that I will cry myself to sleep, longing for his touch and for his strong arms around me?"

"Perhaps," Jane thought.

But how was she to know that during her visit in Austria, that her melancholy thoughts were going come to the surface? How was Jane to know that she was going to get so mellow with sadness, yet comfortable enough with Joseph, that she was going to be able to share with him some of her deepest fears?

Jane did not know that during their many late night conversations, Joseph had the gift of using leading questions and analyzing her. But was it truly a gift or a curse for Jane? How was she to know that during her stay with him, she was going to reveal so much of herself?

Jane did discover one specific thing, among many, about herself during her time in Europe: That she had no business drinking alcoholic beverages! In Joseph's company, Jane was able to let her guard down, although she was feeling quite vulnerable! That was going to be a hard lesson learned...

Around 11:30 p.m., they decided to finish looking at photos. She thanked him for dinner. He stayed downstairs to read some emails and she went upstairs to her room. She opened up her suitcase, got out her toiletries and pajamas, changed her clothes, then went to the bathroom, washed her face and brushed and flossed. She went back to the bedroom, closed the blinds and the white fringed curtains, then she turned on her cell phone. No service. She turned it off, but kept it close by.

She did some stretches for her back and legs, then turned off the light and slithered into the bed. The cushion and pillow were so welcoming and comfortable. *"Ahhh."* Jane lay on her back for a moment, listened to her breathing and her heart pounding in her chest. She thought about the day.

Suddenly, she felt an overwhelming need to cry but was glad that she did not. She turned over to her right side, placing a portion of the comforter between her knees and fluffed the pillow into the curve of her neck. She closed her eyes, took a deep breath and slowly let her breath release and repeated that action several more times. She knew that that act would relieve some of her stress and woes from the day.

With her eyes closed, Pascal popped into her head and she welcomed the thought of him and of them lying together in his bed. In her thoughts, he slowly caressed her with his fingertips. He rolled her onto her back and kissed her so passionately. He kissed down her chin, her neck, her chest and on her nipples, all the while one of his hands was slowly moving down her belly, then stroked in between her legs. In her thoughts, her back arched. She slept well.

"Thank You for another great day."

The next day...

Jane woke up at 7:30 a.m. and heard Joseph in the bathroom, getting ready for work. She ran downstairs, used that bathroom and brushed her teeth, then came back upstairs, grabbed her computer, then went back down to the kitchen table. She started journaling, then Joseph came into the room in a hurried fashion. He verbalized that he was running late. He went to the kitchen, got some bread and butter and some water, then grabbed his things and took off for work. On his way out he asked of her plans and she told him she was going to venture into town. She went to the kitchen, got some bread and raspberry jam and orange juice and continued to journal.

A bit later, she cleaned up the dishes, cleaned the kitchen counter, put the dishes away that were in the dishwasher, then she went upstairs. She took a bath, cleaned out the tub, then got dressed in jean shorts, a pink top and brown boots. She put on makeup, grabbed her camera and a bag of snacks, then went downstairs and took photos of the interior of Joseph's condo and also of his backyard.

Around 11:00 a.m., she grabbed a water bottle from the fridge, then went out the front door, took photos of the front exterior, then she walked into town. On her way, she photographed the fields to the north and the east and some of the traffic signs along the way. For some reason, Jane was relaxed and quite content.

Jane walked down the paved road, with fields and pastures to the right and houses and homes being constructed to the left. Then she passed a side street and four more row houses with tiny front lawns. There was another large house with tall and thin manicured cypress trees that almost completely covered a privacy fence that surrounded the home. She walked over railroad tracks and walked through a parking lot. She passed a house that had a dilapidated garage and a rundown shed, plus there were chickens wandering in the yard. *"I wonder if they only understand German,"* she jokingly thought.

The beginning of the rural road that led out of town continued to the right and then curved to the left. She passed a bus stop, a large grocery store, several side streets and a wide intersection that had a triangular divide with grass and curbing. The divide had a light pole with many signs of towns pointing in multiple directions and a large Jesus on a cross.

There was an Irish pub on the right, an Italian pub on the left and a gas station with a very long name that Jane would not make an attempt to pronounce. She passed many cafes with quaint outdoor seating under canopies and large umbrellas, a long apartment complex with wonderful landscaping and the town's courthouse and police station. There was another grocery store, a couple of car lots and auto repair shops, plus banks, restaurants, pizza parlors, delis, pharmacies, convenience marts and pastry shops. *"This could be Dayton,"* she thought, *"sans the foreign signs and the foreign marquees."*

Jane took many photos along the way, taking her time. She walked down one side of the street going south, then walked the other side of the street going north, upon her return. She went inside a bank, used the ATM and got out 20 Euros. She stopped at a pastry cafe on her way back home and bought an iced tea for 2.50 Euros. The female clerk was basically rude. Despite that, she stayed inside the cafe for shade. It was a beautiful sunny day and the clerk's unsunny disposition was not going to ruin Jane's natural, happy high.

Jane took a caffeine pain pill for her backache and headache and thought to herself that she may regret that later. She looked around and took in the cuteness of the place. It had glass and brass fixtures, wood floors, small parlor tables and chairs, dim lighting and one other patron. The glass display case was filled to the brim with many pastries to satisfy all kinds of tastes. Jane wanted one of those sticky-sweet and sugary pies, cakes or rolls, but opted to avoid them.

She munched on a granola bar, threw away her trash and then left. She found an electronics store and went in. Jane asked for help from the thin and tall, ever-so-cute, ever-so-helpful, female clerk. "Thanks!" Jane bought a electronic power converter for her computer for 19.00 Euros. It was well worth the stop, indeed. For some reason, she was super excited about that. *"Now perhaps, I can contact someone at home via email,"* she thought, *"and they would be elated to know that I am okay."*

Jane was amazed that even though she could not read German, she could still translate the signs and tell what stores sold what merchandise. It was 12:45 p.m. and she was starting to have lower belly cramping. She was still having some difficulty in that area, ever since she left home. *"Dammit."* On the way back, she stopped at a gas station and bought a diet Coke from a cute, tall male clerk. He told her that he was from Manchester, and spoke little English and could not help her find a drugstore.

She was hoping to find some belly medicine, but she did not tell him that. Inside the gas station store, Helen Reddy's *"Leave Me Alone"* was playing in the background. Jane found that to be very funny and did all that she could to stop herself from busting out laughing. She had not heard that tune since…well, forever. By the time she returned back to Joseph's home, she was sweating a bit, but enjoyed the exercise all the same. Jane could not get the lyrics of that old song out of her head for at least an hour.

She got to the house, placed her things on the table, then downloaded her photos onto her computer. She used her new converter, let her computer charge, labeled each photo and enjoyed looking at her creations. Joseph called Jane around 2:15 p.m. on his cell phone that he let her borrow, and told her that he was going to the store and would be home a bit later.

He told her that after dinner, they would go meet some of his friends for drinks at their favorite pub. She told him that she was excited and that she would be ready. After they hung up, she enthusiastically ran back upstairs, took a quick bath, then got dressed in a red top, olive green casual pants and sandals, blow-dried her hair and put on some makeup.

She went back downstairs and finished with her photos. She was still unable to get the internet so she was baffled as what to do next to contact Pascal, her family and her friends.

Around 5:00 p.m., Joseph came home and Jane helped him put away the groceries. She helped get out place settings and placemats and set the table, while he put the food out on a serving plate. They sat across from each other and had dinner. She had to admit to herself that she could get used to being served, so to speak. She could get used to having a very attractive man sitting across from her at the dining room table...for the rest of her life.

Jane tried a bit of everything that he had bought, including the salami (even though she was avoiding processed meats), a slice of real Austrian bread (she loved bread) and a slice of the sausage and sauerkraut pastry. It was all very delicious.

Even as she ate dinner, she knew that eating some of those things was going to kill her belly later. She felt slightly obligated to try every type of food, especially when it was served to her. She desperately wanted to partake and experience everything, but hindsight being what it was, she should have just declined most of what was offered. But she did not want to offend Joseph.

As Jane had gotten older, her strange and confounding digestive system had not been able to handle processed meats, raw vegetables and had rejected dairy products. She was diagnosed with Irritable Bowel Syndrome after her son was born. She had read articles on what worked and what to foods to avoid. She had read somewhere that the main culprit might just be stress. *Great!* She had always said that to tell Jane to avoid stress, was like telling a zebra not to have stripes. Jane had repeatedly consumed the better foods that seemed to work for days and days, then some days later, she had problems with those same foods.

Her belly problems arose around the time of varying degrees of stress. Jane believed that her stress started at the time of her birth! Her trip to Europe was a *super-doozy-stress-provoker* and she was dealing with her belly being distended, with no relief in sight. She was in agony most of the time and could not think of anything specific that was going to save her.

She was limited on what she could bring with her on the flights and she basically had to leave her fiber powder back home. In her own opinion, she looked pregnant and she knew that it was going to take some time before she could get back to normal, whatever normal was for her. She felt that she was rapidly gaining weight, but her clothes fit her the same. Although everything that Joseph brought home was tasty, Jane knew that she was going to pay for it later, in some form or another.

They cleaned up the dishes, then sat around for a bit just chit-chatting about Joseph's day. She felt comfortable in his home and in his company. He let the next door neighbor's cat inside, as it had been pawing at the patio door. Joseph was taking care of it, so he fed it some food in the kitchen. She was a simple, small house cat and quite friendly. They took their time letting their food digest, then they eventually got into his car and took off for the pub. They literally drove around the corner to the Italian pub that was next door to the gas station, that was just down the road from his neighborhood.

The name of the pub was *il sapore* (which translated to *'little kitchen'*). The pub was very small and cute, with a small patio out front, a small bar and glass case with snacks, a few tables and chairs and a long bench along the wall. There were pictures of Sophia Loren, along with some plants, dim lighting and about seven other patrons, other than his four friends from his choir group.

Joseph introduced Jane to Mary, who was a teacher. She met Annemarie, who was a hands-on healer (a kinesthesiologist) and Emma and Karl, who were married. She was a nurse and he was a film-maker.

They were all very sweet, very patient with trying to understand what she was saying and vice versa. They wanted to know all about Jane, her family and her trip and Jane wanted to know all about them as well. They told each other as much as they could in such a short period of time.

During their visit, they told Jane to visit the Farmer's Market on Schulstrasse Street the following day, and they gave her a list of things to taste or to purchase. The list included *Longos* (Fried dough), *Connaught* (Fried dough and garlic), *Kurbisbernol* (Pumpkin oil) and *Kaiserschmarren* (Sugar pancake). They told her that she would truly love it and she believed them. It all sounded very good.

They took photos of the group with Jane's camera and she took photos of each of them. She knew that she would always cherish meeting them and hoped that she would see them again some day. She learned a lot about them, their jobs and families and she felt very comfortable in their company. She was happy that they were very welcoming and greeted her with open arms. They visited for quite some time.

Jane told Annemarie that she looked like the lead singer from The Pretenders and she tried to sing some songs from that band for Annemarie. Annemarie had never heard of that band before. Joseph got on the internet on his cell phone to look up the band and played some music for her. Everyone liked the music that was played. Annemarie expressed a lot of curiosity about the singer. So Jane told Annemarie that it was a compliment.

She told her that the singer was tall and beautiful and very talented and that Jane's boyfriend, Pascal, would love to meet her. He was *"in love"* with her because he thought she was *"hot."* Jane was surprised that she had to explain what she had meant by the word *"hot"* (Sexy, gorgeous, desirable) and when she did, Annemarie blushed.

At that point, Joseph chimed in with a loud, *"You did not tell me that he was your boyfriend!"* Jane told him that it was just easier to say that Pascal was that, than trying to explain to him that Pascal and she were just very good friends. She kept to herself that she had hopes or even some expectations of becoming more to him some day. She kept to herself that she and Pascal were also lovers. Joseph's reaction was quite strange to Jane, but kind of cute, for he almost sounded jealous. He had no reason to be, but it was sort of flattering all the same.

Each of them talked about their favorite music and about their travels. They were amazed that Jane looked so young, when she told them that she was a grandmother. She told them that she had gotten that comment a lot, but she attributed it to good genes, a somewhat healthy lifestyle and a healthy attitude. She also told them that she finally admitting to herself that her marriage was over and that she got a much-needed divorce many years ago. That had added ten or more years to her life! They all laughed at that last comment.

Jane had always envied people with many true friends or for that matter, having one true best friend for life. She had dreams about being invited to their homes on a regular basis, including holidays and having them come over to visit her at her home as well. Jane felt that she needed to belong to another family since her kids were all grown up. She had always wanted to be a part of something bigger than herself, that reached beyond friendship, beyond the blood ties of a family.

There had been so many rifts and miscommunications in her family over the years, that she had been saying all along that, *"I've had strangers treat me better than my own family members."* She remembered working with a woman years ago, who was older than Jane, who would talk about her many trips, from the past to the present. She had taken vacations with her many girlfriends, whom she had stayed in touch with since college. They traveled to various parts of the U.S., together without fail. When Jane heard that, not only did she have a hard time believing it...since that had never happened for her, but she was remarkably jealous of it.

While with Joseph's friends, she briefly reflected on feeling lost, when she thought of being involved with a group of girlfriends from her past, with whom she no longer kept in contact.

That group of women still get together, from time to time, sans Jane, partly because of her divorce. When she was getting divorced and was in a deep time of need and guidance from them, they had abandoned her.

Despite that, she had already forgiven them long ago. Jane had also come to realize that she had no need for people like that in her life, who would be willing to treat her like last night's trash. She felt disregarded, tossed aside and disrespected by them. As a matter of fact, she was quite indifferent towards them, whenever she had run into them after her divorce.

"I am so capable and willing to meet nice people, who would treat

me better than my own family," she would tell herself. *"I deserve better than my previous, toxic friends. I deserve that in this lifetime and everyone deserves that in this lifetime. I do not need anyone like that and I will be making strides to keep that negativity away."* Once Jane had adopted that attitude, her life continuously changed for the better.

Sometime after 10:00 p.m., Joseph and Jane left, with hugs and kisses for and from everyone. Jane's face hurt from all of the smiling and laughing that she did that night. She felt very happy, indeed. They went back to Joseph's place and Jane got settled in front of her computer at the dining room table. Joseph downloaded his internet access onto her computer. Jane almost jumped through the roof with glee as she was able to get her email. She thought that she actually shrieked. She profusely thanked Joseph for his help.

Jane had many letters of mostly concern for her welfare and her well-being. She took a moment to reply to some of the emails and to compose one each to her son, her daughter, Toni and Pascal. Joseph went to bed, but Jane stayed up for a bit longer

Jane was elated as she wrote about her adventures and sent emails to her kids and to some friends. She eventually decided that it was time for bed, so she turned off the computer, petted the cat, turned off the lights and went upstairs. She put on her jams, brushed, flossed and washed her face. She went back to her room, turned off the light and sat on the edge of her bed, folded her hands and counted her blessings.

She prayed for a good night's sleep, for her children to be happy and safe and to hear from them soon. She prayed to have another great day tomorrow and to have some intestinal relief. She felt that that was a bit selfish, but somewhat necessary. Jane thanked Him for another wonderful day on this great Earth.

As she lay in bed, with her head on her pillow and pressed up against her neck, Jane had realized many things: She was very lucky to be alive, to see another day, to be THERE and to be among positive people and positive situations. She was blessed to have been able to laugh and smile and sing and dance in her head. She was fortunate to eat good food, see new places and enjoy the day's warmth and sunlight. And she was lucky to have happy and healthy children. She was the lucky one, indeed. "Thank You." As she drifted into slumber, she cried.

Wednesday...

Jane woke up with pain in her back and in her lower belly. *"Is today going to be a good day for me, regarding elimination?"* she wondered. Why was it that that seemed to be such a preoccupation for her? She was not too comfortable right then, but wanted to know that when she was able to venture out, she would be able to find comfort somewhere close by. Do most people think like that, too? She could hear Joseph downstairs, drinking tea or eating breakfast, as she heard the clinging of utensils against ceramic dishware.

She got up, brushed her teeth, made the bed, put a hair band in her hair and went downstairs. They greeted each other with a *"Good morning"* and then she used the bathroom adjacent to the living room. After that, she went straight to the table, sat across from him and watched him as he read his newspaper, with his reading glasses on the bridge of his nose.

Joseph looked at her, tilted his head down a bit, viewed her over his glasses and asked how she slept. She told him that she had slept okay and that she usually slept for four hours or so, solid and straight, but it was still a bit restless. She told him that she had stayed up to emailed friends, had finished her second glass of wine and went to bed sometime after midnight.

She told him that she had listened to her music on her headphones and thought about her grand babies, but she did not tell him that she had cried herself to sleep. He told her that he slept great for the first time in a few days. She was glad to hear that. He had been going full-throttle since he had picked her up on Monday. At that moment, she thanked Joseph again, for all of his help and for being a great host.

They talked about her plans for the day. For some reason, she admitted to him, again and embarrassingly, that she was still constipated. She thought, *"How humiliating!"* She told him that she had plans to lounge around, exercise and, as she opened up her laptop, she told him that she was looking up home remedies for her current problem. He reassured her that she would be fine, but she disagreed. He admitted having the same trouble every time that he had traveled.

They talked about how it could be possibly deadly to have a bowel blockage. *"Wow! What a subject to talk about!"* she thought. They laughed, because they agreed that that was not exactly her problem, just yet. She told him that she needed more water, etc., to make her feel better. She read to him some of the remedies that she had found on the internet and he told her that he agreed that sauerkraut would help. She needed more water, fiber, a scheduled diet, exercise and better sleep, but mostly, she needed less stress in her life. How was she going to accomplish that?

Jane felt that every day brought on some sort of stress for everyone, but she just needed to find a way to either reduce it or to get rid of it. She also felt that she had to change her attitude and outlook about her life in order to do that. She also felt that would mean that she would have to change her entire personality to do *THAT.* She reminded herself that cemeteries were filled with many people who had no stress.

Joseph got up, handed her a pear from a basket on the floor by the table, then went to the kitchen. He came back to the table and showed her a container of Muesli, which was a mixture of whole grains, which she could add to orange juice or eat raw. *"Okay,"* she thought. *"Something to start with and something that is good for me. I need to do something soon for some relief."*

He finished up his breakfast and went upstairs to get ready for work. Jane went to the kitchen, made some green tea, added some grains to a glass of orange juice, cut up the pear and had breakfast at the table. She read and replied to emails, including one very short one from Pascal. Pascal was a very good conversationalist, but not very good at texting or emailing. His comment of *"Have fun"* was all that she got from him that day. She planned on doing just that.

A bit later, Joseph came back downstairs and grabbed a few things. Jane told him that he looked great in his blue shirt and he smiled, thanked her and wished her to have a great day. She returned the greeting and he left. What he did not know was that he truly did look great in that color and that she told him that for two selfish reasons: To tell him the truth of that observation, and to see him smile after that compliment. He had such a great smile and she needed to see it again.

Jane continued to email her friends, send photos and update them of her journey. She emailed her daughter and sent photos, with the hopes of hearing from her real soon. She finished breakfast, did the dishes, put away the dishes from the dishwasher, cleaned off the counter and swept and mopped the kitchen floor. A bit later, she was happy because she had some immediate digestive success! More than likely, it was the sauerkraut pastry from the day before, but she did not care about the source. She just needed relief and she got some. Now she could face the day, feeling lighter and renewed.

Jane understood that was a bit embarrassing but serious for some people and very typical of travelers everywhere. It was just something that she hated to have to suffer through from time to time. It was quite annoying. Eventually, she finished up with her computer, then went upstairs, got her clothes and toiletries, started her bath water, brushed and flossed, then soaked in the tub for a while. *"Awww. Let go of the stress."* By then, she wanted to take a nap.

While she soaked in the tub, Jane thought of something funny. Months ago, when Jane was visiting with Pascal, they were watching TV, then he told Jane that he had to use the bathroom. One of his two bathrooms was adjacent to the living room and to the two downstairs bedrooms. While he was in there, he continued to talk to Jane, and she to him, while she continued to watch TV. Jane thought it was a bit odd, but also that it was quite funny that he did that. She was impressed that he was able to use the bathroom in front of him and that he had no fear in it. Her other boyfriends were never that comfortable with her, regarding that.

As a matter of fact, it was from day one, after she had met Pascal, that they were able to use the bathroom in front of each other. They were able to undress in front of one another, without hesitation and it was something that she had noted was not the case from her other beaus. That was a few of the many things that she loved about him.

Going to the bathroom in front of a lover was not something that Jane had aspired to, but it was a good thing that Pascal and she were so comfortable in their own skin. They were so comfortable with each other, that they could be just themselves...with each other...no matter what.

When he had emerged from the bathroom that night, he looked

quite relieved and relaxed. And without missing a beat, he stated boldly and sarcastically, with his chest puffed out, *"It is a life-altering experience to have a complete elimination of the bowels."* Jane busted out laughing at his statement, almost to the point of peeing her pants. She was laughing just as hard, as she thought of that, at that moment.

She washed up and conditioned her hair, then got dressed in tan and green plaid shorts and a matching shirt and undershirt. She put on some makeup, put her things away, straightened up the bathroom, washed out the tub, got her purse and then went downstairs.

She turned on the TV then went through the selection of DVDs and found *"Platoon."* She popped it in the player and couldn't get the contraption to work. There were five remotes and five too many for her to figure out. She got the TV to work, but not the volume. She pushed every button she could think of without success.

She left the TV on, went back to the table and worked at her computer again. She tried to listen her favorite Dayton radio station, Mix1077, but that was not going to happen either so she went back upstairs, got her mini-music player and listened to her music, while she typed away at her journal.

She eventually turned off the TV, got some water from the fridge, turned on her music on her computer and listened to Rascal Flatts. She belted out the words to *"This Everyday Love"* and found that it made her a bit embarrassed to sing aloud, thinking that someone may hear her, but she continued anyway. It would be quite embarrassing to be caught doing that, but she did not care. No one was there, she thought, but she and God, and she was sure that He would not mind it at all. It was 12:30 p.m. and she continued to journal.

Later on, she was able to nap in her bed, for about 20 minutes, but got very frustrated as her thoughts drifted to Pascal. She wondered how he was doing. In her waking thoughts, she imagined his hands all over her and vice versa. It was not a good time for her to think of that. It just was not. She got up around 4:00 p.m., remade the bed then heard the worst sound that she could imagine, especially being in a foreign country: Emergency sirens. They sounded more like tornado sirens.

What the hell was that? She looked outside the bedroom windows for some kind of clue. She opened the window and watched for some kind of reaction from the family in the adjacent backyard, who were playing in their pool. Since their reaction was nil, she decided not to worry either. She went back downstairs and continued with writing on her computer.

Joseph came home around 5:00 p.m. and looked quite whipped. They addressed each other, *"Like an old married couple,"* she thought. He went to the kitchen, made himself a snack then came back to the table to read his newspaper. While he had his snack of tea, beer, bread and prosciutto, he thanked her for doing the dishes and for cleaning up the kitchen. She replied with, *"You are very welcome."*

He let the cat in and fed her some dinner. He certainly spoiled her and seemed to love the attention that she gave him. It was nice to have a four-legged companion in the house. They continued chit-chatting about their day.

She told him about not being able to get the sound on the TV and about not being able to watch a movie. He went to the TV and fixed the problem, which was some additional combination of buttons, plus one button that she did not know about...the volume button on the side of the TV. She told him that she would watch a movie another day.

He showed her how to run the stereo and they listened to some music. A woman was singing a different version of a Dixie Chicks song and Jane thought that that was awesome to hear. Then they listened to some music on her computer, including Kenny Chesney, John Hiatt, The Pretenders, Bruce Springsteen, Latin music, Tom Petty, the Talking Heads and The Wallflowers. Joseph's living room/dining area had perfect acoustics for singing. She loved the echo and he was a good singer, too.

He made some phone calls to his friends, to set up a meeting for them to meet one of his other friends, Erwin, from Slovakia, who was a painter. He was needing and wanting Joseph's friends to purchase some of his creations. Jane could not help but hear Joseph's phone conversations, because she was within earshot. She did not know what he was saying, but she did notice that he liked to pace back and forth, in the house and on the back patio, while he was on the phone. She caught herself smirking, while she watched him do that, because she had observed that one of her ex-boyfriends had done the same thing. She wondered if it was a *guy thing*, because she did not do that at all. As he talked on the phone, she played on her computer.

A bit later he came inside and asked if she was ready. She told him that she was, as they debated where to go. He decided since the weather was nice, they would go to a winery, which was owned by his ex-Uncle-in-law, Franz, in Csaterberg. He also mentioned that they could go to Hungary the following day or by the weekend. He wanted to take advantage of the non-rainy weather, so they took off, grabbing their jackets on the way out.

As they drove and toured along the winding streets of Joseph's village and its outskirts, Jane took lots of photos. There were churches, homes, fields, pastry shops and more quaint cafes. Jane thought that if she blinked, she would miss the many cute buildings, for they stood among the many houses and homes. They were packed together like sardines in a can and the buildings were very close to the street. She wondered if there were many children in any of those villages and if anyone would get hit by the speeding cars, if they made one misstep.

They stopped and walked through a cemetery, which was designed a lot differently than she was accustomed to seeing in the States. The headstones and marble structures were placed close together and some were on top of each other, to take advantage of limited space. Nearby, there was a school and a church. The cemetery was on a hill. Joseph liked walking through there from time to time, because it was peaceful.

Some of the headstones were ancient and hard to read and others had precise letters carved in marble or granite. They took pictures of each other on the steps of the small church. Off to the north, Jane noticed a gathering of people, who were possibly celebrating something. They were loud and there was lots of music.

On the drive they saw a couple of castles. The first castle was in the village of Rotenturm. Joseph said that the building was either a castle or a chalet and the village name and castle name meant *"Red Tower."* It was 300 years old.

The second one was in the village of Kohfidisch, named after Earl Graflich Erdody'sche. The castle was a SchloBkellerei, which meant that it was a palace or chalet and it had a cellar where wine was stored. That one was built in 1591.

They were equally beautiful and unique. Jane was in awe just thinking that she was so close to something that was that ancient, that historic. *"These are much older than the beautiful buildings at home,"* she acknowledged.

On the drive, through each of the villages, the roads were narrow and winding. They traveled through hills and valleys, meadows and beautiful countryside. Jane wondered about all of the people who had lived there before, in many years past. What was life like in those villages, as the villages were being built, many years ago?

Looking at the uniquely built homes and chalets, she felt as if she had just stepped back in time. It was a time that she would have loved to have been a part of, even if just for a brief moment.

Jane was of German descent, as well as English, Dutch, French, Welsh, Scottish and Irish. She envisioned herself as a virtuous damsel, strolling in the hills of that country, being flirted with and playfully chased by her courting, handsome sweetheart. She could see that briefly, in her mind's eye and as she envisioned it, she felt childish and smiled. She wondered if she had been breathing as she was daydreaming or if she had been smiling profusely. She wondered if Joseph had looked at her and if he had wondered what was exactly wrong with her.

Jane was overwhelmed from all of that beauty and she felt envious towards Joseph and all of the villagers. She wanted to cry. It was all very surreal. She felt silly and even stupid, for feeling small, like an ant in the vastness of that country. She felt quite insignificant, like she did not matter in the world.

She had to admit to herself that at that moment, she had gotten tired of being such a very sensitive, bawling-at-the-drop-of-a-hat, woman. Most of the time, Jane felt very juvenile and sophomoric and she did not like it one bit. She knew that she was an adult and that she had many responsibilities and carried them out. She knew that she had a great sense of humor, too. But she also knew herself deep down. She was a very passionate, empathic, sensitive and caring person. But she was tired of feeling insignificant at times. She was tired of her most current woes. She told herself to just grow the hell up and face the realities of life.

Jane and Joseph talked about his life in Austria. He told her that he was a happy child and had many friends. He talked about his home village of Altenmarkt, which was 40 kilometers away from his current village. He told her how he got involved in neurology. He told her that in Austria, everyone in the medical field had to take medical training first, then get additional training in the specialized field in which they are interested, including dentistry. He was interested in neurology because of the mystery of it. It was like being a detective, he told her, who solved a puzzle for someone and of what part of the brain was causing the problem. It was very interesting, indeed.

Jane had never thought of it as like being a detective, but that made sense to her after he explained it. Joseph's eyes sparkled as he spoke and she could see that he was passionate about his work. She could see that he loved what he did for a living and more than likely, it was what he was meant to do. A detective of the brain.

She was happy to watch his face as he spoke of his work. She told him that she felt the same way about being involved with special needs children. She told him that there was nothing in the world like witnessing a child learn.

As they continued on their drive, the sun was slowly setting, which made a wonderful wispy, cloudy haze in the sky. They drove through a section of a town that had many wooded areas on either side of the road, which made the trees bend toward the street. It felt as if they were driving through a dark tunnel. It felt a little romantic, Jane had to admit.

Jane was not scared in his car, because Joseph was a good driver. Although he did speed a bit, it did not cause her any concern. She knew that in most cases that she preferred to be the driver and it was a control issue for her. But mostly it made her feel trapped in some way, if she did not drive.

If the hair on the back of her neck did not go up when someone else drove her, she knew somehow that she was going to be fine. She would know that she was safe and that they did not make her feel imprisoned in their vehicle. She felt that it was odd that she was able to sense that kind of danger, but that was a part of who she was.

Jane concluded that her somewhat neurotic attitude or behavior, in her adult years, had originated from her childhood. She felt that it was because of being in her family's station wagon on many long trips from Dayton to West Virginia to visit her grandmother. She felt that her attitude came from feeling trapped in that vehicle, with her many brothers and sisters around her, and not knowing when was a good time to mention that she had a bellyache or that she had to use the bathroom.

Jane felt that it could also be because of being picked on by her siblings, in those close quarters, in a moving vehicle. On one of those trips, she remembered being burned on the leg by one of her brothers, who brought his magnifying glass with him. It was dealing with things like that or dealing with endless hours of feeling cramped. It may also have to be because of having to deal with the smell of someone getting car sick. *Hmmm...*

That attitude may also come from the few times that she felt trapped in a car during high school. She would get rides home with "so-called" friends, who would wind up running many questionable errands. She would get in their car and they would intentionally drive other places and leave her in the car. She did not know what they were doing. She did not know what neighborhood she was in and she did not know how to get home. That was way before cell phones. She could not get the driver to take her back home early enough, so as not to get into trouble with her parents. She would be late getting started on her homework and she did not like that feeling. She did that a few times, then made the wise choice of not hanging out with them ever again. She walked home most days, even in the snow and rain. She preferred that because she was in charge and in control of her own whereabouts. *Hmmm...*

Jane had many experiences being trapped as the passenger in the car during her marriage. With the car moving, she was not able to flee when she was in a full-blown argument and a screaming match with her husband. Without fail, he would insist on insulting her and calling her names for no real apparent reason. Don't get it wrong, she was by far from being innocent in any argument with him. He would call her names and she felt obligated, compelled and justified in calling him names, back to him. Her action was her reaction to his initiated action. She never knew his motivation, other than trying to succeed in controlling her and severely hurting her feelings. Most days he succeeded, hence, why she needed to get out of that possible irreversable toxic environment. And save her children, too. *Hmmm…*

With Joseph, she did not feel trapped. Is that one of the reasons why she hated to fly, too?

Joseph wanted to know more about Jane's interests, so she told him about wanting to go back to school and wanting to get a degree in business, writing and maybe even working with the elderly. She did admit that she was quite confused as to what to do next in her life. She told him that she was concerned about *"the next chapter."* She told him that she was well aware of turning 50 years old soon… and she was wanting something significant to happen before or by then.

Jane told him what it was like being a part of a large family and being raised Catholic, but not being Catholic any more. *"It was chaos,"* she admitted, *"but I handle chaos sort of well. It was fun and it was sometimes not fun."* She told him that her mother told her that she was always concerned about where their next meal was coming from. Jane told him that she never knew that they were poor, until her mother told her so, sometime after she had a family of her own.

Being a part of a large family was all that Jane knew, so she told him that she felt as if being a part of a family was all that she wanted. But she also admitted that she could see herself just drifting through life on her own as well.

Joseph wanted to know about her loves, so she told him about

Pascal. She told him that Pascal was tall, dark and handsome and that she had never had tall, dark and handsome all at once, in her life before. They laughed about that. She told him that she was very happy and giddy to have met Pascal. She told him that he was charming, funny, a good conversationalist and very current on political issues. He sort of liked to instigate debates and conversations that may be a bit edgy. And that he liked to watch foreign films because they always had realistic, unhappy endings, in his opinion. She told him that Pascal had told her that most American dramatic, or even comedic, films were a bit too sappy and that they always had happy endings. *"That is not real life,"* he would tell her.

She had told Pascal that she liked happy endings and that, for about two hours, she could get away from her own problems and her own issues. She could get away from her own challenges and watch others in their struggles or in their happy settings. She had told Pascal that she loved movies of all kinds, except horror flicks and he had felt the same. Joseph agreed that he disliked horror films, too.

Jane told Joseph that one day, Pascal and she had watched a drama/comedy musical and before the end, he stopped the movie, threw his hat at the TV and cussed out loud. He exclaimed, *"It is stupid that the two main actors would wind up together, because he was too stupid to realize that she was a f*cking, stupid whore."* Jane was shocked at his reaction, to say the least.

Jane told Pascal that he should stick with watching the end of that movie, because someone was going to die, but that did not make him feel better. They had eventually watched the end of the movie...

one week later…when Jane had encouraged him and provoked him, and also reassured him that it was not a happy ending. Once the movie was over, he had stated that that was *"more like it."* Pascal never apologized for his reaction or his behavior.

Jane felt that he was too overboard with his reaction, but she also felt that he was a bit embarrassed that those two characters were in love, which Jane felt, was realistic to some degree. It was a musical after all. She told Joseph that she had to share his reaction with her friend, Toni, who had always encouraged her to *"ride the situation out,"* with Pascal. Toni felt that they were meant to be together. Jane did not tell Joseph that she wished and hoped and prayed that that were only true.

Jane continued to tell Joseph that Pascal had two adult children, that he was her age and that he had many friends, but mostly from that damn *'clubhouse'* of a bar of his. She told him that she worried about his drinking and driving habits. She told him that he liked his job, that he wanted to move to Europe and that he was very good at making her feel wanted and needed. But she also told him that she worried that he would cheat on her. *"Why did I mention that?"* She feared that he did not feel the same about her as she felt about him, nor would he ever.

She told Joseph that when he had first met her, Pascal commented that he sensed *"duality"* in her, but not in *a mental-kind-of-way.* Pascal stated to her that he was intrigued by her, because she was a petite grandmother, but she had 17 tattoos. He was fascinated by her because she worked at a school, but she was able to dance like an experienced stripper. That comment made Joseph laugh out loud. Joseph did not comment about the number of tattoos that Jane admitted she had and she was okay with that.

Joseph commented that he must use that line about duality on the next woman that he may find interesting. Joseph said that that would not be actual duality, but it meant that it was Jane just being Jane and how she functioned in her life. She agreed, but he also understood that Pascal did not mean *"duality"* as in a split personality.

She told Joseph that Pascal offered to *"peel back the layers to find out what made Jane who she was,"* so Joseph seriously asked her if that was a metaphor for stripping off her clothes? Jane laughed and told him that it was not, but it was more of a way to say that he wanted to get to know her more. Joseph busted out laughing again, because he admitted that he knew what she had meant. It was very funny. They laughed for several minutes.

A few minutes later, Joseph started a new conversation. *"No offense, but you seem to be like the subject of that Elvis Presley song."* Jane asked what he meant by that. *"Which song?"* So in an Elvis-like voice, Joseph started singing *"The Devil in Disguise." "You're the devil in disguise...Oh yes you are..."* and so on. She looked at him and laughed so hard to the point of not breathing. Joseph was cracking up as well, especially at her reaction. Jane was sure that was what he wanted. He lowered his voice and sang again. It was hilarious.

Jane asked him to sing it again and again and begged him to let her record him on her camera. He would not let her, although she had promised that she would show just a few friends and then erase it. She promised not to put it on the internet. She was a bit disappointed when he turned her down, but she understood, wholeheartedly. Even as she thought of that moment much later, it still cracked her up.

They continued driving until they got to a small village made up of wine houses, that were scattered in various places in the hills and valleys near the road. Those houses were originally built by and for the vineyard owners. The owners could live near by, tend to their crops and store their wines, although their homes and hometowns were elsewhere. Those houses were not much bigger than a large storage shed, but were currently equipped with satellite dishes and internet.

Joseph stopped the car and they got out. Jane took photos of the houses, the nearby vineyards, the setting sun and the fields in the distance. There was a Dachshund dog who seemed to ignore her, but perhaps more than likely he did not understand English. He eventually waddled away, towards the west and in between the rows of grape vines.

They got back into the car, drove a bit then finally made it to the *"Bei Franz"* (By Franz) Winery. They parked and walked down the hill to the entrance. It was getting darker by the minute and she feared that her simple camera would not capture the uniqueness, quaintness and beauty of that small, family-owned winery and eatery.

There were forests and vineyards surrounding the winery. A huge black sheep dog was barking and approached them. Jane opted to try to ignore him. There were two patrons. Each table had lit candles in assorted sized holders and there were more burning candles in sconces on the building walls. There were citronella candles, rustic picnic tables and benches, rudimentary posts and canopies, a teepee, a tree-house with a chaise lounge underneath and antiquated shelters and sitting areas. As they walked down the hill, Jane noted the mud and the uneven, irregular stepping stones along the main path. There were crickets and mosquitoes galore.

They were greeted by the owners, his (ex) Uncle Franz and his new girlfriend, Anita. They shook their hands as they made their introductions. That place was wonderful and she felt like she fit right in. Joseph told her that that place was very busy on the weekends and she believed him. It was quite cozy and inviting.

They sat down and Joseph explained the menu, which offered different choices of assorted meats: *Jausen,* (meaning a snack, not meal)…*Geselchtes,* which was smoked ham, *Blutwurst* (sausage made from blood), *Brettliause* (snack on a cutting board), *saure Presswurst* (Mit Kernoell…with pumpkin seed oil) and a translucent pressed dish made with gelatin, pig skin and spices. *OMG!*

In addition, Joseph explained, there was *Kaese* (cheeses from Emmentaler, from the Valley of Emmen, in Switzerland)…and *Berg* cheese (which was referred to as mountain cheese)…and *Speck* (bacon) was offered, but Joseph did order that item. They also had a choice of wines *(Blaufrankisch or Cubee)*, which were red wines… that were made from a certain kind of grape. Those wines were made from the neighboring winery, next door to the *Bei Franz Winery*.

After Jane hesitantly agreed, Joseph ordered a variety of meats and cheeses, a liter of red wine, water and bread. Joseph had Jane cracking up with stories of others who have visited him, who would not try many things for they were afraid of it. She told him that she was, too, but she was willing to try it all. He commented to her that that was what he liked about her, that she was willing to try anything, at least once. *"So true,"* she said, as she winked at him. And that made them laugh all the more.

While they waited for their dinner, Jane got up and took photos of their surroundings. She hoped that her camera would be able to capture the images in dim lighting. She took photos of the outside and of the inside of the cafe and caught herself *"Ooohing and Ahhhing"* at the many items inside. It was quite adorable.

The interior looked like a log cabin, with framed pictures, antlers, candle sconces and other assorted décor donning the walls. There were antiquated tables and chairs inside, with mismatched centerpieces. There was what looked like a hand-carved fireplace mantel to her right, with assorted sized stones lining the fireplace. The kitchen was to her left, plus a very small bar, which offered a wide variety of beverages. She noted the chipped mismatched tile on the floor.

In her mind's eye, Jane could imagine that that place would be packed on the weekends, with many inebriated guests, with grand amounts of conversations and lots of loud music and dancing. The bar would probably violate health and safety codes, but she got the notion that no one would care. As a matter of fact, she assumed, that the Health and Safety Code Inspector would be there on weekends, too, for the partying that most likely went on and on and into the weekend nights. Jane had only wished that it was the weekend…

Joseph's Uncle Franz and his girlfriend, Anita, came over to their table and lit more candles. The three of them talked for a bit but Jane could capture only one word that she understood: *American.* Joseph explained to them why she was there as he smiled at her. A bit later, Joseph spoke to another patron, who turned out to be a wine maker named Bradl. They talked of his leg ailments, as Joseph had noticed that he was limping. Bradl told Joseph that he was going to have to go to the doctor, for they were willing to drill a hole in one of his leg bones to relieve pressure. Joseph laughed and told him that he could not help him, unless he was willing to come over to Joseph's house and let him use his power drill. That comment caused laughter among themselves and the other patrons. Joseph explained all of that to Jane, after the fact, which was still funny, even second-hand.

They continued to eat, even while Jane was getting full. She enjoyed the sights, the smells and the tastes of everything around her. They continued to talk about everyday things, including how she was excited about her trip. As the sun continued to rapidly set, it was becoming very apparent to Jane that she was getting quite tipsy from the wine.

She was feeling woozy, very relaxed and silly and her limbs were feeling heavy. That had been a problem for Jane, since she only started drinking at the age of 40. She had gotten married the year after high school and since she was pregnant soon after that and then eventually had her two kids, she decided that *"Alcohol and children do not mix."* She was not much of a drinker anyway and she did not *"successfully"* drink currently.

That day at the winery was not going to be any different. Joseph was really enjoying watching that situation unfold, until she got too smashed to function appropriately. It only took a small bit of alcohol to get her in that condition. She made a slight fool out of herself as she was talking out of her head, as she was not using a filter and she was saying everything that was on her mind. That, too, was funny to Joseph, but not to Jane, for she was slightly incoherent.

Mistakenly, she began to talk about Pascal. She talked about how much she cared about him and her woes and worries over him and about her other boyfriends and of being cheated on by them. She told Joseph that she was not feeling good enough, for whatever they were looking for. She talked about feeling inadequate, for being told that she was too fat and too ugly to date. *"Yes, I was told that, by that rat bastard!"* Jane yelled. She talked about being poor, being estranged from family members regarding her dad's will, about being out of a job, and about being in between dress sizes, hair styles and homes. She confessed to Joseph about having some health problems in the past, not having one true friend...and it went on and on. It was quite pathetic and definitely embarrassing to Jane. She just could not seem to stop herself.

By 10:00 p.m. or so, Jane was so hammered that her head was resting on the top of the table. She apologized profusely to Joseph for being embarrassed and for inconveniencing him for the night. He did not need an apology, he told her and he reassured her that she did not need to be embarrassed. It was too late for that. Joseph confessed that he thought that her behavior was a bit entertaining but by then, she could not completely understand him.

Jane could hear the muffled conversations of some of the other patrons and including the conversation between Franz and Joseph, about her state of being. She was not sure how she guessed what they were saying, but there was a tone of concern between the two of them. She asked Joseph what Franz was saying and he told her that Franz wanted to know if she needed help. She begged Franz and Joseph for forgiveness, but was almost crying while she spoke. Joseph paid the bill and then had to literally physically help her get up the hill to the car.

By then, the grass was full of dew and was slippery, which made their trek not only difficult, but quite comical. Both of them and the other patrons were laughing by then. Jane slurred her words, as she thanked Franz and Anita for their hospitality. She could hear their laughter become more faint as they ascended the hill. Joseph was a trooper, by holding on to her and practically dragging her to the car. He was able to get her in the passenger side and she slithered into the seat. Once he got in the car, she did not move much. He buckled her in, then buckled himself and they took off for home.

The drive home was quite a blur for Jane. But the things that she did remember were her goings-on about Pascal. She blurted out comments about her divorce and the endless feeling that she damaged her kids in some manner, by not leaving her husband sooner than she did. She remembered talking about her sadness over being cheated on, by every man that she knew.

Joseph kept her engaged in conversation, by asking a lot of direct questions, including for her to physically describe Pascal and the others. He asked her to put together a reason why she had been attracted to them in the first place.

The drive seemed longer than earlier and Jane wondered if Joseph had taken a longer route home...or...did he drive slow, just so she would talk more? Was the drive feeling longer just because Jane was smashed? Jane told him basically everything, without hesitation. She knew that he already knew what her ex-husband had looked like, so she described Pascal in a nut-shell as tall, dark and handsome.

In a shrilled voice, she told Joseph that Pascal was arrogant, very selfish, loud, obnoxious, mostly politically-incorrect...that he forgot things from too much drinking and forgot things sometimes on purpose, but he was wonderfully worldly and super humorous. *"Did I mention that he was selfish?"* she sarcastically asked. She almost started crying, for she missed him so much already. But she did not know why...

She described both of her first and second boyfriends as nerds and geeks, that they were very smart, somewhat funny, very selfish and very white...with glasses and chicken legs. That statement made both of them laugh out loud. Jane thought she was going to either pee her pants or throw up from the laughter. She even shared some of the details of how they were in bed and began to get mad at herself, for she was somehow unable to stop talking. For some reason, she knew that Joseph did not seem to mind the details. She told Joseph that she was very patient with one of the things that they all had in common.

When Joseph asked what that was, Jane hesitated. She didn't want to say the wrong thing, but it was too late for that. She told Joseph that each of her three boyfriends had trouble...at times... in bed...possibly due to their age. She looked at him and said, *"No offense. But I have to assume that all men at your age have trouble getting it up, from time to time."* There was a pause, then she laughed uncontrollably.

He had the biggest smile on his face, as she continued. She told him that she assumed that Pascal had trouble due to his age and alcoholism...that boyfriend number two had problems because of his age and because of his medication and because of his lack of usage and experience. And that boyfriend number one had trouble due to his age, his stress at work and his medication. Then she added, yelling...*"Possibly also due to his F*cking cheating!"*

Jane began to cry a bit, when she made the assumption out loud, that she was just not good enough for either of them. She stated that perhaps she was the one of the many things in their lives that had caused all of them stress. She assumed out loud that they were just not attracted to her at all…that she was not attractive enough for them.

She said that she never could understand why they even bothered to date her, if only to bang her. *"They can do that with any woman that they could find in a bar or at a damn grocery store!"* she emphasized. She said that perhaps it was because she was the most gullible, the most stupid of all, to accommodate them …to help them…to spend time with them. She was stupid to fall in love with them and be blinded by what was unfolding in front of her.

She told Joseph that she believed that humor was the one thing that they had in common, that was what she liked the most about them and that they were kind and very attentive, in the beginning. She admitted that she worried that Pascal was gong to fall into that category of being a cheater and a liar. She also giggled when she told Joseph that overall, they were good enough in bed and that she was pleased regarding what they could do to her, for her and with her. Sex was not her priority, she told him.

"Falling in love, being in love…and staying in love and being a part of another family…is my intended life," she told Joseph. She also admitted that she feared that it was not going to happen. She told Joseph that she had one shot in her life, and she failed. She did not fail at having kids and raising them to be the wonderful

human beings that they are. She spawned and she was done with that responsibility. What she believed that she failed at, was finding a man who would cherish her and respect her and love her like she believed she deserved. They were not strong. She was not wise.

Jane went on and on…without taking a breath…as she began to complain that her head hurt, her heart hurt, her limbs were feeling immobile and heavy. That part of the conversation made Joseph giggle.

Joseph told Jane that he thought she was allergic to red wine because she never reacted that way when she had beer. He suggested that she should stay boyfriend-free for a while so she could truly heal from being cheated on and being lied to. He told her that those two things were what she feared the most and that there were no assurances with anyone that she would date.

He told her that there truly was nothing wrong with her…that she was not fat and she was not ugly, and that she should take more time to realize that. He told her that she was not a failure as a mom, a grandmother, as a writer, as a homeowner. How could anyone have foreseen the economy? He told her that she was not a failure as a lover or even as a friend.

He told her that men and women cheat and that he believed that it was just a natural part of being human. She got super loud over that one as she wholeheartedly disagreed. She told him that she would never cheat or knowingly be involved with a married man, for she would not *Do to her, what had been done to me.*

He told her that once she got back home, she should sit down and have an honest conversation with Pascal. She should tell him her concerns and that she should go back to school, find a good job, let her house go into foreclosure and forget about it. He told her to forgive and make peace with those family members, about her estranged family issues, but mostly, she should go home and forgive herself over all of those woes and worries. He told her that she should finally admit to herself that she is better than all of that crap that had been dished out to her so far. He told her that it was imperative that she found peace and love within herself so she could function better and regain her confidence.

If Jane could have taken back all or most of what she had said, she would have. But by the time they reached his home and he helped her out of the car and into the living room, she was crying and very embarrassed, indeed. She just could not stop herself from spilling her guts and revealing most of what made her who she was today.

She was reassured by him again, that he would not repeat what was said, nor would he ever think less of her for saying what she did. He told her that he appreciated her honesty, but he emphasized that she should truly stay away from alcohol. She agreed. Pascal popped into her mind for a moment, for he had said multiple times, that he had *"appreciated her honesty,"* too. It was strange that Joseph would say that. It really bothered her that he did, because she was not exactly sure what that meant. Sure, she understood the word honesty...but Jane did not understand what either of them meant behind the statement. She was drunk and said what was on her mind. That was all.

Their conversation at his home had gone on for about another hour or so and then when they realized the lateness of the hour, Jane excused herself to bed. She went upstairs, brushed and flossed, stripped to her underwear and went to bed. As her head hit the pillow and she lay there, sniffing in the aroma of Pascal's cologne, she cried herself to sleep, but not before she had prayed that Joseph would forget everything that she had said. Jane even wished that she had forgotten what she had said, too.

Then she thanked Him for another good day. She truly prayed for *"peace and harmony and good slumber. Amen"*...

Thursday...

Jane woke up around 1:40 a.m. She went quietly downstairs and into the kitchen, downed an entire bottle of water in one long gulp. She went back upstairs, slowly and quietly and plopped back into bed. She was emotionally exhausted, but knew that she would be okay. She tossed and turned, but she thought that she fell back asleep for a bit. She heard Joseph leave and she wondered about the time. Lying there, she stared at the window, enjoyed the sunlight and watched the thin clouds drift by. She eventually got up, checked the time on the cell phone. It was 9:00 a.m.

Jane made the bed, gathered her clothes, went into the basement, put Joseph's wet clothes from the washer into the dryer, then started another small load for herself. She was very impressed that she had been able to accomplish that small feat. When she had been tipsy before, she never had had enough alcohol to ever experience a hangover. She went back upstairs to the kitchen, drank a mixture of orange juice, olive oil and raw grains, then she ran to the bathroom to pee.

She sat at the dining room table and started the computer, downloaded the new pictures, then went back upstairs. She did 30 minutes of exercises, including running up and down the stairs, core work on Joseph's exercise ball, stretches, back arm exercises, twists and punches. She took a bath, shaved, washed her hair, then got dressed in blue and red plaid shorts, a pink V-neck top and white undershirt, gym shoes and socks.

Jane stared at herself in the mirror and observed that she looked tired and old that morning. Her face looked oily, which it seldom did. She looked down at her growing belly and grabbed her chubby center and stood there worrying about how much weight she had put on since arriving in Europe.

She felt chubby, but her clothes fit her as they did before. So why did she feel full? She was constipated and uncomfortable. She stared at herself once more and she could see the wheels turning in her head, as she asked herself, *"How much of our conversation will Joseph remember, and how much will he deliberately forget?"*

She gelled her hair and scrunched it a bit, put on makeup, then gathered her purse and went back downstairs. She listened to Kenny Chesney and a mixture of other music on her computer. She composed a mass-email regarding the fun times she had had the day before and sent that to many friends. Then she replied to other emails and continued to journal her wonderful experiences.

Jane ran downstairs, folded Joseph's clothes and put them in a basket. She put her clothes in the dryer, took Joseph's clothes to his room, then went back downstairs and took more photos out in the backyard.

Jane closed her eyes and listened for a moment. As she stood outside enjoying the warm sunlight on her face, she could hear the kids playing in the pool in the adjacent backyard. She could hear the sounds of construction in the front of Joseph's home. She thought for a moment that she would love to stay there. The neighbor's cat brushed up against her, bringing Jane back down to reality. Jane opened her eyes and leaned down to pet her. She told her that she was not welcome to come back inside just yet. She wondered if the cat understood her. Jane ran inside and had a bit of success regarding her belly.

Afterwards, Jane went to the kitchen and prepared some food. It was 4:00 p.m. For lunch she had salami, a sweet pear, water, green tea, pesto, bread and two different types of cheese: *Hollandischer Maigouda* and *Gouda alt.* Even though she did not think that the cheese and salami was a good idea, it was delicious all the same. She ate, journaled and listened to Jason Mraz. *"A perfect match,"* she thought. She bee-bopped her head to Mr. Mraz's songs and even sang some out loud. She was proud of the fact that she knew all the words by heart. Great music is hard to come by, she thought.

Jane eventually checked on the laundry and the dryer quit working. *"Oh no! Did I break it?"* She pushed other buttons, turned the dial again and nothing. She would have to wait until Joseph got home to figure out what was wrong. She went back upstairs and sang along to the music as she brushed and flossed. Then she went back downstairs, washed the dishes, put some in the dishwasher, cleaned off the counter and went back to the dining area where she journaled again. She drank some water, thought, sang and wondered how her family was doing.

Jane let the cat in, fed her and continued with her thoughts in her journal. A bit later, the cat wanted out. As she opened the back door, she asked the cat, *"Are you sure that you are not a guy? You are in, you are out...You eat and run. Just like a man!"* That made Jane giggle.

Around 5:30 p.m., Joseph came home and they talked about his day, her day and so on. His day was uneventful. The cat was at the back door again and Jane let the cat in. Joseph fed her, then they went downstairs to repair the dryer. He showed Jane that the dryer's reservoir was full of water. How would she have known that? She did not know that dryers had reservoirs.

Joseph emptied it and Jane continued the cycle. Back upstairs, Joseph got himself some food. They talked a bit and he translated some words for her journal and for her photos. Out of the blue, he talked about his daughters' travels to Italy and Croatia. He confessed to Jane that he missed them and had not seen them for a while. Jane noted that he looked somewhat sad and definitely looked tired. He eventually took a shower and Jane continued to write. A bit later, they got ready for their trip into Hungary. It was 7:00 p.m. when they left.

Jane and Joseph grabbed their jackets and on the way to Koszeg, Hungary, they listened to the radio with the volume on low. Michael Buble's *"Save The Last Dance For Me"* was on. They sang along. ...*"And don't forget who's taking you home and in whose arms you're gonna be. So darlin,' save the last dance for me"*... It was fun to do that with Joseph for he had such a wonderful voice. It was a beautiful night for a road trip.

On the drive, there were long winding roads, many farms, pastures and hills and more villages. The sunlight was dancing on the roofs of the towns to the south and east. The sun was slowly setting and it gave off such a warm glow. Jane and Joseph talked about work, about life in general, about their parents and their families. They talked about the strangeness of dating at their age. They agreed that it was something that they never expected to do that late in life. They agreed that they had expected to be married and to stay married, as they had approached their later years.

Out of the blue, Joseph told her that a woman who had a lot of men in and out of her life was like a nymphomaniac, but was also referred to as a *"woman who has a white liver."* Jane burst out laughing. Joseph did not know where that saying had originated. He thought he had read that it came from Jamaica or India and that it meant that a woman had a very high sex drive. It was not meant to be an offensive term, but Jane could not see it as being a positive comment. For a moment, she wondered if Joseph thought ill of her. She quickly let that thought swoop from her mind.

They talked about the many different foods that they liked, including American fare that he loved, especially hamburgers… and…how to spot a Hungarian car license plate. Those license plates had an *'H'* on them, although the true name for Hungary started with an *'M.'* Jane did not know that. She loved the fact that their thoughts were scattered and random. Jane was quite comfortable with that kind of nonsense.

They traveled through the border of Austria into Hungary, which in the past would have been very difficult to do. She told herself later that she should have gotten a photo of the border crossing. *"That was exciting,"* she thought. She also thought of how lucky she was to be an American. It was a perfect summer night as they parked on the street and exited the car, leaving their jackets behind.

Both of them brought their cameras. They started walking and taking photos galore of the many shops around the town. There was a market on the street that sold colorful flowers and foods and crafts. There were assorted businesses and buildings of mysterious, historic origins. Some of the businesses were closed. Joseph did not speak, nor could he read, Hungarian. They saw a synagogue, a castle and more cafes. One of the small cafes had advertising for

Pepsi-Cola. *"Cool,"* Jane thought.

Many sections of that small village were under construction. There was a wide variety of restaurants, churches, a museum, a post office, shops with purses, cookware, bakeware and jewelry. Many of the streets were lined with trees, iron fencing and flowers. Some streets were lined with tiny square bricks, in parallel fashion and in circular designs. It was a very quaint community.

They walked all the way around the town, then into the main plaza, where there were more restaurants. They saw bikers wearing helmets, kids playing on the church steps, some wearing inline skates, some people walking their dogs, couples holding hands, groups of teenagers and elderly folks sitting and relaxing on park benches.

Jane was so happy to have been there with Joseph and to just people-watch. But she admitted to herself that saying the word *"happy"* was not enough of an emotion to describe exactly how she felt. She was overwhelmed...again. *"This is so surreal,"* she thought, for in her wildest dreams, she had never imagined that she would have been in Europe, let alone Hungary. Was she dreaming? She was on the verge of crying, again.

Jane offered to buy dinner, although her lower belly was still quite bloated. Joseph thanked her. They looked around for a bit and found the smallest of small falafel shops, which was recessed in between two larger shops. He told her that their food should be superb. *"Cool,"* she said, for she was open to that idea. They went inside and the interior was very hot from the meat cooker.

154

Joseph spoke to the very short, plump woman behind the counter. He ordered vegetarian falafels and they opted to share an iced tea, which was in a very small refrigerated case, advertising Coca Cola. *"Cool, again."*

Jane took some photos of the woman behind the counter. Although, when Jane had asked her if she could, the woman's reaction was the same as most of the women whom Jane had met on her journey. They were too shy or too preoccupied with what they thought they had looked like. Or perhaps they were too embarrassed. But the woman allowed Jane to snap away anyway. Jane thanked her and paid the bill.

Dinner was around 5.80 Euros. The woman told Joseph that they also accepted Forint, which was Hungarian currency. Jane wanted to see what that money looked like, but did not get a chance to ask. They got their food, thanked the woman and walked outside. They crossed the plaza, then sat down on a bench. Behind them was a large fountain that was encircled with Earth-tone bricks and many stone benches, flowerpots and lit street lamps.

As they ate, they talked about dating. Jane had told Joseph that she was surprised that he was not with anyone, telling him that he was cute, personable and very funny. What she did not tell him was that her only requirements for dating a man was that he needed to be breathing and employed. She giggled to herself when she thought that sarcastic thought.

He told her that he had dated, but would take more time to figure out what he wanted in a woman, with the next one with whom he expects to settle down. She agreed with him on allowing *Time* to take its time, for *Time* to reach out and tell us when it was time. What she did not tell him was that she felt that her *Time* was running out, for her to find true love and true happiness.

Jane told him, without hesitation and almost all in one breath, was that she was hoping that she could get lucky one day and find a man who could do more than just tolerate her. She wanted to find a man who could appreciate her quirkiness, her odd sense of style or lack thereof, and appreciate her duality. He would need to appreciate her sarcasm and humor, he would love her no matter what, despite the fact that she could get chubby from time to time, but mostly in winter.

She told Joseph that she expected to find a man who would understand that no matter what, she would always love him, regardless of the possibly of getting bald, getting chubby himself or even being unable to perform as he got older.

He would need to understand that she loved being loved on, that she loved holding hands and cuddling and also…most of all, she loved having intimate time together, especially getting and giving physical attention. Joseph smiled at her and for a moment, Jane turned pink.

She told Joseph that that man would need to know that she was patient and kind, giving and honest, appreciative and doting, thoughtful and considerate. He would need to accept that she was short and funny, although she could not help either one of those things, and that she did remember things, but she also forgets things and that *"I am only human, too"*...

Jane went on... She wanted and deserved a man who would cherish her, love her and wanted to be with her, even when he was not with her. She wanted a man who would love to travel, take walks, hold hands in public and was not embarrassed by her in any way, shape or form *(especially her shape and her form).*

She wanted to be with a man who was confident in himself and confident in her and who would know that she would never lie or cheat or go behind his back to meet others. Jane deserved a man who would love her family, especially her kids and grandkids and her friends and even tolerate her enemies, no matter what. In addition, she deserved an honest man who would not make fun of her or insult her, even as a joke.

Even with that said, right then, Jane knew that she did not want or need all of those things, all at once. She would like to have them later, maybe not too much later, but when it was right and when God decided that it was right for her.

She told Joseph that since she believed that most people only get one soul mate in one life time, she feared that her so-called soul mate had already died in some other part of the world and therefore could not be reached for comment. They laughed at that.

They continued with their talk for a bit. They finished their delicious dinner, which was a tasty falafel filled with cucumbers, soured cream, a fried cream on top, onions, assorted vegetables and fresh fried bread. When they were done, they took a walk to the west of the plaza. It was too dark to take pictures by then and it was getting darker, so Jane's cautious side came out.

Once she told Joseph that she got worried when it got dark, he told her not to be concerned about it and so she tried. She was happy that he was with her on their little tour. They passed another castle, a pizzeria and another bar that was recessed in a basement of what they assumed was a closed and devastated building. There were beautiful and old homes, winding streets, private courtyards, more flowers and trees. They walked through a darkened area of more construction, but found a couple of restaurants and pubs that were still open for business. They commented that one of those places would have been great for them to have had dinner.

As they walked slowly by, they could see that one of the pubs was small and intimate-looking and had a familiar, cozy atmosphere. Jane felt that that pub could have been a place where she could have worked, frequented and could have become her home away from home. She knew that she was losing her home sometime soon and it would be gone forever. She thought that it would be nice to belong somewhere.

On some days, Jane felt somewhat desperate because she knew that life was passing her by. She had dreamed of belonging with a man, who would welcome her with open arms, no questions asked and who would be very willing for her to meet his family and some day move in together. She was praying for that in some form, when she met Pascal and she was hoping that he would be that man *"One can dream,"* she thought, for dreams and wishes and hopes were sometimes all that Jane had.

Jane could hear people having conversations, somewhere in the darkened paths of their tour. They saw some people touring around or cutting through that area, too, but for some reason, Joseph was oblivious to the idea of being in harm's way. But Jane's senses were heightened. Her eyesight was a bit poor at night, but her ears were wide open. Was it just a woman thing? Perhaps, but rightfully so. Luckily and positively, they were fine, as they made their way back to the car, coming around the neighborhood in a full circle.

Jane told Joseph that his navigation skills were excellent, for she would have been lost within 10 minutes of leaving the car. Not really, for she was a Girl Scout, but she had to compliment him somehow. He told her that his navigation skills were not that great, for he had gotten lost before, and recently.

Joseph told Jane that when he was on his recent backpacking and hiking tour in Italy, he had been lost for about two hours. During that time, he fell and broke his rib, but did not know that it was broken. Once he reunited with the touring group, they tried to persuade him to get medical attention, but he refused. She thought, *"You are as stubborn as all of the men that I have met in my life. Typical male, to not ask for directions and to be too willful to ask for help"...* Ultimately, he was fine on his tour there.

On their way back to the car, Jane and Joseph wound up coming around the bend of a street. She asked him if they could try to locate a bathroom soon, for her unpredictable belly. She told him that they could possibly wait until they got closer to Austria, but he told her that that may be too late. The bathrooms may be in poor condition or really dirty, no matter where they would find one.

He told her that they could find a bathroom and he apologized for forgetting that she had mentioned it earlier. They walked past the car and into the first restaurant adjacent to the plaza. There was no time to waste, as he asked the bartender if she could use the facilities. The young and quite attractive bartender pointed towards a narrow hallway to his right. Joseph located the woman's restroom and Jane went inside. That restroom was so small, that one would have to exit it, to change one's mind. Now that was tiny.

Although, she was sort of tiny herself, she was having trouble maneuvering inside the bathroom. She had to step up one step to get inside, where there was a small sink (everything was small there) and then she had to step up two steps to get inside the stall. She wiped off the seat, did the sign of *The Cross,* prayed that there were no germs, sat and did her business.

She thought that it was funny that she was pooping in Hungary and for some damn reason, that thought cracked her up out loud. She sat and sat, waited and waited, feeling quite dumb and ass-numb. She was quite embarrassed and thought, *"Of all the time in the world that this could happened...Why here? Why now?"* Despite that thought, she continued to laugh. She wondered what Joseph was thinking, as he waited for her in the bar.

A bit later, she met Joseph back at the bar, where he had finished having a cup of coffee and had been reading a newspaper. Now, she did not take that long or did she? *"Why is this an embarrassing thing, when everybody does it?"* she thought. *Hmmm...* They thanked the bartender and left.

They got into the car and she thanked him for driving them there and for giving her that wonderful, once-in-a-lifetime tour. He told her, *"No problem"* and they drove home.

On the way back, somehow the conversation came up again, about the guys that she had dated. *"Why was Joseph so curious?"* she wondered. She told him more about her former boyfriends, and of course about Pascal. They talked more about how devastated she was when she was cheated on and lied to. It was horrible to be told that she was fat by one of them and was told that she was not pretty enough by the other one. She confessed to him that she was called a *Bitch* multiple times by her ex-husband. She also told Joseph that life was too short for that kind of crap.

During that revealing conversation, she got a bit melancholy but ultimately, she was okay. Joseph made an interesting comment to Jane about what he had heard her saying, most of all. He stated that she had a tendency to conform to the guys that she had dated, but that she should be more independent of them. He asked her if he was wrong and she told him that he was not. She told him that she found it interesting that he was able to come to such a conclusion in a short amount of time. *"How observant,"* she thought.

And he was right. He was...and that was quite irritating. Not because of him being right, but because it was what she did: *Conform.* Because that was who she was, and she could not seem to help it.

Jane accommodated everyone in her life too much and she knew it, but she did not know why. They talked a bit more about that, but they sort of agreed that she should be more aware of that…or not. Joseph told her that perhaps that was just who she was: *The female giver, the female nurturer.* Joseph told her that was also okay. *"I truly have not been harmed by my own character, my own actions, my own personality, have I?"* she wondered. *Hmmm…*

They eventually made their way home, coming in from around the north of the town. They went inside, sat down at the table with their computers and he checked on emails, as she downloaded her photos. Her belly started making noises and she felt a bit uncomfortable. Joseph was a doll and did not acknowledge the loud noises that she was making. How embarrassing.

He was checking on a bus schedule for her, to possibly travel into Graz early the next day. She could tour the town and take photos and sight-see, taking in the sights and sounds, shopping at the markets, etc. Then later she could meet up with him after work, to see a concert there in the evening.

They stayed up until 11:30 p.m., Joseph went to bed, then Jane helped herself to some pink and white wine mixture. As she sipped her beverage, she continued to journal regarding the day's events. Earlier, Joseph had told her that there were only two buses from Oberwart to Graz. One was early in the morning and one was late at night. He said that he would call her, after talking to Mary, to see if she knew of another way for Jane to travel to Graz before the Jazz concert at 8:00 p.m.

Jane had told him that it was quite okay for her to miss sightseeing there, for that would give her an opportunity to see more of the town of Oberwart. She mentioned that she could possibly walk an hour to the mall or see more stores that were formerly closed on her previous visit into town.

As Joseph went to bed, Jane thanked him again, for the tour of his favorite town in Hungary, for showing her around and spending the evening with her.

After he went to bed, she sat and sighed. Another day was over and that put her another day closer to going home. It was something that she thought she did not want to do.

Did she fear the plane ride and the possibility of delays and missing her flights and sitting near an annoying stranger? Yes...

Did she worry about being the annoying stranger? Yes...

Did she fear the search for a new job and being poor and starving to death, if she did not find employment? Yes...

Did she fear losing her home...becoming homeless...and was she feeling helpless about what to do next? Yes...

Did she worry about going back to school and failing? Yes...

Did she wonder if Pascal was missing her, longing for her...or was he just hoping that she would disappear altogether? Yes...and yes...

Did she wonder if she would ever see her family again? Yes...

Did she know or feel that she knew, that they did not care about her? Yes...

Did she not want to return home, because she would be that much more farther away from her granddaughters? Yes...

Did she fear going home, because she might have to admit failure, in all areas of her life...possibly including, her own love life, again? Yes...

Did she want to stay, with the hopes of finding love in another country, since she could not find it in her own hometown of Dayton? Yes...

Did she want to remain in Europe because she was scared to go home and face the problems that awaited her...and that she would have to deal with them head on? Yes...

Did she want to stay because she was somehow feeling at home and comfortable in Joseph's company? Yes...

Did she miss Pascal...and did she fear that he would cheat on her? Yes...and most definitely, Yes!

Jane was scared...she freely admitted it...but to pinpoint exactly why, she did not immediately know. Except she was coming to the conclusion that it was all of the above and much, much more. Jane wished on a daily basis, that she would stop worrying, and she wished that her brain would quiet down. She also knew that her brain was unique to her and wanted so badly to love her brain. Her brain, her mind, was what made her loving, creative, empathic, compassionate and patient. And there should never be anything criticized about that. Never.

Jane turned off the computer, put her glass in the sink, turned off the lights and made her way upstairs very quietly. She brushed and flossed, used the restroom, put on her jams and plopped into her soft, albeit borrowed, bed and just lay there thinking about the day.

As she drifted off to sleep, she thought of the sights, the sounds, the smells, the tastes, and the feel of all that had taken place before her. She was just one lucky woman that day, for she felt as if she fit in. She felt that she would do well, if she stayed and that somehow, if she took up residence in Europe, it would find its way to love her.

Deep down, she had always felt that she was somewhat lucky, for she had not died from her mistakes, although she had felt as if she wanted to. What she thought was in spite of her shortcomings and of her flaws and quirks, she had found some love, if only temporarily. She had been lucky to have had many friends throughout her years, who had stuck by her in her time of need.

She had been lucky to have those same friends stick around and still find time to appreciate her and not take advantage of her kindness and her dependability. She had been lucky to have met many people along the way, with whom she had shared her life… and therefore, she sometimes felt as if they were the lucky ones. That may sound arrogant, but it was not.

As she lay in bed, she thought…that all of their lives had been enriched somehow by meeting, conversing, sharing stories, loving each other in some way. But somehow, for her, it always came to an end, even as friendships came and went. It was so hard for her to let go because she had been so happy, at least for a time.

Is happiness overrated? Was what she was feeling true happiness or was it just a false state of being, that she failed to truly recognize? She was happy with boyfriend #1...and boyfriend #2...and now boyfriend #3, Pascal. So then why did she let Pascal worry her so much? She told herself that the worry was because of her brief life experiences with those other men and how those situations turned out to be quite devastating. She forced the negativity out of her mind.

It was a great day, indeed, despite the fact that she could have benefited from more elimination. *"Thank You, again, for allowing me to be here. Amen."*

Friday...

Jane woke up around 6:00 a.m., but lounged in the bed, while she heard Joseph get ready for work. She did not want to interrupt his routine, so she waited to use the bathroom. She thought she drifted off to sleep again and when she awoke, she felt a bit refreshed, hopeful for another day.

She got up, looked at the cell phone and it was 8:00 a.m. She made the bed, gathered some clothes, put them in the bathroom, started bath water, used the toilet, went back to the bathroom, brushed her teeth, stripped and soaked for a bit. *"Ahhh"*... *"I do need a back and a neck massage,"* she thought.

She washed up, conditioned her hair, got dressed in tan Capri pants, sandals, a while undershirt and a long pink, white and gray argyle top. She put on makeup, cleaned out the tub, blow-dried her hair, styled it and put in some clips. She grabbed her purse and went downstairs.

She went to the kitchen, got orange juice, oats, and water and she cut up an apple. Then she sat at the table, turned on the computer, read some national news and ate. She returned some emails and sent photos and journaled.

Around 10:45 a.m., she straightened up, cleaned up the kitchen, successfully had more belly action, then she gathered her things and took off for the mall. Although she did not know exactly how to get there, she had faith that she would somehow find it. She would jot down her thoughts on the way, stop and write like a crazy person, as ideas would pop into her head. When she would return to Joseph's home and to her computer, she would journal the day's excitement. She was nervous as she walked out of the front door.

Whew! Around 6:30 p.m., Joseph had started dinner and she could smell the lamb baking in the oven. Yummy! He went into the backyard to do some weeding, after he finished in the kitchen and taken out the trash. She had heard him whistle his little happy tune after he sang a bit of it, while he had prepared the food. "I can see clearly now, the rain is gone…" She finished making the salad and then they waited for dinner to cook. He stayed busy with things around the house and she sat at the table. She had kicked off her shoes, sat on her bum and she had typed away about her great day…

This was what had happened:

It took Jane around two hours to walk to the mall. She had headed west from the house, which was the only way that she could go into town, then she walked south. Within fifteen minutes, she had regretted her choice of footwear. *"Dammit,"* she thought, *"Why didn't I just wear my sensible gym shoes that I had brought from home?"* *"Oh well."* She kept on walking.

She walked down the left side of the street, the opposite of what she had done on Monday. She took more photos and took her time. There were more cafes, car dealerships, shops galore, beautiful homes recessed within and between the businesses and a post office that she did not see the other day.

She passed the courthouse and made her way west down the side street that lead to Joseph's place of business, near the hospital. She went inside the apothecary (drug store) to inquire on belly meds, but she changed her mind quickly because the place was packed and the pharmacists looked tired and impatient. She walked a few stores down and took a picture of a cute pizzeria delivery car.

When she turned around, a tall and very plump man was staring in her direction. As she approached him, she asked him if he spoke English. He told her that he did. She asked him if he could give her directions to the mall. As she looked at his puzzled face, she corrected her question by saying, *"The Shopping Center."* Then, his face lit up for then, he knew what she had meant. He immediately started speaking quickly and he mentioned that he was confused as to why she was taking pictures of his delivery car. Jane told him that she took the picture because it was cute and unique. He smiled and told her that it was okay then. He asked her where she was from. When she told him that she was from America, his smile could not have been any bigger.

He was the owner of the pizzeria. He invited her to come back and to join him later in the week at his home for dinner. When he asked if she was staying at a hotel, she told him that she was staying with a friend, who was a doctor and for some reason he looked so pleased. He invited Joseph, too. He was happy and quite insistent. She told him that she would think about it and she would check with Joseph.

He smiled a lot and looked Jane directly in the eyes. She liked that about him. She admired his animated face and his honest demeanor. He gave her the directions to the mall. Jane was aware that for some reason her eyes were very wide, as if that would help her understand every other word that he was saying. She finally understood some of what he was saying. *"You turn right at the hospital…at the street lamp (traffic light)…then go down to the next street lamp and turn left."* She hated to admit that she had forgotten some of what he had said, as soon as he had said it. She was better off reading directions.

He asked when she was returning and she told him that she was not sure. She thought that he wished her luck and she thanked him for his help. She thought that having dinner at his home could be very interesting and possibly a wonderful learning experience. She wondered, if she could have talked Joseph into going back that weekend and to meet that very animated, large man and the rest of his very large family. She had forgotten to ask his name, but thought that she might run into him upon her return.

Jane went on her merry way, aware that she was sweating bullets, but not really caring about that. She forced herself to stop thinking about her belly issues for the moment. She passed by a swimming pool, that was surrounded by high, well-manicured bushes. It was busy with the sounds of happy children. It was a great sound; a sound that she had deeply missed. Jane love kids and would miss working with them, since she lost her job working with preschoolers. *Sigh…and life goes on, now doesn't it?*

She took photos during her walk, including one of a creek. *"Water under the bridge,"* she thought. She walked over that bridge and took photos of more restaurants, a couple more cafes, a kindergarten school, then she walked towards the hospital on the corner, at a traffic light. She turned right and stopped to take photos of Joseph's place of business.

She wondered if it would have been an okay time for her to stop in, but she regretfully changed her mind and kept walking. Joseph had said later, that it would have been okay to stop by and meet his co-workers, if she had wanted. By then, she was at least an hour out and had developed sores on the top of her feet.

"New sandals. What was I thinking?" She passed by another cafe, a cemetery on a steep hill to the left and an area of tilled up dirt to the right that was being readied for construction of new

buildings. There was a small billboard that stated as much. She saw advertisements on other billboards of many things that she did not understand. She admired the small, quaint beautiful homes with flowers galore, flower pots, iron gates, small cars parked on the street and in the driveways.

She saw homes decorated with 3-dimensional sculptures on the outside, with window boxes, live pets in some windows, small lawns and trellises. She was in heaven for the entire walk because each of the neighborhoods were as enchanting as the next.

The day was bright, warm and welcoming and even though her feet hurt and she was sweating like crazy, she was aware of how alive she felt. She felt safe overall, but was still a bit worrisome. Was it just a female caution or just an American caution?

She saw kids on bikes, a man pushing his disabled motorcycle and people in their cars at the cemetery parking lot. She thought, *"I wonder if they are making out?"* She saw a woman who was arguing with a man about something, and a business that sold cemetery and garden monuments.

Then for some reason, she turned right at the light, where the street stopped. She passed another creek, car repair shops, more cafes and a restaurant. It occurred to her that somehow she knew she was going the wrong way. Jane felt comfortable enough to ask for help from a young woman who was walking in her direction. She was pretty, had platinum blond hair, a bright yellow shirt and was pushing a small toddler girl in a stroller of sorts, that looked more like a tricycle with a basket on the back. *"That looks so handy,"* she thought. Jane asked the woman if she spoke English and she indicated that she spoke a little. She told Jane that she spoke German, Hungarian, Italian and Romanian. *"How exciting and how envious I am at this moment"* Jane thought. *"Okay, this is going to be a challenge."*

Jane asked where the mall was located. The woman just stared at her, but when Jane said *"shopping center,"* the woman knew what she needed. Jane said, *"Oh, thank goodness!"* She told Jane to go back from where she came, as she pointed west and *"after three street lamps, turn right. The shopping center will be right there."*

Now, bear in mind that the woman did not say it just like that, but Jane knew what she meant. She thanked her and did just as she had suggested. They walked the same direction for a block then they parted ways. Jane thanked her again, crossed the street and kept walking.

Jane saw more beautiful houses, a man walking her way, an elderly woman with groceries walking her but from across the street and also, a boy bumped into Jane, as he was coming up behind her on his bicycle. He never said *"pardon me"* or anything indicating that he was in the wrong.

She passed the second light and still wondered where the mall was. After coming around the bend of the street, the area opened up with more businesses, more developed area, another traffic light ahead, bigger street signs and highway signs and finally, there was the mall to the right. *"Thank goodness."*

The outside of the side of the mall was labeled 'EO' (actually lowercase eo). Jane did not know what that meant, but she did recognize it as a mall. She walked just a few more steps and entered under a canopy of a mezzanine area. There was a huge parking lot to the left and many stores on the first level, with outside entrances and merchandise on display in front of their doors. She walked under the canopy and got instant relief from the shade. It was 12:40 p.m. and she was happy to have finally made it.

She stopped at a shoe store and looked through the sandals on display on the main floor. She found her size. She went inside and paid 8.95 Euros for the new, form-fitting blue-strapped sandals. She went back outside, sat down on a round bench, put on her new shoes and continued looking around.

The mezzanine level had about four sets of round benches, an open-air Italian ice cream shop with seating, large leaning posts to hold up the canopy, rectangular areas of grasses and pots of plants and flowers, trash cans, cigarette cans and an *'up-only'* escalator. There were many patrons coming to shop for the day. *"This is the perfect place to people-watch."* she thought.

She saw many families and groups of teenagers. She saw couples, some of whom were fighting or at least arguing, some unruly children, behaving children and infants. There were women shopping alone, men shopping alone and some men with man-purses. There were over-dressed women, under-dressed women, some women in heels, flats and gym shoes, and some with large and small purses.

Some of the people were on their cell phones or using hand-held computers or listening to their mini-music players. With some of the patrons, she could not tell whether they were female or male. There were elderly folks walking with a pep in their step, and some with a distinct gait and some with walkers and canes.

She saw some patrons with special challenges, wheelchairs and so on and also families that looked like they just got done at sports matches with their kids, like soccer or basketball. Some people were thin, too thin, fat and too fat, average in size and some average in shape and not so average in height.

To be perfectly honest, sans the different languages that they spoke and the foreign signs to Jane, that sure could have been a mall in any part of the world, including America, including in and around Dayton. It was perfect.

Jane went inside the main entrance, which had a extraordinarily wide revolving door with window displays inside the door itself. *"That is unique."* As she entered, she thought, *"Once you've seen one mall, you've seen them all."* There were stores galore. She saw electronics, phones, school supplies, clothing of all kinds with some on sale and some on clearance. There were purses, camping equipment, hair supplies and a hair salon, accessories, watches and so on.

She followed the universal signs to the bathroom, which was past the escalators and past an irregular-shaped fountain and a small body of water. She walked to the right, found the ladies bathroom, went inside and did her thing. The sound system inside was playing a Jason Mraz song and Jane sang along in her head. When she came back out, she heard The Backstreet Boys on the PA system inside the main mall.

She walked to the left and saw Hooters, which was across a walkway and a driveway. She thought, *"Well, I have never been to a Hooters, even in Dayton, so why not now?"* She went inside and was greeted by the very cute, petite and helpful waitress, Elizabeth. She told Jane to sit anywhere she wanted. At least that was what Jane thought Elizabeth had said, for her accent was heavy.

Jane found a table that had two high chairs and a portion of a booth. She opted for the booth and sat down, relieved just to be in some shade and shelter. Elizabeth came over to her, Jane asked if she spoke English and Elizabeth said that she did. Jane told her what she wanted, which was just a hamburger, fries and a diet Coke. The waitress told her that it came with a salad and Jane agreed to try that. She left to get the order and Jane sat there for just a minute and took a deep breath.

The sunlight was hitting her directly on the face, but she was determined not to move. She was being bugged, literally, by two or three bees, which she had to bat at continuously. *"How annoying."* She looked through the photos on her camera and then Elizabeth brought the food a few minutes later. Jane had to take a picture of that ridiculously large hamburger, which she, unfortunately, was able to finish off. *"Dammit."* For some silly reason, she was now worried about her cholesterol, among the many things that were already worrying her. *"Seriously, Sweetie"* she thought, *"Why would you think of cholesterol at a wonderful time like this? Who really should give a crap about that?"*

Jane ate mostly everything, leaving some of the fries and the bun. She drank all of the pop and then downed the water that she had brought with her. Familiar American music was playing in the background, including Richard Marx, Elton John and strangely, Dolly Parton's *"9 to 5."* She was happy to hear it...well, mostly all of it. Even at home, she did not hear much of that latter song.

Another couple came in and sat in the booth next to her and that was her first encounter with cigarette smoke. Apparently, there was no ban there. *"Dammit!"* She watched the different soccer games on several huge TVs, not knowing who was who *(Haifa vs. Genk, Zurich vs. Bayern, Odense vs. Villarreal)*. Jane loved to watch most sports, although she didn't know all the rules. She loved soccer, basketball, baseball and football, but for some reason, her true favorite was hockey and she was not sure why.

As she was growing up, all of the students in her grade school, including her siblings, were offered free Cincinnati Reds tickets (in the *"nose bleed"* sections) and also were offered free Dayton Gems hockey tickets at Hara Arena in Dayton, as long as they were able to get straight A's. Jane and her dad were always going to the Reds' games, because she was basically a good student.

She remembered going to the hockey games with other parents and her friends a lot, too. Despite the fact that Jane was never comfortable in cold weather, she loved going to the games and watching them skate and fight. She once owned a hockey stick with all of the Dayton Gems signatures on it, dating back from the

1970s. It was stolen and broken and thrown away by her ex-chubby hubby. Why did he have to be so mean and do that?...and ...Why did that butt-head have to pop into her head, at that moment?

Perhaps the true reason that Jane loved hockey so much, was because she liked to watch the men beat up each other or fight with each other. She could live vicariously through them, as she imagined pounding her siblings and classmates who picked on her. Perhaps...

Jane told Elizabeth why she was visiting Europe and they asked another waitress to take their photo together. She got the impression that Elizabeth was used to having her picture taken, because she was so enthusiastic and quite photogenic, plus she stuck out her boobs when the picture was taken. *"Oh well. After all, I'm at Hooters"* Jane told herself. *"If I had boobs like that, I would stick them out, too."*

Jane paid the bill, which came to 10.20 Euros and thanked her waitress, then walked around the rest of the mall, looking at the pretty clothes and shoes and jewelry. Then all of a sudden, she was happy to make her way to the restroom and finally, some more success. She listened to the music and sang along and did not care who listened. While she sat in the stall, she sang, *"She's a devil woman, with evil on her mind."*

A bit later, she walked around again, took more photos, then decided it was time to go home. On her way out, she saw a drug store, so she went inside. With the help of the female clerk, she bought some constipation meds, to use at another time or another day, for she knew there would be more trouble some time. She also bought raspberry jelly for Joseph, since they downed the rest of his that week. She walked outside around 2:30 p.m. and could see that a storm was brewing in the west. *"Great!"* Now that was sarcasm.

Jane sat and waited for a bit, debating with herself whether she could possibly get back home before it hit. She did not know the quickest route, so she opted to wait it out. The clouds were low and dark and the wind was picking up tremendously. She went inside a shoe store and bought some soft wool socks, came back to the round benches and put those on to cushion her blisters.

The footwear combo of wooly socks and sandals looked stupid on her feet and she thought, *"I now have joined the elderly grandma club."* But she just did not care. Comfort was her ultimate goal and she got it. Besides, it was more than likely that she was never going to see that area of the world again and she hoped no one was judging her on her choice of footwear.

She watched the wind pick up and the lightning strikes in the distance. Many people were coming and going, scrambling for safety as the storm approached. She continued to watch the storm and people-watch. And within a few minutes, the rain and the wind hit the mall.

Everyone who was sitting on the benches had to get up and run closer to the store fronts. She looked up and there were round hole designs in the canopy, so rain was inevitable to come in. She watched as some people ran to their cars and from their cars, with skirts whipping, umbrellas whipping and jackets billowing. The PA music continued to play, as she heard Patrick Swayze's song from

Dirty Dancing … *"She's like the wind"* … and *"Georgie Girl,"* among others.

As the rain pelted down on all of them, she scrambled to the safety of the up escalator and its balcony. She sat on the floor, watched the rain, watched the running patrons coming into the mall and some as they ran out. She watched the storm in the distance as it stayed in full force for some time. She had to admit that she not only felt safe in her temporary perch, but she felt cozy.

At that moment, she had wished that she had a better camera to capture the darkened storm clouds, the lightening and the rain. She wished that she could have captured all of the shiny traffic lights, car lights and streets lights that were illuminated against the threatening darkness. It was dangerous, but oddly welcoming, because rain was needed, but it also made her feel alive to witness it. She enjoyed the people-watching. She enjoyed the smell of the rain. She enjoyed watching the busy-ness of that moment.

Jane left a message for Joseph on his cell phone, of her whereabouts and of needing help getting home. She just sat and waited…watched and listened…as many patrons ascended the escalator and began their shopping inside the mall. She also listened to the many patrons who came through the doors behind her, sounding disappointed to discover that they could not descend those same moving stairs. She could not completely understand German or many of the other languages that she had heard on her trip. But there was also one distinct guttural sound that most people make when they are upset. And most of those people made that sound and even cussed, if she were to guess, when they could not take that exit to run to their cars.

For the rest of the night, the storm lasted for quite some time and Jane was glad that she did not walk home. A bit later, Joseph called and told her that he got her message and that he was on his way. He apologized for not getting her message earlier. He had taken his bike to work, rode it home quickly and got soaked in the process, then he washed up and changed, then jumped in his car to come and get her.

A few moments later, she saw his car pull into the parking lot. She ran inside the mall and went down the escalator and met him at the curb. She jumped inside and thanked him for coming to get her. He asked her how was her day and she told him. She asked about his day and he told her that it was good.

Joseph told Jane that he needed to stop at the grocery store. While they were there, she sarcastically asked him if Austria had fruit. He had a puzzled look on his face, so she told him that she had observed that most of their diet consisted of meat, cheese, bread, wine and pastries...so...where were the fruits and vegetables that she could buy? He showed her the produce section of the store and she bought grapes and strawberries, plus some spinach.

She told him to get what he wanted, for she felt as if she needed to treat him to something, due to all of his hospitality. He did not want to accept, but she was glad that he did. She wondered if he felt guilt of some kind, but he did not need to feel that way. She told him that she felt she could never repay him. She wanted to help in some way, to earn her keep, so to speak. He thanked her, they made their purchases and then left.

Back at his home, they fixed dinner together and ate as if their lives depended on it. *"Why does food taste better when someone else fixes it?"* she wondered. They had salad, fruit, raw vegetables, cheese and beer for dinner, as they chit-chatted about their day. After they cleaned up, she journaled and also showed him the photos from her adventure. Because of the storm, they decided to skip the concert and watch a movie instead.

Later on, Joseph let her know that they would be having a female friend of his joining them for beer and to watch the movie, *"Platoon."* *"Cool,"* she told him. She was always looking to meet new people. Alisa arrived a few minutes later. She was tall, thin and quite, quite beautiful. She instantly reminded her of someone famous, but she just could not remember who.

They shook hands at their introduction, she petted the cat then she and Joseph went outside, had a beer each and talked for some time. Jane continued to type away on her computer. What they did not know was that Jane was observing them from the reflection in the open double patio doors.

She could tell that Joseph liked Alisa, based on his body language, the sparkle in his eyes and his massive smile. Jane wondered what was the deal? *"Why did he not make a move on her before now. She's gorgeous!"* Sarcastically, she thought, *"If he does not ask her out, I will...for him."*

Jane hoped that all would go well for him or for them, once she went back home. She wondered if she was supposed to offer to go upstairs and give them alone time, but she just did not know what to do. She felt as if she was infringing on their time together, or at least, that she was putting a damper on his bachelor moves. She also felt like a voyeur. She loved to people-watch and that situation was no different. Their body language was something at which to marvel.

In addition, Jane hated to think that she sort of wished that Joseph looked at her the way that he was looking at Alisa. Not for him to fall in love with Jane, mind you. But who wouldn't...who couldn't...fall in love with a short and funny beauty from Dayton, Ohio?

But what Jane wished for...was for any man to gaze upon her like he did just then, and prove to her that he admired and loved what he saw. Jane had never had that before. No man ever looked at her, the way Joseph looked at Alisa. *Why was that?*

Lust was what she had received...perceived...and recognized... from the facial expressions of the men that she had known, and it had taken her a long time to realize that. Anyone can lust after another. However, true admiration and eventual love was what Jane was hoping for. She looked upon that situation that was right in front of her, as a moment of hope for her and for Joseph. She hoped that being there was not going to hinder whatever may blossom for him.

Quite a while later, he came back in and asked if Jane was ready to watch the movie. She quickly closed the computer, got up, sat on the couch and was ready. He had the movie started, then Alisa announced that she had to leave to cook for her father. Alisa and Jane told each other, *"It was nice meeting you"* and Jane could see that Joseph was disappointed. He walked Alisa to the front door. *"How sweet and how unfortunate."* Jane was not sure what had verbally transpired between then, and she felt that it was none of her business, but…she had to admit that she wanted Joseph to tell her.

He came back to the living room and they watched the movie, while he remained working on his computer and as she was slithered down on the couch, waiting for the bad parts to happen. He was preoccupied with whatever he was looking at, in addition to checking bus schedules for Jane to travel into Vienna the following day. She made a comment or two about how much cussing there was in the movie and Joseph acknowledged that.

Overall, Jane enjoyed the movie and she was amazed on how young all of the actors looked, especially the ones that she had recognized. She told him that that was not as bad as she had expected, regarding gore and graphics. She turned down the volume, then turned off the movie. He put away his computer then went downstairs to get his laundry. Jane got out her computer at the table and returned some emails and journaled. When Joseph returned back to the living room, they said goodnight and Jane went upstairs to bed.

It was around 11:30 p.m. Jane was hoping for a good night's sleep. She changed into some jams, brushed and flossed and stared at her reflection for a moment, realizing that she needed to color her hair.

Sarcastically, she thought that she needed a face lift, for the wrinkles had surfaced two-fold. She realized, despite her stress there and at home, and despite her constant worrying and sadness over many things that she could not control, that she looked pretty damn good for a tired grandmother. She asked herself, *"Why doesn't Pascal love me?"* Then she answered her own pondering...

It was not her...but him...and he was scared, just like she was. He was denying himself true bliss by not getting to know the real her. Even as she thought those thoughts, she knew that she was lying to herself. She knew Pascal, like the others, did not know how to just let go and love unconditionally, without forethought, without prejudice...without conditions.

"Are there any men out there who can do that?" She did not know, but for a moment she thought that she was willing to find out with him. Somehow she knew that when she got back home, her life was going to make some drastic changes (again). She was going to fight those changes, kicking and screaming, into the next chapter of her life. She was not sure how she knew that, but she did and dammit, being right, some of the time...was quite exhausting!

She finished up in the bathroom, went to her room, turned off the light, got in bed and found the baggie with the shirt and cologne, that was hidden under her pillow. She opened it and took a deep breath. *"Awww."*

She was in aroma heaven. A reflection of thoughts and experiences from the day, came to the surface of her brain, as she drifted off to sleep. She had a smile on her face, as she was feeling lucky, if only for one more day.

"Thank You for another wonderful day of heavenly senses. Amen."

Saturday...

Jane had awoken around 6:00 a.m., and as she lay there for quite some time, she thought, *"Wow, I still haven't heard from my daughter."* It was hard for her to believe that at that moment, the majority of her trip was almost over. She had to face the true reality of life when she got back home. She had to find another job, which was scarier than her trip. She had to pay some bills, that she would not be able to afford.

She would lose her house, work all the hours that she could, if she found a job, send out more resumes and check on the status of other resumes. She would continue writing and possibly take up her friend's offer to stay with her in Arizona or to stay with her *cousin near Akron, and in both places she would be looking for work. Whew!* It was lot to absorb early in the morning, but *"Oh well"...*

She listened for the sounds of Joseph arising, but heard nothing more the sound of a fly bopping on her bedroom window. She got up, opened the window and gently coaxed him out. *"It had to be a male,"* she sarcastically thought, *"since he was quite irritating this early in the morning."* She brushed her teeth, started her bath water, gathered her clothes and took a quick bath. Jane locked the bathroom door because she did not want Joseph to walk in on her. *"That would be horribly mortifying,"*

She got dressed in a purple V-neck top and brown shorts, gelled her hair, put on some makeup, cleaned up the bathroom, went back to her room, gathered her purse and her new cheap canvas bag, that she bought at the drug store for one Euro. She filled it with her mini-music player, tissues and some granola bars and went downstairs.

Jane got some orange juice and oats, journaled on her computer, sent out some emails, then around 8:30 a.m., she put a bottled water and a bottle of tea in her bag and headed for town for an ATM. Jane needed to get Euros for the bus ride into Vienna. She still did not know how much it was going to cost her and she had forgotten to ask Joseph the previous night. She expected or at least hoped, that he would call her soon on the cell phone. She thought, *"He may not even be in the house. He may be out on a bike ride or running errands."* She just did not know.

Jane expected to be an hour, but it only took her thirty minutes on the walk to get what she needed. She asked one of two women who were waiting at the bus stop at the bottom of Joseph's street, if that stop was the right place for the bus to Vienna. One of the women confirmed that it was, then she asked how much one way would cost and she told Jane that it would be 20 Euros. Jane thanked her and took off into town to get money.

On her walk, she wondered where those two women were going. The one woman who spoke was tall and pretty, young and had short blond hair. The other woman was much older, had brown hair and was much shorter. She wondered if they were friends or acquaintances. She knew that they were not going to be there when she got back to the bus stop.

Jane wondered how differently the day would have turned out if she had just been able to get on the bus with them at that moment. She wondered if they would have been able to sit with each other and talk about their lives, about their plans for the day. *Sigh* and *"Oh well…such is life."* Jane stopped at the first ATM which was inside a bank, but the door would not open. A beautiful dark-haired woman appeared from around the corner and she offered to open the door for her. Jane asked if it was open for business and she said something, pointing to the machine inside. Jane had gathered from what she watched, was that the patrons of the bank had to have a card to activate the doors to get inside. *"Okay."* Jane thanked the helpful woman.

Jane got some Euros from the machine then walked back towards the bus stop. She stopped at a gas station to buy something, in order to break a 20 Euro. She bought a chocolate covered, cinnamon cream-filled pastry for 1.60 Euros and thanked the clerk for her time.

Jane had to explain and re-explain what she had meant for the clerk to *'break'* a twenty. Since she still had some time to kill, she headed back towards the house, where she got some grapes, then took off again for the bus. She had not even made it into Vienna yet and already she was breaking a sweat and feeling the burn in her calves. *"If this does not get me into shape and make me have successful bowel movements, then I don't know what would,"* she laughed at that thought.

It was 9:30 a.m. By the time she got back to the bus stop and settled down on a bench, she called Joseph. She apologized that she had woken him. *"I was getting up anyway,"* he told her. He could not believe that he did not hear her leave...twice! He double-checked the time of the bus and she was right on schedule. She thought that he had told her the night before, that the pick up time was 10:00 a.m. and she was right. He told her that she would be dropped off at the street market at the Sesassion Location, around 11:45 a.m., then he told her to look for Oberwart/Gussing on the bus for her return.

The return times were starting at 3:15 p.m. on the quarter hour, but not at 8:15 p.m., but until 9:15 p.m. *"Thanks."* She mentioned to him that she hoped that she would be okay and he told her that he knew she would be. She was glad that he had faith in her, too. They wished each other a good day and hung up.

Jane took a deep breath and waited. She ate some of her slightly smashed pastry, that had ended up in the bottom of her bag. It was still delicious. She cut her fingernails. She stood up...sat down and then she saw the bus. *"Awesome!"* She got on, asked the amount, it was 19.30 Euros. *"Perfect."* She paid the male driver and sat down on her claimed seat, which was in the middle of the bus and at a window. It was a double decker bus, so she told herself that she must ride on the top level when she returned.

When Joseph told Jane that the buses into town were like charter buses with a toilet, she was a happy woman. The bus was comfortable and clean. The driver drove like crazy, through the small town of Pinkafeld and beyond and crazier on the open highway. *"Is he even going the speed limit, whatever that was?"* Jane wondered.

Jane popped in her ear-buds, ate some grapes and listened and bee-bopped her head to a wonderful variety of music: Rascal Flatts' *"Everyday Love"* and *"While You Loved Me,"* *"Oklahoma-Texas Border"* and many more. She listened to many Brad Paisley songs (which never disappoint)…Sugarland's *"It Happens"* (and *IT* does!)…some Bob Dylan songs (can never go wrong there)…*"Say Hey (I love you)"* by Michael Fronte and Spearhead (that was a song that she had for a ring-tone for a certain ex, but had not cried lately when she heard it). She listened to Garth Brooks' *"The Dance"* (that song made her sad, but she managed to hold back the tears).

She heard *"Life in the Fast Lane"*…Jo Dee Messina's *"That's the Way It Is"* (a great song about Jane's life…and Miss Messina's)… She listened to Sting….Keith Urban… Dierks Bentley *(Sexy on a Stick!…I will take one of those to go, please!)*…The Doors' *"Under Waterfall"* (Love it)…and Kelly Clarkson's *"Already Gone"* (so true)… She listened to Jason Mraz's *"Make It Mine"* (Love it)… *"Horses"* from Due South…everything Gaelic Storm (she so wanted to get up and dance in the aisles of the bus whenever their music played in her ears)…Kenny Chesney's *"California"* and *"Crazy Last Night"*…Michael Buble's *"I've Got The World On A String"* and many more songs. Jane loved her variety of music.

On the drive, the sun was shining and the sky was periodically dotted with puffy clouds. She realized at that moment that she had forgotten her map of Vienna and an umbrella, in case it rained and she *did not have any sunscreen to put on her delicate, sensitive Irish skin. "How stupid of me...how silly of me?"* She was slightly sunburned from the other day's walk to the mall, so why would she not have remembered to ask Joseph if he had any? She did not include that in her carry-on luggage. What was she thinking?...and *"Oh well...too late."*

Jane was in awe, as she saw numerous pastures, with rolled up straw or hay, rows and rows of trees that were tall and fat and thin and short. There were cows in the fields, houses and chalets galore, varying in sizes and colors, decorated with window boxes full of colorful flowers. Through Pinkafeld, there were many cafes with large multicolored umbrellas, a place called The Café Daytona *(Cool!)*...narrow winding streets, with railroad tracks, hotels, cyclists, people on motorcycles, many shops including ice cream, accessories, clothing, etc. There were striped and solid-colored awnings on store fronts and some gazebos.

They drove through a lot of 2-lane, winding rural roads. A few of the times that she was able to turn around, the valleys opened up to allow her to see many villages and rivers below them and beyond them, among a vast number of trees and mountains. It was spectacular, picturesque, almost indescribable. It was more than beautiful.

Jane was reminded of a moment...a scene...in the movie *"Contact"* when Jodi Foster was finally in space. Her face was filled with emotion, and at one moment it was distorted to reveal her childhood face, being in awe of that once-in-a-lifetime moment of seeing the most beautiful thing in her life. She was at a loss for words to describe that beauty before her, as Ms. Foster says, *"They should have sent a poet"* (to describe that spectacular view). That was how Jane felt. She actually shivered, when she realized all of its beauty.

Megan and Sawyer's mother should have been a poet.

Once on the highway, Jane saw gas stations, bigger outlet stores, repair shops, etc. Even on the drive, she was overcome with emotions, for she felt all alone and temporarily lost. She did not know what direction her life was going to take...today, tomorrow... or when she got back home to Dayton. She wanted and needed, to have had someone with her at that moment...to share in that once-in-a-lifetime event. Somehow she felt abandoned. She held back tears as best she could, but found that a few ran down her face and she quickly wiped them away, hoping no one saw.

On the bus, was a middle-aged couple who sat in the back and a boy of about 9 years old (eating something from a container), who sat in the very front. There was a chubby, 50-plus-years-old woman, who wore a black skirt, a silvery long-sleeved top, with glass earrings and matching necklace and she had black and purple hair. Jane asked her to take Jane's picture, which she did, then she asked the woman if she was heading into Vienna for lunch, because she looked very pretty. Jane gestured 'eat' and 'beautiful' in sign language and the woman nodded her head, confirming her plans. She nodded her head again and said, *"You are a very nice girl."* *"Thanks."*

Around 10:45 a.m., Jane started to get sleepy. *"No!"* She took a caffeine pain pill with some water and was happy that the caffeine had kicked in just a bit later. *"I have one more hour to go,"* she thought, *"And I must see all that I can see."* She was nervous and excited, and somewhat scared.

The bus arrived into Vienna around 11:45 a.m. She thanked the driver, who agreed to let her take his picture, then she exited the bus, after she took photos, even while the bus was still parking. She ran into two young men, who she heard speaking English. She stopped them to inquire if they were from America. One was from New York and the other was his Austrian guide. They talked for a moment. The New Yorker was traveling around Europe for the summer and for fun and for the experience *"of a lifetime"* and the Austrian was there to help him out. She told them her reasons for being in Europe, too. She wondered if somehow she could make arrangements like that in the future, whereby she could get a guide to tour Europe again.

She took their picture with their permission, wished them luck on their travels and vice versa, then said goodbye. She headed directly into the Marketplace, which spanned several blocks, with dual aisles and so much to see. It was buzzing with many people of varying nationalities and dialects and languages. It was breathtaking and colorful. Jane wound up taking over 300 pictures that day.

Jane had seen many people on her travels that week, in the airports, the train station, the bus station, the mall, downtown Oberwart, now Vienna and so on. Some of those people looked similar to those she knew personally and those she had seen on TV. She could have sworn that she saw Conan O'Brien, Allyson Janney, Bruce Willis and Arte Johnson, although she thought he was no longer living. She thought she saw one of her former boyfriends (now that would have been weird) and some friends and family members, TV personalities from home and acquaintances from long ago. *"It was amazing how similar many people are, even all the way in Austria. Amazing."*

The Marketplace was the perfect place to be on that wonderful Saturday. It had *cafes, cafes, cafes,* etc. There were shops that sold raw and cooked meats, many different cheeses, raw and dried fruits and even fruits that she had never seen before. There were vegetables, spreads, spices, coffees, specialty foods which she couldn't pronounce. She heard many conversations and many people were taking pictures also, of the many items for sale. There were shops with International fare, Chinese and Japanese foods and clothing, Indian shops, Italian shops offering foods and many other items and many crafts. There were many teas and fruit smoothies to entice anyone's pallet. The colors and displays were vibrant and welcoming.

She continued to walk around and people-watch, take photos and literally bumped into people of all kinds. Then eventually she heard some music and gravitated toward the sound. She snapped a picture of two men playing musical instruments and singing in a different language. They smiled and stopped to pose when she took their photo. *"Thanks, guys."*

It was hot. It was sunny and it was a perfect day for sightseeing. The Marketplace opened up onto the next block. The fare changed from newer goods and foods to more like a large yard sale of many items, which included wallets, jewelry, silverware, kitchenware, lamps, crafts, knick-knacks, books and household goods, etc. Jane called those things *"dust-ables."*

She traveled north. She separately asked two different men for the directions to the Opera House. The first man was on a bike, he was much younger than Jane and he had stopped to look at his map of Vienna. The second man was plump and older. Both of them did not know how to help her, because they both told her that there were at least four Opera houses in Vienna. *"Oh,"* she did not know that. Although she did not speak their language, she mostly understood what they meant.

Well that changed everything, for she did not know which Opera house she was looking for or where it was. She only had in her memory a glimpse of it, as Joseph had shown it to her in the rain, when she first arrived. She basically gave up on that journey.

She continued to walk north and took more photos. When she finally decided to take a break, she crossed the street at a huge intersection, made her way across a small park and to the steps of a church to sit and recoup. She ate her snack of grapes, water, bread, tea and a granola bar. It was 1:00 p.m. and she was getting sunburned again. After her snack, she looked at herself in her small broken mirror (to check her teeth) and although her teeth were clear of food particles, her eyebrows were in desperate need of plucking!

("Note to self: On my next European trip, bring a better pair of tweezers and a magnifying mirror").

While sitting on the church steps, Jane observed many couples and families. There was a chubby man with mismatched clothes, white hair and a red toupee. There were friends and family members walking about and even a little girl carrying a wrapped present as she was on her way with her daddy to a birthday party. *"Awww."* She saw graffiti on walls, she saw trams and buses and many people on bikes. She wanted to call her dad and check on him and she could not figure out exactly how to do that. She figured that since he popped into her head, she had better call him. She finally saw a pay phone and gave up after a minute of trying to figure out how to use it.

After people-watching and resting for a few minutes, she walked back around to the main street and eventually headed west, up a long street named *Gefreidermarkt*. That street had buildings under construction and had beautiful architecture, a bike shop, cafes, an ice cream shop and so on. She stood at the next big intersection and just watched. She met a couple from Bonnyville, Alberta, Canada, who were also traveling around Europe. They were very nice and tried to be helpful regarding the Opera house, but ultimately could not help her and that was okay.

She continued south on *Maria Hilfer Strabe* (street), which was a heavily trafficked street filled with shops galore, more cafes, grocery stores, restaurants and at least two fast-food restaurants that she recognized from home. That street was overflowing with visitors and cars, cyclists, travelers and patrons who were in and around the many shops. She saw children with their parents and siblings, teenagers with backpacks, shoppers, beautiful women and gorgeous men. It was a wide assortment of people from all over the world.

She could smell wonderful foods being prepared throughout her walk and she just could not get enough photographs. She went as far as her little legs could take her, into an area that opened up into another plaza that was filled with resting people, buses, a stadium and more shops. *"This is the end of my journey,"* she thought. Jane was very disappointed that she had no more energy to go any farther. It was 2:30 p.m.

It took Jane around two hours or so to walk that street, with many stops and picture taking. She felt alone, although she was surrounded by many people. In a way, it was nice to travel alone. She did not have to wait on her travel companion…to take photos, to have to go pee and perhaps having to pee a lot. She did not have to worry about their well-being. She did not have to worry about them wanting to shop, when she could care less about that most days, especially when she didn't have any money, and did not want to have to pay to have gifts shipped home. She did not have to worry about when they would need to eat, sleep, rest, etc.

But as Lorraine had told her when she went shopping for

luggage, *"At least when you travel with someone, you can share those experiences with that person at the end of the day, recapping your adventures."* Lorraine was right. Jane thought of Pascal for a moment and wondered if he would have wanted to travel with her some day. Jane was alone and that was the way that it should be... for her...for the time being.

Jane needed to hoof it back to the bus station if she wanted to make the 3:15 p.m. or 4:15 p.m. bus, so she did just that. It was a whirlwind of colors and smells and sounds, as she scurried back in that direction. She saw different things on her return, including a theater, a jeans shops and an adult store (now that was interesting). She saw more pigeons. She saw a protest or a demonstration of which she had no clue of what was being said. She even saw some street performers and musicians. She watched some people eating at the outdoor cafes and saw one man almost get hit by a car.

She was disappointed in not seeing the Opera House or the Diplomat's Hotel, but she did see it, she thought, on that rainy day with Joseph. She just would have to be satisfied in knowing that, and she would just have to come back to Vienna another time and see it in the bright sunshine. Another time to visit with Joseph and his friends sounded good to her.

Jane realized that she was in love with Vienna and she did not want to leave.

By the time she made it back to the intersection where she had met the Canadian couple, it was 3:00 p.m. Her belly was bloated, her head was pounding and her calves were screaming. But despite that, she turned left, instead of right, which was the direction of the bus stop. She headed north. She decided that she could last just a bit longer and go the other direction to take more photos. So she did, taking pictures of a museum and a university. Both of those places were a-buzz with many visitors and photographers and she was happy that she did not miss it.

The university campus was filled with many people. Some were probably visiting and some were probably residents, she concluded. Some were busy walking about and some were resting on the steps of various buildings, as they were taking their breaks. The campus grounds were colorful with bright green grass, flower beds and flowers in planters. There were many statues and grand steps to the different buildings. There were many trees, plenty of benches in the shade and lots of paths leading to this way and that way. At one moment, there was a photographer taking pictures of a pretty woman posing next to a huge statue of a horse.

A bit later, Jane headed back down the street to the bus station. She saw the bus in which she needed to head home, per Joseph's instructions and ironically, she had the same bus driver. They smiled at each other and said *"Hello"* then she went up the stairs to ride in the upper level.

She sat behind two very cute and leggy, 20-something-year old girls. They were dressed in mismatched-colored shirts and leggings, they had large purses and colorful bands in their hair. Jane was sure that it was irritating to them, but she took more pictures on the return to Oberwart. She asked them if it was okay and they told her that it was. *"Thanks, girls."*

On the ride home, the highway was very busy. They made five stops to pick up and drop off more passengers. Jane saw gas stations signs that she would have seen back at home. She listened to her music and again, bee-bopped her head to Kenny Chesney, Jimmy Buffet, Latin music and some of Dana Owens' Jazz music (Love it!). She heard Rascal Flatts' *"Love You Out Loud"*...*"Georgia Rain,"* *"Bring Back Your Lovin' To Me"* and *"Wild Blue Yonder"* by John Hiatt. She listened to Jim Morrison and John Lee Hooker's *"Rock House Blues,"* *"Start A Band"* by Brad Paisley...plus John Mayer, Keith Urban, The Dixie Chicks, The Pretenders' *"Break Up The Concrete,"* and many more.

Jane felt as if music set the tone for her life. She identified and reminisced with some songs that she heard when she suffered through her heartbreaks (*"Red Light"* by David Nail. Perfect and so true). When she heard John Denver's *"Take Me Home, Country Roads,"* she thought of her mother, for her mother loved that song so much. In addition to that, her mother loved Elvis Presley, so when Jane heard anything by him, she always smiled. Jane identified with music that she heard when she was young and when she traveled to her grandmother's home in West Virginia (anything from Carol King). She could also pinpoint happy moments when she heard music that reminded her of her high school years (*"Drop the Bomb on Me," "No Parking on the Dance Floor").*

Music was good for Jane's soul, even when it was in torment. She could listen to some songs now, that had made her cry in the past. She was always happy when she had finally gotten to the point of not crying. She wanted to always eventually find something positive from a song that had somehow brought on negative connotations. Music was everything to Jane.

Jane was aware of how tired she was. Her head was pounding, she wanted a massage and she wanted a bath. She was exhausted, but thoroughly happy that she had survived her trip to and from Vienna. She able to follow the directions and take the right buses on her own. She was feeling elated.

She had met some people, she had participated in the day, she had seen so many beautiful people and shops and things. She had done that despite her fears. Jane was a changed person and for the better, she had hoped.

Jane had spoken to the girls for a moment on the ride home and they spoke a little English. She had asked them if they were aware of the stop into Oberwart and they were not. One of the girls told her to just listen to the announcement. Jane agreed, but she did not tell her that the driver spoke too fast for her. *"I can do this,"* she thought.

The ride was smooth. It was a beautiful day, sunny and quite warm and she was ready for home. The hours flew by. Jane heard the announcement and she got off the bus along with two others. She took a deep breath and walked downtown towards the Irish pub that she had seen earlier in the week, for she wanted to check it out. It was still closed. *"Dammit."* She headed back towards Joseph's house.

Once inside, Jane found Joseph in the living room. She greeted him, as he was lounging on the couch. He asked how her day was and she told him that it was *"Perfect."* He told her that Mary was having a gathering at her home later that night and they were invited. Jane was so excited about that. He told her that it was a small party with his friends from his choir group and that they could get ready and go anytime. *"Wonderful."* He had had a busy day, too, and she could see that he was exhausted, so she left him there and went upstairs and prepared for her bath. She needed to relax, as well.

Jane gathered her clothes, ran the water and got in the tub. *"Awww."* She soaked for a while, with her eyes closed and thought about her day and smiled. She was one satisfied and proud woman. She thought about her kids, about her dad, about Pascal and at that moment, she had realized that he had popped into her head only twice. For some reason, she got a smile on her face, regarding that.

It was around 6:15 p.m. when she got done. She got dressed in a very pretty pink dress and cream-colored, long over-vest, along with a wide belt and sandals. She put on makeup and blow-dried her hair and was thrilled to have been able to dress up a bit. She went downstairs and had to smirk to herself when she got to the living room because Joseph was flat on his back on the couch and snoring. She just stared at him for a moment, smiling and wondered what to do next. She was ready to go, but he needed sleep. *Hmmm...*

Jane grabbed her computer and went back upstairs, sat on the floor with the computer on the bed and wrote about her day. She had gotten up to use the bathroom, when she noticed in Joseph's girl's bedroom, that he had done some laundry and had hung some of it on drying racks. There was a basket on the floor and she was compelled to check it out. Jane's suspicions were right. The clothes in the basket were damp and he obviously had forgotten about them.

She used the bathroom and then for the next thirty minutes or so, she hung up his clothes, precisely and quietly on a drying rack, using the first drying rack as her example on how he preferred to place his clothes.

Even though she felt as if she was helping, she was worried about doing it wrong and did not want him to be upset if she had. She finished up and then went back to her journal. He came upstairs to get ready and told her that they could have leftovers for dinner. *"Okay."*

Jane went downstairs and met him moments later in the kitchen, where they prepared the food, then sat at the table. They ate lamb and vegetables and talked about their day, among other things. She told him that she hung up his clothes and he thanked her, commenting that she did not have to do that. He told her that in the past, he has left his damp clothes in the baskets for days at a time and that they did not get moldy, but they were a bear to try to iron. Jane giggled at that.

Somehow their conversation lead to talking about her travels and about her son and daughter, which instantly caused her to get moody. Jane told him that it might be best not to talk about her daughter and her granddaughters, for her arms felt empty, her heart felt empty and her soul felt a bit broken.

They dropped the subject and continued about what she saw in Vienna. She thanked him for having faith in her, that she could go there on her own. He told her that perhaps she was meant to travel more, so she could see the world and she agreed. She thanked him for dinner. He told her that he wanted her to tour a castle before she went home, so they were to go there the following day. Jane was so excited about that. They put away the dishes and headed out the door for the party. It was 10:45 p.m.

As they got into the car, Jane quietly breathed in Joseph's cologne. She closed her eyes for a moment. She found that his cologne was like alcohol to her, which was quite intoxicating and she loved his smell. She could not help but have Pascal pop into her head, for he smelled wonderful, too. She wondered what he was doing at that moment and she got a bit upset with herself when a mysterious woman popped into her head as well. *"Damn! Why did she show up?"*

They drove a short distance to his friend's home. They drove up his street and down another, in the quiet dark of the night. She was not wearing her glasses, but she still could see the lights of the road, the lights in the distances, down in the valleys and into his small village of Oberwart. There were plenty of stars and it was a beautiful night. They talked about the road signs, the drive, the night sky and about his friends. *"He is a lucky man,"* she thought…*"to have such caring friends, who lived so close.*" She envied Joseph, regarding his intelligence, his travels, his driven spirit and it made her believe that there was hope for her, somehow. She wanted what he had.

Not his money, not his home, not his things, but his determination, his smarts, his education, his adventures and his command for attention. She knew that if she wanted all of it, she could have it. All she needed to continue to do, was to believe in herself and know that even after this adventure into Europe, anything was possible for her.

Jane knew that her mistakes and her misfortunes and her quirks did not have to define her for the rest of her life. Most of America was going through that hard economy. Many people that she knew were losing their homes, losing their jobs and many of the women that she knew, had lost their friends, some family members and boyfriends, so there was nothing unique about Jane.

She not only thought that life was going to get better, but she believed it. She was a very happy person that day and she so wanted that feeling to continue. Everyone enjoys and thrives on happiness, whatever happiness means to them. She may have had many downfalls and short-comings throughout her life, but she had been happy, regardless of it all.

She had been told in the past, that she was *"sickeningly chipper, always happy, always positive,"* which was meant as an insult and more than just an observation. That has not always been true, but she had always tried to be positive around company, despite being quite sad. Many of her good friends had heard her wail, cry, bawl, etc., over her break-ups, over her mother's death and over the loss of many things, so she was not always happy, all of the time.

But she could find the good things about life, eventually and mostly, find the time to laugh about it later. That was one thing that she loved about herself. Her positive outlook and her positive spirit. How could that ever be viewed as a bad thing?

Joseph parked the car. They got out and looked up at the millions of stars in the heavens. It was a cool, crisp night and she was thrilled to be out and about and in his company and the company of his beloved friends. They walked up to Mary's house and went around the side to the backyard patio. Jane could feel the damp grass beneath her feet and they could hear laughter and see dim light around the corner. They greeted everyone who was there, on Mary's small patio.

It was an intimate setting at her round outdoor table, with candlelight, snacks, bushes, trees and starlight. Emma and Karl were there, plus Mary and Annemarie and another couple, Bernard and Carli. Joseph presented Mary with a bottle of wine and Jane felt silly that she had not thought of getting her something earlier. She could have gotten her a Thank You gift for hosting, but she did not know about the party until after her return from the day's events.

They ate snacks of breadsticks, tuna, curry, cake and wine. Joseph insisted that Jane not have the red wine, but he said she could have Aperol, which she gladly drank. It must have had less alcohol, but she did not bother to ask.

Joseph told the group of their trip to the winery and how blasted Jane had gotten and everybody laughed. Mary served beverages and they talked about Jane's trip into Vienna. They talked about politics, but Jane just listened, for she never got involved with any political conversations.

They talked about the wedding that the choir had performed on that day and they commented on how fake and superficial it seemed. Jane asked what they had meant by that. Most of them chimed in that the wedding was too huge and it was just for show. The couple did not seem to be in love and it did seem more like an obligation or some sort of arrangement. It was very gaudy. *"How sad,"* Jane thought, for she loved weddings.

They talked about the stars and specifically about the North Star. During their outing, Joseph handed her his sweater, because she was being bitten by mosquitoes and she was a bit cold. She thought that Pascal would not have offered up his sweater or jacket for the world. *"Why did she think of that?"* She thanked Joseph and thought that was a very sweet, selfless gesture, indeed. *"Thanks!"*

They talked about the earwig bugs that were crawling around the table and Karl looked up information about them on the internet on his cell phone. He read aloud about them, how years ago, they were ground up and used in deaf people's ears as a remedy, hence the name. Karl was very smart and Jane could tell that he was, just by looking at him. She told him that those bugs were in America, too.

She was having a hard time taking photos in the dark, so Bernard took some time to adjust her camera with the right settings and Jane was able to successfully capture their time together that night. *"Thanks."* They told funny stories, which made everyone laugh, taking the time to explain some things to Jane... slowly. Joseph asked where everyone else was and Mary told him that everyone from the choir group had waited as long as they could and were tired so they went home. Jane was slightly disappointed in not meeting the rest of Joseph's choir group friends.

Joseph commented that he was tired, too, and had been sleeping on the couch. So, reluctantly, Jane asked Joseph if he knew that he had snored, which she imitated, jokingly. Everyone laughed. He told her that he had been told that before, but without proof, he would not believe it. Jane told him that she had recorded it on her video camera, but he gave her a smile that indicated that he knew better. Strangely and sarcastically, he asked if she would still marry him, despite his snoring and quickly and sarcastically, she told him that she would. Everyone laughed. Now, that was funny.

For a brief moment, her thoughts went immediately to the men with whom she had been involved. Her ex and her ex-boyfriends and Pascal all snored. Another thing that they all had in common: Humor and having some trouble in the bedroom sometimes...and snoring. The snoring was something that she did not find out, until she had been already heavily into knowing them and eventually had been asleep in bed with them. It was something that she had just realized at that moment. *Hmmm...* She wondered why each of them snored. Her ex was heavy, so that was obvious, but the others were much thinner. He had had Sleep Apnea. She wondered if she snored, but gathered that she did not, for no one had ever mentioned that one before.

The night went on for some time. Mary's son and Annemarie's son, who each were around twenty years old, came out of the house and were getting ready to go out somewhere. They introduced themselves to Jane and soon they took off.

She could tell that everyone was getting tired. Bernard and Carli got ready to leave. She was quite tipsy and mostly non-functional. Jane told them that it was nice to have met them, but she knew that Carli would not remember meeting her. A little while later, Karl and Emma left. Jane had told them that it was nice seeing them again. She got a little sad knowing that she would never see them again. But perhaps she actually could some day, if she was able to visit.

She wondered what the protocol was in Austria or Europe as a whole, for that matter, on whether or not hugs would be accepted and reciprocated, when just meeting people for the first time. She waited and when they did not initiate a hug goodbye, she came to the assumption that it was not acceptable. Perhaps, they thought the same of Americans. It could have truly been nothing more than a thought that had never crossed their minds. The fact that everyone was just too tired to do anything else, but go home and sleep, was possibly the real reason.

Jane felt she needed a hug from somebody, for it had been a while since she had been touched. It was not more than a passing thought, but Jane was aware early in life, that hugs were important to her, since some of her family members were *'huggers.'* She remembered that her parents hugged her a lot and since getting and giving hugs was a good memory, she made sure that her kids got lots of hugs as they grew. Somehow the thought of her kids popped into her head and she smiled, for she knew that they would pass that happy tradition onto their kids.

She remembered one particular incident whereby her son was around six years old or so and her daughter would have been around three years old. Her son mentioned to her that he had noticed that his grandpa (Jane's dad) had stopped hugging him as much, but somehow hugged his sister more. So Jane, being the mom that she was, encouraged Sawyer to ask his grandpa why that was, even though Jane had to admit that she had not noticed such a thing. She believed her son, for he was adamant about it. He would not have mentioned it, if it had not bothered him. Sawyer brought the subject up and his grandpa apologized and all was well with the world.

From that day forward, Sawyer and grandpa hugged each other every time they saw each other and to this day, they still hug each other when visiting. Jane made that observation right away, as she tried to be more aware of such things. She also observed that her kids got hugs more often than her other nieces and nephews, but that was okay, too. Not everyone likes to give or get hugs. Jane could not imagine her world without them. Bear in mind, she only accepted hugs from people that she knew or at least with whom she felt comfortable. She never would have hugged the two men that helped her find her hotel. She never would have hugged the cute clerk at the first hotel. She never would have hugged the Italian family on the train. But she would have hugged Julietta, if her parents had allowed it. At that moment, her arms and her heart felt empty.

Those that remained at the party cleared the table, blew out the candles and took items to the kitchen. Mary's home was very modern, with large windows, pastel and sheer window treatments, overstuffed chairs and couch, wood floors and shiny silver light fixtures. She had earth-tone accents and knick-knacks. Joseph and Jane thanked Mary for her hospitality for opening up her home for the gathering and then they left.

Jane assumed that they were heading home, but excitingly, they were not. Joseph had driven a different way into town. Everything was a different way for her, since she had no clue exactly where she was. As he drove down the main street of Oberwart, he mentioned that there was a party going on at one of the local pubs and wanted to know if Jane was interested in going in. He must have gotten a second wind. *"Oh yeah!"* she exclaimed. Joseph was excited that she had agreed. He wanted to see the band that was playing, for he had seen them before. Jane was all up for staying out all night, if possible. She did not know where her energy was coming from, but she guessed it had something to do with the excitement of it all.

They parked on the street and walked just a block to the pub. It was perfect. The pub was a-buzz with drinkers, some drunk already and some just getting started. Joseph and Jane claimed a high table, next to the long white tent, where the stage was set up, then she left to go pee. On the way to and from the restroom, she had to take pictures of the back patio that was filled with picnic tables and benches, with table settings of candles and flowers, as well as the overhead trellis that was covered in grape vines. *"How quaint,"* she thought.

She had to walk past the men's restroom, to get to the women's restroom and unfortunately, the door was wide open. She got to take a brief gander (not on purpose) of several men standing at the stalls, with their pants slightly down, as they urinated.

"Great!" she thought, sarcastically, *"Men's backsides! What I always wanted to see in Europe! But wait!"* she thought, *"I will take what I can get,"* as she laughed and thought of Pascal's cute bum. She used the restroom, after she locked the door, ensuring that no drunk man was going to walk in on her. A moment later, she returned to the table.

Joseph asked what Jane wanted to drink and she wanted red wine, so he allowed her have some, telling her to have just one. He commenting that it should be a pretty good-tasting wine. Their waiter came to the table and they ordered drinks of wine and beer. As the waiter left, Joseph and Jane grinned at each other, as they had noticed that the waiter was fancying Joseph. He told her that he suspected that the waiter was gay and that did not bother him. When the waiter came back with their beverages, he stood there, then leaned on the table, leaning *'into'* Joseph, as they chit-chatted about something in German.

Jane was loving that moment, even though she could not understand what they were saying. She eventually snapped a picture of the waiter, telling Joseph later on that she had gotten a picture of *his boyfriend.* That comment made Joseph smile and chuckle, which was ultimately what she wanted to see and hear: his genuine laugh and his beautiful smile.

As they stood there, the band named Oberwart 3, began to play and she was in love with that moment, above all else that night. They watched as many of the patrons sang along, loudly and drunkenly. Many of them got up to dance and one man, who was with a group at one of the picnic tables, whom Joseph dubbed *"The Truck Driver,"* kept smiling and winking at Jane. He was the one who sang the most and the loudest and probably was the most drunk.

He was cute, despite being drunk, with his dark tank top and tattoos and slightly balding head. She winked back at him and his smile got even bigger. She enjoyed the flirting. She was glad he did not assume that he could come over and talk to her. It was fun to be there and she was happy that Joseph had made the suggestion.

Joseph could tell that the alcohol was now getting to Jane a bit, so he suggested they to sit under the tent, which they did. Joseph pointed out to Jane, two special needs adults who were there, which he noted were at a lot of the musical venues in town throughout the many years that Joseph had lived there. Jane got very excited that she actually knew some of the songs and sang along. The band was very good and she loved listening, swaying and singing. They stayed for quite some time, then eventually called it quits after 1:00 a.m. He drove them home. Jane was able to walk upright. They went inside, said *"goodnight and pleasant dreams"* and then they went their separate ways to bed.

Jane went upstairs, brushed and flossed, washed her face, then changed into some lounging clothes and then she plopped into the bed. She was happy and excited, satisfied and content, with one of the most rewarding and fascinating and wonderful days of her life.

Jane lay there with her pillow snug into her neck and another pillow between her knees. She put another pillow firm against her back, as to fool her all night that she was lying against another human being. She drifted off to sleep, with a smile on her face, as she thought about the day, as she thought about seeing Pascal soon and sharing her adventures with him. She thought about how proud she was of herself and of how much fun she had had that day.

For a brief moment, before she was sound asleep, some silly thoughts popped into her head of why Joseph did not want to take advantage of the tipsy Jane. But then she remembered that he was a gentleman…

…That he probably did not view her as *his type*…

…That he already knew that she was constipated and that her belly made terrible noises…

…That she had already bawled in front of him and that she looked very ill when she cried…

…That he probably did not want to risk seeing her naked, then throwing up, therefore insulting her…

...And that it would have been very awkward indeed...for future visits...

She thought that she actually giggled out loud after those thoughts, for she knew that she was kidding herself and she did not mean any of it. Really.

"Thank You for letting me know the wonder of the world around me and thank You for another wonderful, unforgettable great day!!! Amen."

Sunday...

Jane took her time getting up that next morning. She suspected that it was around 6:00 a.m., but she had left the cell phone downstairs. Did she do that on purpose? One would think so. She got up, made the bed, got dressed in black Capri pants, a black and purple cowl-necked, sleeveless shirt and black sandals. So far the band-aids were helping her blistered feet.

She folded some clothes and packed them in her suitcase. She put her gym shoes, socks and an extra shirt in her new cheap canvas bag for walking to the castle, then she went to pee in the tiny bathroom. She went into the main bathroom where she wet her hair, conditioned it, wrapped her head in a towel, then washed her face, brushed her teeth, put on makeup, combed out her hair and popped on a headband. She gathered her things and went downstairs.

For breakfast, she had a small slice of bread with raspberry jam, a sliver of goat cheese, a handful of grapes and orange juice with oats, mixed with a small amount of sauerkraut juice. She hoped against all hope, that that additional ingredient wouldn't *"kick in"* when they were walking to and from the castle. She ate and journaled, then she petted the cat and let her outside, per the cat's request.

She emailed an ex-boyfriend's mom and almost cried as she wrote to her, letting her know how she was doing and how beautiful of a time she was having. Jane hoped that she was well and she missed talking with her directly. She missed her. They emailed occasionally, as she continued to give her support and letting Jane know how disappointed she was with her son for hurting Jane and letting her go.

She had reassured Jane that she and the other family members loved her, enjoyed her company and were sorry that things ended as they did, with his horrible insults and lack of compassion and tolerance. She let Jane know that deep down, she knew that she was going to be okay and she wished her the best of the world, telling her that she loved Jane, always. Whenever Jane communicated with her, she thought of how much she missed her own mother.

Jane heard Joseph get up. She continued to read the world news on the internet, she laughed about some things posted on Facebook from some friends and she checked her emails. She replied to Pascal's email of *"How's it going?"* and she responded with *"Very good, indeed."*

She was baffled that although that man was a wizard with opinions and conversation and dynamic expressions, he sucked when it came to typing, writing and emailing. She supposed that she could not be too picky, for he did write…at least something. She cleaned up the breakfast dishes, then Joseph came downstairs. It was going on 10:30 a.m.

Joseph was dressed in his white robe (dressing gown) and he looked well rested. They talked as he prepared his breakfast of tea, bread and jam. He offered her some tea and she took him up on his offer. Since Jane was a bit less stressed out, they wound up talking in depth about her daughter and her family. They talked about how and when they moved in with her and her brother. They talked about her son-in-law, about Jane's worries over him being in the military, from a mom's perspective, regarding his safety.

Joseph got a phone call and his friend Erwin, a painter for Slovakia, was coming over quickly to return a camera that he had borrowed, that he used for photographing his creations. Joseph started straightening up a bit, even grabbed a broom to sweep up the cat hair. He said that he was going to hurry and get dressed because he did not want his friend seeing him in his gown. Joseph told her to open the door when it rang and as he was about to dart up the stairs, the door bell sounded. *"Oh my"*…

Joseph did not have time to change, so he answered the door and Jane could hear them talking. She got up, went to the door, Joseph introduced her to his cute artist friend and they shook hands. She said, *"Hello and it was nice meeting you,"* and then went back to the table. A bit later, Erwin left and Joseph came back to join her for a moment, showing Jane his very nice, very expensive camera. It was a beauty. Jane thought of how nice and how trusting Joseph was to let Erwin borrow it.

A bit later, Joseph rushed upstairs to get ready for their adventurous and busy day. Jane took pictures of herself with her camera, near the patio door, with the bright sunlight coming in and bouncing off her pretty shirt. She used the bathroom and was so beyond tired of waiting for more results. She feared that there would be more later, but she just did not know when.

Joseph came downstairs, put on his shoes, asked her to help remember to feed his fish at the office and she told him that she would try. They gathered their things, including some bottled water and a snack for Jane later on. They got in the car and took off for some festivities at his favorite Italian bar, *il sapore.*

Joseph told her that they were to make a stop there, before driving to the castle. He wanted her to see the costumes, hear the music and taste the foods at that Austrian gathering, that was a fund-raiser for an animal shelter. She was so up for it, so *"Okay!"* It was around 12:30 p.m.

It was a hot and humid day, with people from all over, dressed casually, dressed-up and dressed in traditional Austrian outfits. The event was held in the parking lot of the bar and it was packed. The band was hopping and she knew that it was going to be a great day. Joseph told her that the music being played was their form of Country music.

They found a tall round table that was unfortunately in the sunlight, but near a white canopy over the bar, which was buzzing with many drinkers. There were many people hiding from the sun, having many conversations, all of which she did not understand. He knew mostly everybody there and vice versa. It was considered a small village.

Jane gave Joseph some money and he got two white wine spritzers. They stood at the table and had a great casual conversation about everything and nothing. Jane laughed a lot, which she loved to do and was grinning from ear to ear as she observed his gestures and made observations of the people around them. She took photos of her surroundings and of the two of them, as they goofed in front of the camera. He looked so good in his sunglasses. *"What a handsome man,"* she thought. *Sigh.*

They eventually found a spot at a picnic table under one of the four tents. They sat and talked and she took more pictures. He left for a moment to put his camera in the trunk of the car, as he had realized that he had left it on the back seat. He returned with her granola bar, per her request. She ate it, as they talked more about the music, the costumes and the food.

Most of the waitresses were in costumes and they were mighty busy. There were families, singles, people with challenges and couples galore, a few pets and some babies. He interpreted the lead singer's very tacky jokes that were made in between sets of music and not everyone was laughing. Joseph was laughing, as he commented that it was all bad. *"Two worms slithered past a plate of spaghetti and one worm said to the other: Look. Group sex." "Oh, that was bad,"* Jane said.

"One man asked the other, Where do you think the light goes when you turn off the switch? The other man responded with, I am not sure, but I think it goes into the refrigerator." Again, very horrible. There were many more and some cracked up Joseph. It was fun to see him smile and laugh, as he did the interpreting for Jane.

Joseph said that he had a headache, so she gave him some Ibuprofen. They flagged down a waitress and she took their order, telling us that it was about an hour wait. *"Okay and good."* Jane was willing to wait as she observed everything, talked more to Joseph, took notes and took more photos. There was a small girl around three years old, who was rocking and dancing with the band. There was boy around five years old, who was eating melting ice cream, which was mostly on his face and even some of it dripped to the ground.

She saw a young girl and her grandmother play a hand slapping game, and she watched the flustered male waiters and female waitresses wait on and serve their hungry and hot customers. She recognized some of the music, including *"Beer Barrel Polka"* and a Latin tune, which for some reason surprised her that it was played. She was not sure why she was amazed by that.

During the time that the band played, they had to sit very close or at least lean into one another, in order to hear what each of them was saying. She had to admit that she enjoyed that closeness, because she could smell his wonderful cologne. It was a welcoming scent, as always. She could feel his leg against hers and she could feel his arm against her arm. She watched his face closely, watched his lips as she leaned closer, to better hear him. She wondered about her breath and she wondered what he thought of her. It was so hot, that she wondered if she smelled. What a strange thought to occur, but it had occurred in her brain all the same.

Jane continued to listen as he recognized and pointed out some of his friends, patients and acquaintances, including his personal trainer and the local veterinarian. He left the table to talk with his trainer for a bit, then came back when their food arrived, which was around 2:00 p.m. He was not too hungry, so he told Jane to eat as much of their salad as she wanted and he would finish the rest of it later.

She had to admit that it was hard not to eat all of it. It was so delicious, but as always and always being a woman, she did not want to seem greedy and piggish. However, somehow that day, she did not care as much. The cheese was rich and creamy and she was sure that she would pay for that sometime later.

"Life is short, get constipated anyway," she would say…*"and deal with the dirty and agonizing results later."*

According to Joseph, they were eating something called *Bird Salad,* which had bird salad greens, sheep cheese, horseradish, onions, *beetle beans* (he did not know why they were called that) and it was drizzled with balsamic vinegar and pumpkin oil. It was delicious and for a brief moment, she thought she was in heaven as she ate it. She wondered if her eyes were crossing, with each bite.

A bit later, they got a *wiener schnitzel,* which was a first for her. Jane did not want to tell Joseph that she had heard of that dish, but she never knew what that was anyway. It reminded her of a pork tenderloin and she could have gone the day without it. It was also very good, but it was fried, served on top of a bed of French fries, with a single lemon wedge and a single packet of ketchup. For many years, Jane had been trying to stay away from fried foods and processed foods, dairy and processed sugar and anything with high cholesterol. So far, she had not succeeded with that, since she left Dayton.

When she had met Pascal, his diet consisted of food from the bar that he had frequented daily, and fast food while at work. He had American/Mexican fast food late at night, cheese and crackers and hummus occasionally and beer, vodka and red wine. She drank some of those beverages while in his company.

She had not started drinking until she was older, so just a few sips of any alcohol, any time, made her very tipsy, indeed. That was very comical to Pascal, because she would get woozy and very talkative, saying anything and everything that came to mind. Jane was almost always embarrassed by her behavior, every night she would be at his home, but he did not seem to mind. On a couple of occassions, Pascal observed Jane's consumption of vodka, and timed it, as soon after she would be loopy. It took exactly seven minutes for her limbs to go limp. It was quite comical.

Joseph and Jane had sparkling water with lemon and they

finished their spritzers as well. It was ghastly humid, but they stayed under the tent for shade. They agreed that whoever had put up the tents, should not have closed off the back side of those tents, which more than likely would have provided all of them with a nice cross breeze. *Oh well.*

They continued to watch the festivities, including a *'best couple'* contest, a dancing contest and a race where the men carried the women on their backs. Jane told Joseph that that was going to be a bad idea and she was right. As the three couples took off, one couple hit the ground, as the man tripped over a raised sewer grate. It was horrible and the entire crowd gasped as they witnessed his fall. He landed full-force onto the concrete, on his shoulder, with the woman still on top of him. She was lucky not to have slammed her face into the ground. The race was halted while the medics checked him out and ultimately, they assumed that he was taken to the hospital. She hoped that he was okay.

There was also a fund-raising raffle, which Joseph's band director won. He went up to claim the prize for his friend, who was not there. The prize was a gym membership valued at around 400 Euros. Jane thought, that at raffles at home, one had to be present to win. You had to prove who you were and no one else could claim it for you. You had to give blood and your first born child in order to receive it. Not really, but she was surprised that he could claim it for his friend all the same. Like he had told Jane before, everyone there knew everyone there. *"I would love to belong to a small town like that,"* she thought. She would love to be accepted, with no questions and she would love knowing everyone that lived in her village. *"How lucky Joseph is, to have had that wonderful upbringing,"* she thought.

In the meantime, Jane made another observation about the patrons, like she had done when she was in Vienna. Some of them looked similar to those she already knew. Joseph had told Jane that human beings as a whole, put people in categories in order to feel welcome, to feel like they are at home, to feel like they belong and that no one is a stranger. That was an interesting thought and she agreed.

At that festival, she could have sworn that she saw Angelica Houston, Ron Perlman, one of the actors from *'NCIS,'* Janeane Garofalo and Justin Bieber. *"It could happen,"* she thought, although she was more excited to have seen Arte Johnson the other day, but did not know why.

They finished their food, the waitress took away their dishes and she excused herself to the restroom. She watched a woman go into the 'one toilet' room and as she waited, a little boy came over and tried to open the men's bathroom door. Jane opened it for him and apparently his dad was in there. She was embarrassed and apologized for opening the door, because he was still *'going.'* The dad spoke with his son, she guessed that the boy needed to *'go,'* too, so they both went back inside. Her embarrassment did not last very long.

It was finally Jane's turn in the women's restroom and that was definitely the smallest bathroom that she had experienced yet. It was so cramped that her knees came close to hitting the wall when she squatted over the toilet.

She thought that the Europeans must know something that Americans don't know: That one has to be thin or at least small to fit inside their bathrooms. So, it would make sense to eat right and exercise to be fit and trim, just so one could use the bathroom in comfort. Is that what life is all about? To be thin, just so one can poop and pee in a comfortable small space? *Hmmm...*

She finished up and rejoined Joseph under the tent. He mentioned that he, too, needed to go and they agreed to meet out at the street, a few minutes later, so she could finish her water. It was 2:30 p.m.

They finished up and as they walked towards the car, they realized that there was a huge bike race coming through the main street in town. They watched as several bikers rushed by with SAG wagons trailing behind. They quickly crossed the street and as they got into the car, a man spoke to Joseph about turning immediately left from the curb, and advised him of what streets to take to get around the race route. They watched more bikers fly by, then he quickly turned on a dime. They drove up a side street and up the hill at its peak and traveled south.

They talked more about her kids and his kids, etc. and she got a bit nervous because their conversations began to get a bit more personal. But that seemed to be okay with them. They took some back roads, including a gravel road and eventually made their way to the highway. She had no idea of what adventures were awaiting her.

On their drive, they talked about traveling, touring, visiting and what was expected as informal manners in some countries and with some friends. They talked about how some people refuse to be paid back in any way, as they consider it hospitality and may be offended if money is offered. That heightened Jane's curiosity. Joseph told Jane not to pay him back in any way, shape or form. He told her that her company was reward enough. *"Thanks and cool."* Jane did tell him that she did want to repay him, but she was not sure how and when she was able to do it. She offered for him to come and stay with her, if he was ever in Dayton again. He agreed and thanked her for that offer.

Since they had an hour drive, she told him in detail of how she got to be there exactly, from start to finish, with her dad's financial help. She got misty-eyed and a lump in her throat with the thoughts of never being able to completely repay him for everything that he and her mother had done for her. They had helped her so much over the many years since her divorce. But especially for his help after her mother had died. She told Joseph that she and her dad and her brother suspected that it was this trip that started another rift within her family.

They had concluded that it was a form of jealousy of some kind, based on the amount that their dad had afforded to help her. Jane and her dad had never told anyone the amounts that were borrowed or given, but also her dad had given money to all of his children, from time to time. She was truly baffled. She had a *"why now"* attitude and could not figure out why she was the current target and topic of conversation, between her other siblings.

She was also made aware of a conversation that took place the previous year and she was told that it was very bad indeed, very derogatory and quite unforgivable, for the topic was about Jane and her children. She asked Joseph to never repeat any of what was being said. He agreed.

She was sure that he could hear the sadness in her voice, as she told him that she was not doing well financially lately, as they talked about the cost of things in general. It made her a bit uncomfortable, but he asked. He basically gasped when she told him the cost of her last-minute plane ticket. She, too, was ticked about that one. It just should never cost so much.

They talked about friendships, about her many supportive friends, about betrayal in their relationships, hurtful friends who are now in the past and should stay there. In addition, they talked about how one of her sisters had instigated a meeting with other family members. She let Jane know that they intended to sue her after their dad's death, to *"force"* her to pay back all the money that she had to borrow over the years. That included just the general cost of living, groceries, car repairs, etc. Joseph gasped.

Although everyone in her family knew that she was losing her job and was having a hard time finding another one, and therefore having a hard time paying any and all of her bills, her sister decided to tell her that that did not matter. She told Jane that they would hire a lawyer after her dad had died.

She told Joseph that she had cried for three hours after that phone call and that it took her a month to tell her dad about it. When she did, her dad told her that he was sick of the rumors and of the other stuff that was going on. He told her that he was upset with her sister for starting those rumors and he told Jane that she need not worry about any of it.

Jane let him know how sad she was that her sister had done that to her, for she had expected to have her sister and her other siblings around for quite some time. She was sad that that was not going to happen. Jane never expected, in a million years, to ever have been blindsided by her sister and the rest of her family. Joseph was floored by that kind of nonsense and from that kind of betrayal, and told her that he was not sure of what to say at that moment, other than he was sorry to hear about that.

Jane told him that was one of the worst things that she could have ever experienced in her lifetime, for she believed that no matter what else would happen, she would have some of her family around to support her. She fully expected them to be there for her, in her time of need and grief, and she believed that they would always be in her life, but now she knew better.

It was hurtful being called ugly...and being called fat...but a family insult of that magnitude, was far worse. She got very upset that she could be viewed that way and that it was so easy for her family to dismiss her.

Jane stopped herself from crying in front of Joseph, as she told him that it had been hard to concentrate, sleep well and eat right since that phone call. It had been difficult having to deal with the thoughts of her daughter and her family going overseas. It was a bit stressful as she was preparing for her son's wedding. She had not been eating well and sleeping well, since having to deal with a short dating period where she came to love another family and then that breakup happened. Added to, of course, that massive and unforgivable family betrayal, a pending foreclosure, a job loss and her woes of traveling alone.

She got a bit loud as she told him that she was not going to take any crap anymore, from anyone. He told her to just be herself, pray and be happy that *"You are You."* She was struggling with that daily, but she agreed with him.

Joseph was not only a great conversationalist. He was also a great listener. That was his job and she wondered what he thought of her after they had conversations like that. She had dished out a lot, in a short period of time and vice versa, but she also did not expect to do that, nor wanted to do that. He did make her feel safe about it, but she felt a bit alone, even when she was in the car with him or in the same room with him. She felt as if he was keeping himself distant on purpose and that had to be okay. It may be just who he was and that was okay, too. She wanted him as a friend more than anything else. She could see their friendship blossoming until the end of time, if he let it. Her thoughts drifted to Pascal.

As he was driving, Joseph remembered that they had forgotten to feed his fish at the office. He called the cleaning lady for his building and asked her to do it. It sounded as if she could, willingly. A bit later, Jane had to confess to him that it was time for her to use the restroom, *"Dammit!"* He told her that there was a place to *park in a wooded area* and after much more dialogue, she came to understand that he meant a *rest stop*. They came upon it in a short order.

As she had exited the car, she sarcastically commented that she was scared of what she might see in there and he quickly and sarcastically commented that she should be. She laughed as she walked toward the very small building. Inside was everything that she had imagined and more. It was dirty, filthy, gross, smelly, the seat was wet and the last person did not flush. *Yukky.* So she had to clean it up a bit, in order to feel comfortable enough to use it. *"Damn,"* she thought, as she sat there. *"I just can't seem to catch a break when it comes to my belly."* She hoped against all hope that that would be it for the day. She should have brought her Metamucil. *"Airport security, be damned!"*

At least two other people tried to open the door, but they just had to wait. When she emerged from the WC (water closet), Joseph was outside the car, resting under a nearby shady tree. They got back on the road immediately. She thought that she had been in there for about thirty minutes and now she needed a shower.

They continued on the highway for about 10 kilometers, then they drove through valleys and rural roads, and through another small village, quaint as the previous ones that she had seen the other day. She took photos through his windshield and their conversations continued.

She asked him how he came to choose his great Italian sports car, an Alfa Romeo. He explained that it was good-looking, fast, easy to drive and hugged the road. He fell in love with it, after taking it home for a weekend, as one of his friends worked at the dealership. She asked him about when he got started smoking. He told her that he was sixteen and that he would have continued to smoke more if he had not become a doctor. Although he knew the dangers, he only had a cigarette from time to time, for it helped him sit calmly and think clearly. *"I would have thought the opposite,"* she told him.

She also told him that Pascal smoked like crazy and was going to try again to quit soon. They agreed that smoking and alcohol mostly go hand in hand, so it was not a surprise to Joseph that Pascal smoked, since she told him that he also never missed going to his favorite bar. She told Joseph that she worried about Pascal driving home from the bar, but nothing more was said about that. She wondered if Joseph drove when he had been drinking, too. She only hoped that he never did that.

Joseph was surprised to hear that Jane had never smoked, although she admitted to him that she had tried it once when she was younger. But for some reason, the thought of paying for something, that she could become addicted to was not appealing, plus she did not like it. She told him that in the beginning, she viewed it from a financial standpoint and nothing else, but as she got older, she knew her decision was right for her.

It was hard for her to understand why anyone would continue to risk their health like that. *"Although we do that every day when we wake up and step out our front doors,"* she stated. As she told him that it was just unhealthy for him and he should quit, Joseph stated, *"No one wants to die healthy."* She laughed and that lead to the conversation about one of her brothers who had cancer, but who was currently okay. They talked about others that they knew who had cancer, including his brother and so on.

And then, she told him that she had a cancer scare and that she had a surgery regarding that, but currently, she was fine, too. She told him that she also continued to worry about Pascal and the health of his his lungs, heart and liver. She also worried about him driving home from his favorite bar every night. *"Why did I mention that again?"*

That seemed to always be on Jane's mind. She told Joseph that being involved with Pascal, made her think of what it would be like being involved with a police officer or a fireman. Because, every time he would be away (at the bar, like a civil servant being on the job), she wondered if he was going to make it home safely. She wondered about whether he considered the concerns from his adult children and possibly causing them to drink and smoke and/or worrying them as well. She wondered if they wondered if he was going to make it safely back home, too.

She was not sure that what she was telling Joseph was getting through to him, or if she was making any sense at all. She also knew that she did not always make the best choices when it came to talking on her cell phone while driving, or even when she would walk out her door at night to go shopping or to go dancing, etc. She wondered if that was a concern to her loved ones, as well.

The subject was quickly halted as they continued to drive

through the villages and small towns to the castle at Riegersburg. She began to talk about the beauty of it all. They parked the car in a diagonal parking space near the shops at the base of the mountain. They grabbed their cameras and water and exited the car. Jane was very excited.

The road was curved and circular, ascending the mountain. They stopped and turned around several times to take photos of down the mountain sides and of the many shops and chalets. Joseph stopped several times to point out the clothing shops and shoe shops that were closed, but had items marked for sale and on clearance. Each shop was decorated in some manner with plenty of flowers and flower pots, planters full of assorted colors and greenery, multi-colored flags, signs of sales and of their hours of operation, and some advertisements of festivals and upcoming events.

They walked slowly but with determination, as they got closer and closer to the castle entrance. They were walking up and at a steep angle. The day was very sunny, hot and humid, and they were horribly sweating even before they got to their destination. They walked past tiny cafes, an ice cream shop and a few bars. They walked up a grassy and narrowly paved path, sometimes holding onto a rail when they could and walked around other patrons, who were walking much slower.

Joseph made a comment to Jane that she was the first American that he had brought there, who never slowed down or even stopped to catch her breath. He told her that he had brought many friends there, including his original American host family, and each of them had to take a break, for they were panting so much.

That did nothing for her but to confirm his statement and gave her every confidence that he was correct. As she was walking backwards in front of him and he was walking forwards toward her, she told him that she walked a lot at home, that she exercised almost every day, that she had strong *cheerleader legs* and that she loved a challenge. She pivoted on her heel and continued to ascend the mountain, knowing full well that she could have petered out at any moment and embarrassed herself. But because he had made the comment, she was determined to prove that she could do it. And she did. She was very proud of herself for not giving up.

As they continued to climb, Joseph took 219 photos and she took 489 photos of the castle's exterior and its surroundings, including a bistro which had picnic tables on the outside patio. There was a huge draw bridge, a dry moat, the sun setting in the west and the many small farms that dotted the distant countryside. There were cannon holes in the protective brick and stone walls, many vineyards and a swampy area, on which Joseph commented. As a child he was always afraid of that swamp, for he felt as if he was going to fall in and drown. *"Awww."*

They took pictures of the many flat levels, which included a cemetery with large headstones, that Joseph was able to translate the markings, as they cited the history of the fallen. They read about the history of the castle, that it was built in 1100 A.D. and that it was built atop an inactive volcano. That level was Jane's favorite, which had the greenest grass that she had ever seen. It had a great vantage point for photos of the main part of the castle and of the villages below.

However, the surrounding circular wall was not very high and her fear of heights kicked in. She could not get too close to the edge and she told Joseph that, as he continued to get closer, perhaps to see what she might have done about it, as a joke. They smiled at each other, but in actuality, she wanted to smack him. She did nothing and nothing happened. Thank goodness for that.

They continued on their walk upward, then after Joseph paid for their entrance at the gift shop, they were able to take a self-guided tour of the interior of the castle. Photos were permitted, which surprised Jane, but elated her as well. They took their time, taking pictures of the many sculptures, antique furniture, a ballroom, paintings, mannequins dressed in clothing of the times, including chain mail and armor.

One room had a wide and tall ceramic furnace, which was quite innovative for its time. There were also jails and torture rooms with many torture devices. That room made Jane shiver. She was in awe of the colors and sights around her. It was so surreal to be inside a castle, with its history. She was sure that it had many ghosts. She would have loved to spend the night inside that castle, especially on Halloween, which was her favorite holiday.

They went up stairs and down stairs, past interior and exterior balconies. They walked through a tiny courtyard, then back outside and walked along a path that was lined with trees and more vineyards. There was an huge elevator, angled at the backside of the castle, for physically challenged patrons. The upper landing of the elevator was made of thick plexiglas, so they went inside and took more photos from that vantage point. That was very cool.

Around that time, Joseph informed Jane that they needed to get back to the car as soon as possible, for they were invited to his parents' home for dinner, at around 6:30 p.m. *"What the hell?"*

"Why did he keep that bit of info to himself?" She was astounded that he did not mention that before and besides, they were sweating like crazy. *"What kind of impression was that going to make?"* She was baffled, but excited at the same time. Thank goodness that she had brought an extra shirt. Afterall, she was a prepared Girl Scout.

Joseph was a typical male, having pertinent information and waiting until the last minute to share. *"What in the world?"* They took more photos as they walked back down, including an area which she assumed was for shooting more cannons. There was another area of the castle that was perhaps for housing horses, a wooden walkway with a partial roof and more trees than one could imagine. There were plenty of drop-offs that were surrounded with more stone walls. The sun was setting and the light was at its best for perfect photography. Everything looked serene.

They were not the only ones taking in the wondrous scenery. The castle was abuzz with many patrons with their cameras, children, backpacks and water bottles. There was even an area of the lower exterior of the castle, that was set up for rock-climbing enthusiasts, which was very steep and treacherous. *"No thank you!"*

Around 6:30 p.m., they got back to his car and took off to see his parents. When he was able to get cell service, he called them to tell them where they were and that they were on their way. She told him that she was glad that she had brought another shirt and asked his permission to change in the car, while he was driving. He told her that he would keep his eyes on the road. Jane was not sure if he did and she was fully aware that she did not really care, but she was a bit concerned and embarrassed, as she changed.

Jane had gotten a bit bolder as she had gotten older, when it came to changing clothes in front of others. She felt that since she was very vulnerably exposed when she delivered her two children, many years ago, that it did not matter as much, if anyone saw her tiny boobs, even as they were housed in a *fancy-shmancy* lacy bra.

She got her clean shirt ready, unfastened her seat belt, held in her belly as to appear smaller *("Why did I bother to do that?"),* took off her sweaty shirt and put on her fresh shirt. She was able to complete that task within just a few seconds, then put back on her seat belt. She thought that she actually turned a bit red. She wondered if he had glanced her way, but if he had, he would not have been impressed by anything that he had seen.

On the drive, he told her a bit about his childhood and about his parents. He seemed to have a good upbringing and seemed happier for it. They drove through a few towns and villages, then through his parent's quaint, little town. It had a fountain near the square, cafes, grocery stores, etc. They drove down an alleyway, then parked in a carport at his childhood home.

As they walked through the backyard, he told her that it was his mother who had set up the garden. It was so pretty and petite, as she was able to make her plants and flowers and climbing vines flourish in such a small space. There was a tiny fountain, benches, sculptures, an arched trellis that they walked under, a gazing ball and a birdbath, along a paved walkway that bordered the postage stamp-sized yard.

As they entered through the back door, his mom and dad greeted them in the kitchen. His father was tall, with a slight build and Joseph looked just like him. His mother was shorter than her husband, but taller than Jane. She was very stout and plump and had the most animated and excited face that she had ever seen. She was so thrilled to meet Jane, and both his parents hugged her so tight. She was instantly welcomed and she felt at home in their company. By the end of the night, Jane did not want to leave.

They decided to eat first then take a small tour of the house. They would look at photo albums of Joseph and his other siblings after dinner. His parents had the food ready, as they had waited for their arrival.

They sat in the kitchen, at a very small table in a corner, that had two benches, one against the back wall and window, and the other at a side wall. Jane sat on the bench closest to the window and his father sat on the other bench. Joseph sat to her left and his mother was across from Jane. She offered up wine and Joseph explained to them...in German...that Jane should not have wine and why. They busted out laughing, then his mother commented to her...in broken English...that she needed to have wine at every meal. Jane agreed and was elated, as his mother poured the wine for everyone.

Joseph let out a *"Ho Hum"* sound and that cracked up his parents all the more. In his native tongue, he commented to them that, *"If Jane gets tipsy, we may have to spend the night because I am too exhausted from our outing, to carry her to the car."* They laughed. He had to translate to Jane everything that he was saying to them. It was very funny.

They had a variety of meats, cheeses, liver pate', shredded horseradish, bacon grease *(Yes, that was what Joseph had said),* tomatoes, green peppers, hard-boiled eggs, wine and sparkling water. His dad had a beer. Yum. His mom spoke some English, but his dad hardly spoke at all. She got the impression that Joseph's mother spoke for the two of them and his father did not seem to mind.

Jane had gotten full rather quickly for the food was very good. She was sure that it was going to affect her in some manner later, but she did not seem to care. After their meal, his mother wanted to have iced coffee, with ice cream and real whipped cream. When Joseph told her that Jane could not have dairy, she became not only genuinely concerned, but she also was disappointed. Jane saw that immediate reaction and wondered if she had offended her.

Jane told Joseph's mother that she would take some medicine for her belly and she would try the dessert anyway, for she had never had iced coffee. His mother slapped her hands together in excitement and satisfaction, said something in German, then jumped up from the table and prepared the dessert.

Jane got up and got some meds from her purse, came back to the table, swallowed the pills and had one of the best desserts that she had ever tasted. The ice cream was real vanilla bean and the coffee was sweet. Typically, Jane did not drink coffee, but perhaps she would give it a whirl someday.

Joseph's mother stated, *"I think you are girlfriend."* Jane looked at his mother straight in the eyes and told her that she was not, but she told her that she was very fond of him. She winked at Jane, which forced Jane to smile back at her, and his mother gave Jane a great big grin, too.

Joseph told them how they had come to know each other and they continued with other conversations about their families, about her visit and why she came to Europe. She showed them a picture of her granddaughters, which prompted his mother to comment on their hair and how beautiful they were. His mother got up and got out photos and framed pictures of her children and grandchildren. For some reason, his mother brought up the subject of Jane's height and they talked about how hard it was to reach things high up on shelves. That made everyone laugh. Jane realized that Joseph's humor was just like his mother's. It was all very good.

After they finished with the food, his parents would not let Jane help clean up. They went into the living room, sat on the couch and looked at more photos. They talked more about family and his mother was astonished to hear that Jane had so many siblings. His mother got sad when Jane told her how her mother had died and then she hugged Jane again. Jane wanted to cry, but she was glad that she did not. She thought that it would be nice to come back and visit with them, get to know them more and to get more hugs like that from such nice people. Jane missed her mother at that moment.

She got a tour of the house and took some photos, then Joseph and Jane decided that it was time to go home. They were tired. His mother hugged Jane again and told her that she was a very nice lady. She told her that she liked her and told her to visit again. Jane told his mother that she liked her, too. Jane said that she definitely would try to visit again some day.

His dad hugged Jane, but surprised her a bit, when his hand slid down to her lower backside. Then he lightly patted her. She knew right away that that was not an Austrian custom, but she did not blame him for wanting to touch her cute butt. She was a bit offended, but she let that slide. Besides, what was she supposed to say at that moment?

She squinted her eyes at him, as if to facially scold him. She could tell that he knew that she disapproved of what he did, but he probably knew her well enough (as an American or just being a woman) to know that she was not going to speak up. She thought, *"Now that was certainly not a gentlemanly thing to do."* Despite that, it almost made her laugh.

They walked out of the back door. Jane noticed right away that Joseph's parents did not hug him...nor he them...and she thought that that was a bit sad. She felt as if she had sensed a bit of tension, but decided that it was none of her business. Besides, there were still many aspects of his life that she knew nothing about, for if he was not willing to share, she was not willing to press the issue. She knew from personal experience that families can suck and all families have conflict from time to time.

She thought that they may not be close and that would have to be okay. It was his life and his experiences and his childhood and his issues. *"We are a product of our parents,"* she would say, *"And we are a product of our experiences."*

Jane was going to have to believe that they could be just like any other family, who show their best sides in public and can be the opposite of kind and giving in private, much like her own family. It was good to know that they were normal. They were on the road at around 7:45 p.m.

Their drive home was a bit quiet. They listened to some music on the radio. They were exhausted from the castle climb, the sun, the hot weather and they were full from the delicious food. Once home, Jane started some laundry, took a hot bath, got out her computer and emailed some concerned friends. She emailed Sawyer, whom she asked to relay a message to her dad that all was fine. She journaled and downloaded their photos. Joseph had a headache. He drank a beer and they talked a bit, recapping the day and their visit. He went to bed. Jane finished the laundry, then went to bed around midnight.

It had been another great day. Besides Vienna, visiting that spectacular castle was the best thing she had done all week. She had profusely thanked Joseph for taking her there. She had thanked him for letting her see something that even in her wildest dreams, she could have hardly imagined that she would have seen...in her lifetime.

As Jane lay in bed and she had reminisced about the day, she was in awe of how wondrous the world can be. She had stood atop a high peak in Austria, viewing a castle and then touched a real castle for the first time in her life. *"It is amazing where life can take us, even though we may not know the intentions and the thoughts of our Pilot,"* she thought.

She was so happy to be alive at that very moment and expected to have wonderful, appreciative dreams. She said a prayer for her safe return in two days and for Joseph's well-being and for his family, too. She said a prayer for the continued safety of her children, her family and for Pascal.

She asked for guidance upon her return home, to help her with better decisions, to help her understand others better and to continue to be patient and a better listener. She asked for help, to guide her in the right direction, so as to have a better understanding and a more fulfilled life.

She asked for clear signs to get her wherever she needed to go and she asked for minimal sadness to come her way. Now, she understood that that last request was a bit selfish, but she was selfish at the beginning of her adventure, so she did not think that it was too unreasonable to be that way upon her return home. *"Thank You again for another great day...Amen."*

Monday...

Jane woke up with a strange dream about a former friend. She had not heard from her in years, so she wondered why she would think of her. In the dream, Jane was at a pool with many friends. It was a beautiful sunny day and she felt very pleased to be out and among a variety of people. She ran into a man whom she had recognized from school or perhaps from her childhood. He and Jane spoke and then her friend came up to them and she was happy to have seen Jane. They hugged and then Jane realized that her friend and that man were a couple. They told her that they were married and she was so happy to hear that. They talked for a bit, then Jane woke up. That was weird.

When Jane had dreams like that, she felt inclined to call that person, with whom she had not seen in a long time. Something compelled her to think of them in her deepest of dreams, so therefore she must contact them to see if they were doing okay. She thought that she would do that when she returned home.

She looked at the cell phone and it was just before 6:00 a.m. She had lay there for a minute and realized that she had not moved from her right side all night. When she had awoken, she had been rocking. As she had gone to bed the previous night, Jane had remembered that she had whimpered herself to sleep. She knew that she was concerned about her flight, as always, and she was concerned about going home and facing her life and continuing something new and exciting with Pascal. But she also feared it. Those thoughts apparently worked on the deepest part of her brain, so much so, that it affected her physically. She was getting tired of having all of her worries follow her, especially at night, in her dreams.

It was baggage, luggage...and a suitcase full of woe, that she was so desperately trying to rid herself of, and soon.

She got up, made the bed and opened the blinds. There was mist and fog dancing at the base of the mountains. The sky was overcast and she somehow knew that it was going to be a beautiful day. She used the bathroom, got dressed in denim shorts, a white tank top and an orange V-neck shirt. She popped on a headband, brushed her teeth, went downstairs, brought the laundry back up after folding it on top the dryer, then sat on the bedroom floor and packed her suitcase. There was nothing like being as prepared as possible. Somehow Jane knew that the motto *"Be prepared"* had belonged to the Boy Scouts, but was it also the motto of the Girl Scouts? Probably...

Jane rolled some clothes, stuffed small items inside her shoes, including her costume necklaces, squeezed the air out of zipper bags that were full of miscellaneous items and so on and placed those items in her suitcase. She heard Joseph get up during her chore, he went downstairs then went to the bathroom to get ready. Jane finished up with packing, balanced her funds, grabbed her purse and went downstairs.

Before sitting down at the table with some food, Jane went to the kitchen, put away the clean dishes from the dishwasher, refilled it with dirty ones from the sink and got some water and grapes from the fridge. She turned on her computer and read the international news and checked on emails.

Joseph came downstairs, looked quite model-esque as usual. *"Damn, he's good-looking,"* she thought. They greeted each other, then she asked if he was needing her to help him with the car or his bike. He said that she did not need to help then asked if that was why she was up so early. She stated that it was not, that she was just up already, but wanted to be ready if he needed her. She asked if she could have the rest of the tea in the carafe and he said that she could. He smiled that beautiful smile, which made her melt every time.

He was running late for work, he grabbed his things and wished her to have a great day and vice versa. As he exited the living space and went up the flight of stairs to the foyer, he asked of her plans that day, so she told him that she was hoping to go back into town and try some new foods. He repeated what she had said and she verified the statement, adding that she was hoping to rest as well. Then he was off.

His cologne lingered in the dining area and as she heard him take off in his nice sports car, she sat there and she closed her eyes and breathed in his comforting and welcoming scent. *"Damn,"* she thought. She missed Pascal. *"I sure could have been comforted with some cuddling last night."* By then, it was 7:30 a.m.

A bit later, Jane made some breakfast and photographed her

food, for it was quite colorful and inviting. Everything was small in size. She had two pieces of toast with raspberry jam, two scrambled (brown) eggs, some grapes, three slivers of cheese, the last leftovers of the sauerkraut pastry, water, tea with sugar (leftover from the festival from the day before), plus orange juice with oats. *Yummy.* She ate, journaled and when she emailed some friends, she cried her eyes out, for she confessed that she was sad that her trip was coming to an end.

Jane thanked each and every one of them for putting up with her long-winded, descriptive emails, her extensive photo sharing, as she shared her experiences on the mountain and at the castle the day before. She shared that she was very happy to be alive.

Around 12:00 p.m., she was done with writing and ready for a nap. She put away the dishes, loaded the dishwasher, then went upstairs to try to sleep. She wondered how Joseph was faring, after he had popped into her head, and as she reflected on the endless adventures from the day before. She took a quick moment to clean out the tub, clean the sink and mirror, then combed out her hair, put in clips and plopped onto the bed.

Jane fell asleep for a moment or two, curled up in a ball and rocking, as she drifted off to thoughts of Pascal kissing her and more. She found herself awake and crying some time later. She lay there for a moment, listening to the sounds of the construction that was going on in front of the house, and of the sounds of the kids in the pool in the neighbor's backyard.

The warmth of the sun peeking through the window was resting on her body. The rays were dancing in a bright pattern on the hardwood floor. She could feel her heart pounding in her chest. It was noticeably pounding more than it should be, after resting for quite some time. She thought that it could be the lack of enough water or too much sugar or just too much build up of caffeine in her system.

She knew that latter thought was not true. She realized that she had been crying and she knew that she was feeling sorry for herself again. Jane felt sorrowful, but then she realized that she had also been thinking of her own death or the thoughts of being dead and gone and no more.

Why did that cross her mind on such a beautiful day? In her thoughts, she was watching or at least feeling, that her very soul was drifting out into the vastness of space and finally dissipating over time. Is that what death was really like? She kind of hoped so, with the pain and the sorrow quickly leaving her physical being and drifting out into another dimension of its own. That somehow her soul would find ultimate peace. Jane cried some more.

Jane did not know what she had been expecting from her trip, but she felt that she had gotten a lot from it, in spite of her fears. Jane had gained the confidence and trust and never-ending friendship of her dear friend, Joseph. She had shared with him the many sad and scary and happy thoughts and times with some of her dearest friends. She had shared stories about her children. She had met new people, all of whom had been nice and very patient and she had experienced things that she thought she never would have…ever.

As she cried, Jane thought about her flight, getting lost, bumped, being late, missing the next flight and so on. She wondered if her kids and granddaughters were okay. She thought about Pascal and then thought of him kissing her and more, again.

She wondered where their relationship was going to lead, if anywhere...

She wondered if he missed her...

She wondered why she was somewhat obsessed with that man...

She truly wanted to remain friends with him and she felt as if she knew that he felt the same.

Jane had come to love him in such a short period of time, but felt as if nothing would come of it, as far as the deep commitment that she had wanted from some man. She was not sure how, but she knew that it would go nowhere, for that was what they wanted. Nothing more than good friendship (or was it)? She tried to convince herself that she would take that any day of the week, as long as she did not get hurt.

"It is inevitable," she thought, *"that I will be the one to get hurt again."* She had already felt as if she loved him and when he would get to the point of not reciprocating, in the manner in which she felt that she wanted, needed or deserved, she would suffer. She had reassured herself, from time to time, to expect to suffer, because that was all that she have ever known. She continued to think of him touching her.

248

Jane got a bit aroused with the thoughts of him and decided that perhaps that was what she needed: A release. So, she took it upon herself to complete that task and was very surprised at what seemed like never-ending, much-needed, much-appreciated results. She was surprised at how much stress she had built up in that area, so to speak. She thought, as long as her limbs were able to continue, she would continue until she was exhausted. She was glad that she had some upper body strength. She finished and lay there, completely, if temporarily, satisfied.

Jane cleaned up, changed into longer shorts, put on some makeup, went downstairs and started a small load of laundry. She went back to the kitchen, got some grapes, water and bread, then sat at her computer and journaled for a while. She needed caffeine and also desired something salty, crunchy and perhaps some chocolate. She took some headache meds and realized that she was missing a wonderful sunny day.

With that thought in her head, she grabbed her camera and decided to take a walk. She thought that it would be nice just to travel the opposite of town for a bit, then double back to home within a half hour or so. Out the door she went and headed east up the hill, past the construction site, then she turned south to take a walk along a half-paved road in an older type neighborhood.

She took pictures of flowers, signs, houses with small yards and some bigger yards. She heard dogs barking, kids playing, the birds chirping. She heard some construction tools, and the sound got fainter as she walked farther from Joseph's home.

The neighborhood of houses abruptly ended. To the east was a farm with a large pasture, grazing cows way out in the field, a small house and a brown barn. There was a dense wooded area, that bordered that property. Then she saw a narrow, tree-lined path, that, if she had blinked, she would have missed it. She wanted to walk down that overgrown path, but she hesitated out of fear. The thought popped into her head that no one knew where she was. There were no signs that she saw that indicated if the path was private property, or if it was leading to a public park, or if it was closed further down.

Besides, if there had been a sign, would she have been able to decipher it? She was very curious, so she walked a bit closer, dipped slightly under the brush, then she heard a whisper in her head, *"Just go. You know you want to."* She felt as if she was being enticed by a troll…or a garden fairy…or even if she had walked one step further, she would have fallen into the rabbit's hole.

She was able to get herself just to the edge of the trees, where the pavement ended and the dirt, dust and rocks began. She experienced a bit of a shudder… She could have sworn that the birds stopped chirping, that the sounds around her had hushed and that the world stopped spinning at that moment.

Jane just could not do it. She just could not bring herself to take the risk of walking down that hilly trail in that foreign country and to possibly never be seen again. She somehow knew that even after she would get back home, she would regret her decision of not traveling down that road. Jane was tired of feeling like a chicken.

She walked back to Joseph's house, still hearing the birds,

children and the busy noises of the workers at the site. Once back in the living room, she burned several of Joseph's CDs onto her computer, with his permission that she had gotten earlier in the week. She put the clothes in the dryer, went back to journal at her computer then she downed a bunch of water and chewed on some gum. She thought of food, but avoided it.

Around 5:15 p.m., Joseph called to tell her that he was going to the store, hoped to pick up some trout, and that he would be home in 30 minutes to start dinner. *"Okay and thanks."* She knew that she had never had trout before, so that would be exciting. It was a good thing that he was a good cook and it had not hurt that he was truly good-looking. Not only did she like to watch him eat, but she liked to watch him cook as well. *Sigh...*

Jane turned off the computer, then straightened up a bit. She sat on the couch and vegged until he came home. Once he was home, they greeted each other as usual, as he darted into the kitchen to start dinner. She offered to help and he declined at first, telling her that she could help with the salad. She could hear him in the kitchen, with pots and pans banging...chopping and moving things around, etc. A bit later, as she could hear the beginning of searing and cooking fish, he came to the doorway with a glass of wine and as he leaned on the door frame, he looked at her with a small smile.

With tired eyes, she looked back. He had a strange smirk and asked her what she had done all day. She thought, *"What is his smirk about?"* Hesitatingly, she told him that she did nothing much more than journal and laundry. He quickly commented that he was surprised that she would do nothing more than that on her last day there.

What he did not know was that she did do a bit more, but she decided not to tell him about chickening out of walking down a somewhat mysterious path. She did not want to tell him that she had pleased herself on his futon and right then, she was exhausted but relaxed from her stresses. She did her best not to smirk back at him.

He sort of slowly leaned his head sideways and down and he asked if there was something wrong. She told him that there really was not anything wrong, but that she was aware of some heightened anxiety due to the thoughts of her departure. She told him that she was aware that she did not want to leave and that she was concerned about the flights, her unemployment, and everything else, etc. It was the 'etc' that worried her the most...

He had a look on his face that she had a hard time identifying. She immediately thought that maybe he knew...or at least he sensed...that she had pleasured herself, but how could he have known that? She felt just a bit uncomfortable. She wondered what her face looked like, as it could have looked flushed from her brisk, exciting walk.

Or that it could have looked flushed after her much-needed release. Did he have the ability to sense her *pheromones?* Or was it that her face could have looked flushed from her slight paranoia. Her face could have even looked a bit red, because of how she thought that she was looking at him. Was it obvious on her face of how much more attractive he looked to her at that very moment? How embarrassing!

He told her that she should really try not to worry about such things. Jane told Joseph that she had tried to nap soundly, but could not and she just wanted to relax and did. He said that in his opinion, the best thing that she could have done, was to have gone into town, walk around, take more photos and get exhausted. So when she had gotten on her flights, she could possibly sleep better, longer and so on. She told him that that was a good idea, but it was too late. He smirked at her again and then went back to finish the cooking. She felt as if in some way he was trying to scold her and for only a brief second, she felt hurt.

Jane went upstairs and finally took a moment and drafted a letter to him. She had brought a blank card with her on the trip for the sole purpose of that moment. She started out with the usual *'Dear Joseph,'* but had a hard time putting into words of her thankfulness for his hospitality.

After sitting there for a moment, she started with… *'My words cannot express the deep appreciation that I have for the opportunities that you have given me on this trip…'* and so on. She wrote that she loved him dearly as a friend, that she would take with her and share with others, the wonderful adventures that she had had and that she did not want to leave. She wrote that she was hoping that somehow she could stay, but home had called her back. However, she would leave with a new life-altering experience of strangers who have become friends, of kind and patient people and of the beauty of his homeland.

She held back many tears as she poured out her heart to him. She put the card in the bathroom, where she knew that he would find it.

A bit later, Jane went downstairs, washed her hands and helped with tearing up the salad leaves. Joseph worked on dinner. He cut up garlic, cut up onions to add to the salad and they added balsamic vinegar and olive oil, salt and pepper to it as well. Jane set the table. He asked if she wanted wine and she agreed to the white. She put the salad on the table, then he got the plates out of the oven and served the fish and potatoes.

They sat in their usual places and they ate, drank and talked. The food was delicious, but he commented that the fish was too dry. He told her that the trout looked too funny so he picked up cod instead. He got up and got some cocktail sauce, but it was not American cocktail sauce. It was more like cocktail sauce mixed with a mayo of some kind and it was good.

Then, much to Jane's regret and as usual, Joseph was able to get her to open up. *"Dammit!"* He told her that he had made some observations about her and she told him that she was not willing to be observed, but she also told him to say what he needed to say. He told her that she got very mellow, very melancholy when she drank, that she opened up easier, although he admitted that she was able to talk a lot even without the alcohol. He told her, without exactly saying the words and not meaning to upset her, that she liked to talk, but that she had a hard time *listening.* Jane agreed.

He was laughing at that, for he told her that she had asked

him several times about how his day was, but did not give him enough time to elaborate on his day. He suspected that Jane had asked everyone how their day was, because she was a very curious individual. He wondered if she was concerned about what he was going to say.

Jane told him that she did not think so. But she also told him that when he answered *"Fine,"* which was almost all the time, that she possibly assumed too much, that he was finished telling her about his day...and since his pauses afterwards were quite lengthy. *"All men that I have met have done that,"* she told him...adding, *"They just say...Fine."* That comment caused them both to crack up. She was right and he knew it.

She told him that she had been told several times by many others, that she has done that. However, she had been told so, in a hurtful, possibly even loud, angry manner. That reaction had caused her hesitation for quite some time. She told Joseph that she had asked the question most times out of deep concern and also out of sheer small talk. She told him that when she had asked him throughout that previous week, she was always asking out of concern. She told him that most of the men that she knew always answered with *"Fine"*...so she never knew how long to wait for more.

She apologized to him for not being a good listener, for not slowing down and thinking before she spoke. She told him that she had many thoughts racing through her head all day and all night and that she did have a hard time processing her thoughts, most days. Especially when she was under a lot of stress, like she had been for many, many months.

He wondered about things…out loud, throughout their conversation…as she told him about her sadness of her family moving away and moving apart…and of missing her grandchildren already.

As they talked, she told him that she wondered how he was going to ultimately view her, as she was worried that their conversations were possibly going to change some things in his life, regarding her.

They talked a little about sex, life, death, loss of many kinds, cheating and betrayal. She told him that she was not mad. He told her that he thought that she should have been and still may be mad, when her former boyfriend cheated on her. *"You should be mad. The bastard cheated on you!"* he exclaimed. But she told him that being mad, in her opinion, served her no purpose and that she believed that ultimately it was a waste of her time and energy. She had more important things to do and more important things to worry about.

He disagreed. He believed that she was missing the grand purpose of being mad and of hatred. He told her that it was a natural part of healing and that if she dismissed it, she was not understanding its purpose. He told her that its purpose was a step, a phase, and that when she was able to get over it, she would heal. She disagreed.

He told her that when she drank and got mellow, she brought up those sad things a lot. He could see in her face, that their betrayal hurt her deeply and how sad she was that another ex-beau had told her that he did not love her and told her that she was fat. That lead Joseph to think that she had not resolved those problems in her head.

She sort of agreed, however, she also told him that she would never have the answers as to why these men betrayed her, nor did not love her enough. Or that she was not enough for them not to cheat on and not to love her. He asked her *"Why not?"*...and she answered, *"Because, they will never tell me the truth...for they are all liars."*

Jane told him that she was told by two of them (separately and not all at once), that she was intimidating, for she always had said what was on her mind, most of the time. They told her that for some reason, she commanded some attention when she walked into any room. They stated in so many words that she had a *"kick ass now, ask questions later"* attitude and that she talked to anyone, at any time and never seemed to view anyone as a stranger. She told Joseph that she had never viewed that part of herself as being a negative thing, but apparently they did. *Negative and irritating.*

She continued to tell Joseph that she was told by them that she was able to talk without hesitation, telling all about herself without embarrassment, mostly all in one breath and that she told the best stories. Both of those ex-beaus had commented that they were envious of her for all of that and more.

She told Joseph that a former friend had told her that she had agreed with what those men had said and that since she was such an intimidating force, even in her opinion, that those men had to find some way to *"put you in your place."* What they did was strategically, lightly insult her at first, commenting that they were *"just kidding"* regarding her height and weight among other things. Then they pounded Jane with more hurtful comments later on, to ensure their place in their relationship as the alpha male. Joseph had a strange look on his face by then.

And in addition, Jane's friend told her that because she had always come across that she was so confident in her own skin and that was evident everywhere she went, that she had *"emasculated"* them by just being who she was. *"Wow,"* was the look of surprise on Joseph's face. Jane continued to tell him what her friend had said.

She had told her that when they had insulted Jane, especially in private, it was their only way of getting back at her for being confident and outgoing, carefree and optimistic. In her friend's opinion, they were jealous or envious of Jane, for they were not any of that at all. They did not know how to handle their own insecurities. Her friend said that they were weak and she was not, and they did not like the fact that she was not needy. She told her that men want to be needed and Jane was too strong and stubborn of a woman, too strong of a force, for them. She was most likely doomed to never find a strong enough man.

Jane told Joseph that her friend's comments had made her cry for three days straight. Regardless of those comments being true or not, she still never came to the understanding of them needing to cheat on her, regardless of how they subconsciously viewed her. And whether they were jealous, envious or not. Jane believed that all they needed to do was to tell her that they wanted to end the relationship, for they had found another woman that they were interested in.

It would have hurt like hell, either way and it did hurt tremendously, but being upfront and honest was the better way. It was the adult way of handling it, according to Jane. Even as Jane said those things out loud, she knew that she was fooling herself, for they and she, were never completely honest all the time...every day...all damn day long. Joseph told her that it was not realistic to see the world that way.

Jane knew that she had the *"problem"* of saying what was on her mind a lot and that she lacked *"a filter,"* but she also knew that what she has said was not always what anyone wanted to hear. She knew that her opinions were just that...*Opinions*...and not anything written in stone. For most of her adult life, she had been working on trying to stop talking, but for some reason, she had never been able to accomplish that.

Joseph told Jane that the cheating was just a symptom of something else and she agreed with him. He guessed that perhaps they cheated because they found something else in that other woman or women, that they thought that Jane had lacked. He told her that perhaps they took advantage of the opportunity of the other woman's attention, feeling as if her attention was easier and perhaps it was just a way out for them.

He told her that when someone cheats, they are not thinking clearly or logically. They are not thinking of the other person at all, even though they may actually care for that person, even if temporarily and superficially. Perhaps they felt rejected or ignored in all aspects of their lives, like with work, home, children, friends, etc. They would justify what they were doing, no matter what and perhaps they would find ways of blaming her for their insecurities. Jane let Joseph's opinions and comments sink in. She did not want to respond to him, before she could think about what was being said.

Joseph told her that she needed to finally get to a place in her heart and soul, mind and body and not only think, but *believe*, that their cheating and lying was not her fault. Jane agreed, but she also agreed that she was not sure why she had wasted so much time wondering *why*. She told him that she was very tired of having her brain always being *"on"* with thinking, suffering, wondering and being anxious over things that she cannot and could not control.

She told him that she was so happy at the time of being in her relationships and that she felt blind-sided and therefore felt duped, foolish, naive and damaged. He told her that she needed to stop giving away so much power to these men and that she had more control over things than she realized. Jane wholeheartedly disagreed, regarding the control part.

But, Joseph also told her that what he had observed mostly during that entire week, regarding all of that, was that she brought up her first ex-boyfriend a lot, especially when she was tipsy. He felt that on some level, Jane had *never* recovered from his betrayal, even compared to the many betrayals in her marriage. Joseph told her that he sensed that her hurt was much deeper than even compared to her hope of a future with Pascal.

He felt that since she had gotten married at such an early age, that it was (perhaps) inevitable that their marriage would end and that they were both too immature in the beginning. He said that since change would inevitably happen to the both of them in some capacity, they drifted apart, for their interests became different and that was okay.

But, Joseph told her that he felt that after her divorce and after waiting seven years to date again, that when Jane had met and fallen in love with her first real boyfriend as an adult, that she had fallen in love truly for the first time. And that was why his betrayal was the most profound, the most hurtful, the most unforgivable…in her heart.

Jane could not believe her ears! She believed that Joseph had hit the nail on the head. He was right and she knew it, but now, she wondered, *"What do I do about it?"* Jane knew that somewhere deep down that she had always known that about herself, after all of these years had drifted by.

They talked about the fears of each of them getting involved with another person. They talked about Pascal and of how much she had come to care about him in a short period of time and that she feared and felt that it would not last. Joseph commented that she was more brave than she had realized, for she had been able and was willing to open up with another again, even after lots of heartache and sadness. He told her that that was something he had not done yet. He stated that she was willing to take the plunge and that was a good thing, however, he also asked her that if she feared being cheated on, why would she bother with getting involved ever again?

He told her that statistically, cheating was inevitable. He then asked, *"So why risk it at all?"* Why not go through the rest of her life, not getting involved with another and do the things that she can do, like work and save and travel, like she did that week? Why not step out of her comfort zone and take on challenges that would not involve another human being?

Jane told Joseph that she was a social person and that she loved being with others, at parties, going out for walks, etc. She told him that she loved being loved on and that she loved cuddling and holding hands. She loved learning about the lives of other people, of another person. She loved to watch the faces of people and of her current beau, as they told their stories of being involved with their kids, being married, even going through the hard times of a divorce or even a death. She loved to listen to them talk about their families, their parents, friends, etc. She liked to watch their faces light up, including Joseph's, as they told their stories about their children when they were small.

Jane told him that she liked to tell her stories to anyone who would listen and also to get their feedback on the things that she had been through. She told him that she loved being involved with someone, that she loved being in love, she loved the physical attention and the feeling of love being reciprocated, even though most men are hard to read. Isn't that at least *ONE* of the purposes of life, to be with another human being, at death's door?

Jane also knew that she was not willing to admit defeat to herself (again). Jane somehow knew the moment that the relationship was over and that she hung on for too long, for hope that she was wrong. She admitted to Joseph that she had hoped somehow they would change their minds. But Jane told Joseph, that she was never wrong, when it came to seeing in their faces and observing their reactions that proved to her that they did not love her, at least any longer, or even at all.

Jane got loud and could not believe that she blurted out that if and when her relationship with Pascal had ended, that she just could not do it again. *"I just cannot try one more time, in this f*cking lifetime, to try to find love with a man who would understand me and love me unconditionally. I just cannot tell one more f*cking story or try to read another man on whether or not they would accept me and my children and my family as they are."*

"I just cannot exercise one more minute with the hopes of being in shape, with the hopes of being thin enough for the next guy and the next. I am just not willing to find a man who would be man enough to not give a red rat's ass about my stretch marks. I just cannot put on one more ounce of makeup, to look pretty enough for a man, who may say what he thought I wanted to hear....that I was beautiful, that I was pretty enough until he found another. I just cannot put one more man's d*ck in my mouth!"

With that last loud statement, there was long awkward pause and then Jane got such a comical look of surprise on her face. Her eyes were as big as dinner plates. Joseph's eyes bugged out, too. She put her hands over her mouth for a moment, then all of a sudden, both of them laughed boundlessly.

After the laughter stopped and after calming down a bit, she apologized to Joseph about what she had said. She told Joseph that she would take under advisement, his ideas about travel, etc. Jane realized that that was not a bad idea. As a matter of fact, it was a great idea, indeed. Joseph told her not to worry about it, but somehow he knew better.

Their conversation took a strange turn as they talked about the loss of her mother and about the unconditional love of (most) mothers. They talked about their dads and they talked about their children. Jane was nervous, shaky, agitated, squirmy and crying. So much so, that she could not answer him as to why certain things made her deeply sad and cry...a lot...as he got up and handed Jane a tissue. Jane was quite embarrassed and seemed unable to control herself during that conversation.

Joseph made her feel a bit at ease when she talked to him, which agitated Jane. But he was a very good listener, very good at probing and asking the right questions. But what he did not know, was that Jane was observing him as well.

Joseph was leaning forward, then leaning back, with his hands clasped together at the back of his head. He was leaning side to side and had looks of confusion and genuine concern. He was probably wondering why his friend, this strange and little grandmother, was so moody and so messed up and he probably was wondering what he had gotten himself into.

However, she thought that he had offered her the wine and knew that she would accept, in order to get her to talk more anyway. He told her that he was always analyzing people, for that was his job, his detective nature, his genuine curiosity as to what makes people tick. He was a man, as well, and he had a look on his face that Jane could not identify. Or perhaps that she did not want to identify.

She felt a heightened sense of vulnerability, with crying and weeping and many moments of not being able to look him in the eyes during their very lengthy (inebriated) conversation. She sensed that he knew it. If he had been any other man, he would have taken advantage of that helplessness and she was very grateful, very happy that he was not any other man.

Joseph was a decent man, to be able to listen and respond with great concern and not to use her and taking advantage of her weaknesses. That was what a good friend was all about. She was very thankful for his sense of morality and for his decent nature.

She felt confident that he would remain her dear friend for life, in some capacity. That was what made her sleep better, as she drifted off in slumber at the end of the evening. She was content in knowing that she had someone to love her, to care about her, as she is, without being judgmental…on the other side of the world. It was a great feeling and she was blessed for it.

They admitted to each other that it was getting late, that they needed to get some sleep, because of how early they needed to get up. They cleared off the table and Jane started the dishes. He told her that she did not need to do that. She told him that it was the least that she could do. They talked a bit more, as she cleaned up the counter and finished up. Jane looked over her shoulder for a brief minute.

With a drink in his hand, Joseph was leaning in the doorway of the kitchen again, looking as handsome as ever, with what she interpreted as a provocative look on his face. She hated the fact that she could still smell his cologne even from that distance and it smelled so good.

With her back to him as she faced the sink, Jane smirked and admitted something out loud. She said, *"Joseph, I don't want to leave. I feel that I have nothing really to go home to."* There was a bit of a pause. She continued to speak softly. *"I'd love to stay more... visit with you more...get to know you and your parents and your friends and your hometown better, but I am afraid that I would drive you crazy."* His response was typically comical of him, perfect and dead-on. *"We have gotten past that already."* Jane's head spun around to look at him. They smiled. There was a brief pause and then they laughed so hard for the next few minutes. It was a perfect ending to a perfect day.

That lasting laugh and his beautiful, precious smile was worth her trip alone. She finished up the dishes, as Joseph was exiting the back patio doors to smoke a cigarette. She followed him to the doorway, then she asked him why he smoked. He told her that he liked the way smoking went directly to the pleasure part of his brain and when he smoked, it gave him clarity. It helped him think and figure out an answer to something. It helped him relax for the moment. What did he need to figure out? Why did he need to relax?

He had told her earlier in the week that he had not smoked for weeks, maybe months, but did so occasionally, just to work out a problem. She wondered if her visit or at least that last conversation, had pushed him to the brink of smoking again.

Jane wondered if she disturbed him, which she knew she did a lot to others. Jane wondered whether or not she had agitated him... stressed him...or even possibly, aroused him in some way. She did not necessarily mean to think, in a sexual way. She wondered if she had aroused in him, a deeper sense of curiosity about her, for he had not really known her for many years past high school.

Much time had gone by and they had gotten older. They had changed and they had been through a lot. They had gotten married, had kids and had gotten divorced. They had met many people throughout their lives and she thought that most people, like them, thought about the *"What if's"* and the *"Shoulda, Coulda, Woulda's"* in life.

She wondered if he had as much curiosity about her as she had towards him. She liked to people-watch while trying not to interrupt, whereas he liked to talk and probe. She wondered about all of that and more, as she grabbed her camera and snapped away. She was able to capture him with smoke in hand and as he was outside in the moonlight, looking up at the stars. It was a great moment, she thought, of capturing him in deep thought. Those are some of the photographs that she would always cherish, among the many that chronicled her adventure.

They told each other goodnight, after they established the time that they needed to get up and get started. Joseph stayed outside and Jane went upstairs. She brushed and flossed, washed her face, went to her room and changed into her jams of girly blue boxer shorts and a simple tank top. She finished packing up her computer and suitcase, then she found some extra Euros and excitedly went downstairs to offer them to Joseph.

He was sitting at the table doing something on his computer. By the time she approached him, she had realized that she was not completely appropriately dressed, in the presence of her gorgeous single friend. She thought that since he had not grabbed her up, thrown her up against the wall or on top of the dining room table and kissed her passionately (or more), by then, that it was never going to happen and that it should not. Besides, she did not even feel sexy. But she had been told on more than one occasion by Pascal, that when she was in her jams and sans makeup, that she looked absolutely beautiful.

Jane had to admit to herself right at that moment that as she looked at Joseph, that she had thought about that more than once. She wondered what her face looked like, when he looked at her. Did he know what she was thinking? *"That one single act of passion, of lust, of temporary desire, would have been great,"* she thought, *"But it also would have messed up our friendship for life."* She did not want that to happen at all. She loved him and needed him too much for that.

As Jane offered the Euros to Joseph, he told her to keep them, for she may need them for breakfast at the airport. She had over 8

Euros and she could not imagine eating that much food, but she kept them anyway. She agreed with him and went back upstairs, wondering if he had checked out her cute butt. She turned off the light and plopped into bed, and as she lay there flat on her back, she prayed for her safe journey.

She prayed for everyone who would be traveling. She had not heard from her daughter, so she prayed that all was well with her and her family. Somehow, she knew that all was fine, for she did not sense anything differently. She prayed for her son and his fiance and she prayed for everything else in her life to be calm and peaceful. She slowly drifted off to sleep, thinking about kissing Pascal and wondering about her kids and her grand kids. She thought one last thought of Joseph, his incredible smile and she thought of how truly blessed she was to call him her friend. She smiled and fell asleep. *"Thank You again...for another wonderful day. Amen."*

Tuesday...

Jane was awake at around 3:00 a.m. *"Why?"* she thought. She got up, stripped the bed of its sheets, but then could not collapse the futon. *"Dammit."* She wanted to be able to do that, too. She went to the bathroom, washed her face and brushed her teeth, put on a little makeup, then went back to the bedroom. She got dressed in jeans, a white tank top and green patterned shirt, threw on a headband, put on her boots, packed up the rest of her clothes and quietly hauled her stuff downstairs. She put it in the foyer and then went to the kitchen. She got two water bottles and put them by her bags, then went back to the living room and sat on one of the overstuffed chairs…and meditated. It was still dark, it was quiet and peaceful and her time in Europe was over. She realized that she was most definitely sad.

She heard Joseph get up, take a shower, then come downstairs. He greeted her, by asking how she slept and why she was up so early. She told him that she had slept solid for a few hours, she just woke up on her own, and that she did that a lot more lately, as she had gotten older.

He told her that he was surprised how well he had slept, as he prepared his breakfast of toast and tea in the kitchen. His cologne was still wafting in the living room air. *Mmmm…* He started singing a song that she did not recognize. *"I want to be, under the sea, with you, in an octopus garden in the shade."* Jane smiled, giggled, and asked where that had come from and why he just started singing it. He smiled. Again, that welcoming smile, that she was going to miss.

He told her that, from time to time, that song popped into his head and he was very surprised that she had not heard it. He went to the shelf of his extensive CD collection and found The Beatles' CD and put it on the table. He sat and ate. He offered her breakfast again, but she declined. They basically sat in silence for a moment, then they started humming that happy tune at the same time and started laughing. She had to admit that it was quite catchy.

Around 4:15 a.m., they gathered her things and put them in the car. They got in and took off for the airport. She did her best to stay quiet during most of the trip. As they drove away from his home, she got very mellow. He popped in the CD and started the song, singing along with The Beatles. She smiled, and she knew that she was going to miss listening to his beautiful deep voice.

She wondered, that if life could be just that simple. To just appreciate things, to appreciate his deep voice or any man's deep voice and live with the knowledge that that was enough for her. And for that man, in turn, to just appreciate her entire uniqueness. *Period.*

They drove past the darkened hills and valleys to the north of his home. She was going to miss those hills and valleys that she admired and soaked in, on her walks into town. She was going to miss those beautiful and green hills and valleys that she could see out of the window of the bedroom that she called home for the past ten days.

They drove over the railroad tracks, the tracks that they drove over many times down the hill from his home. Those were the tracks that she walked over many times, as she walked into town and back, and to the bus stop on her way to Vienna. She was going to miss those tracks.

They drove up the hills and down the hills, through rural towns and villages, filled with sleeping people. The headlights of his sports car seemingly danced off the black pavement and around the curves of the roads that they were traveling. She smiled and thought, *"How fitting"* as they listened to *"The Long and Winding Road"* and *"Let*

It Be" on the CD player.

They quietly sang along to all of the tunes that they knew and she could feel such sorrow overcoming her. She closed her eyes and fought tears as she allowed herself to drift off to sleep, feeling safe in his car and in his care, as he drove her to their eventual departure. That was a perfect moment for her. She was going to stay quiet to make sure that she was not going to mess it up.

Occasionally, she would open her eyes and see nothing more than the highways and byways and many confusing signs and the cars and trucks that shared the road. He pointed out the refinery and told her that they had about five kilometers to go until they reached the airport. He asked her for the second time if it was okay for him to drop her off, so he could go right to work and she told him that it was okay. Sooner than she wanted, they were at the airport. It was well-lit and it was abuzz with many travelers.

Joseph parked against the curb and popped the trunk. They got out, he helped her get her two bags and then she looked at him. They paused, they smiled, then they moved in close and hugged each other very tightly. She did not want to let go. She thanked him for all of his help and he told her that she was welcome. She looked at him one last time. He had a look on his face that she could not read. She got that smile of his for one last time. *"Thank you so much for that, Joseph."*

She tossed her computer bag over her shoulder and popped out the handle of her rolling carry-on suitcase. She sighed, then pivoted on her heel and walked through the automated doors. She wondered what her face had looked like and if it showed sadness and slight discontent. She wondered if Joseph checked out her butt and that thought made her smile, for she knew that she had a cute, round cheerleader bum.

She also wondered if he wanted to kiss her goodbye, especially just for the heck of it. She knew that she wanted him to, and she would not have stopped him if he did. That would have been the cherry on the top of the ice cream sundae of her European adventures, that she had experienced those entire ten days. It was okay that he did not. Because, after all, she was lactose intolerant. But...she did wonder. And just like that...

Jane got inside and assessed the confusion and the chaos and headed straight for the information booth. The clerk directed her towards the boarding pass kiosk. She was happy to be successful in finally figuring out that contraption. Especially after that thing had rejected her and her American passport three times, noting in big letters on the screen that it did not recognize her.

She thought, *"How fitting. I would not have recognized me either, for I am returning home as a wonderfully and remarkably changed individual."* She got the three boarding passes and seat assignments that she needed, then found a volunteer, who helped her with directions to the right concourse for her first flight. *"Thank you, Patti, the Vienna Airport volunteer."*

After much walking and scooting around other patrons, and after going through security again, Jane finally got to the gate and waited as she heard three separate announcements. The flight had been delayed for boarding, from 7:15 a.m...then 7:30 a.m...then 8:30 a.m. She went to a nearby cafe and bought two chocolate doughnuts. For some reason the female cashier verbalized her surprise that Jane wanted two of them. Jane looked at her with a furrowed brow and thought, *"It is just none of your business, whether or not I need two doughnuts...you skinny, young, tall juvenile!"* Okay, okay, that was not necessary for her to think that, but she wanted two, dammit, and she got two.

Jane went back to the gate area, sat and ate. She remembered at that moment that she had forgotten her water bottles in Joseph's trunk. *"Damn."* She still had plenty of Euros left and she knew she would just be returning home with money that she could not use. *How strange was that?* As she sat there, she observed again, how many of the people had looked like many other people that she had known. She could have sworn that she had seen Billy Bob Thornton, William H. Macy, Drew Carey and Thandie Newton. *It could have been them.*

Around 8:45 a.m., the announcement came and they boarded a bus to the plane. On the ride, she spoke with an older couple who were on their way back to San Francisco. They had just been returning from weeks of traveling to many countries abroad. They were going to miss their connection and had to wait another day to get home. She told them about her adventures, too. They were very happy for her and she was concerned and happy for them. *"How fortunate and exciting,"* she thought, for they had the opportunity to travel together and to share their experiences together.

She got on the plane, secured her suitcase and finally sat down. She was happy to have had an aisle seat and had no one sitting next to her at the windows. Jane wanted to personally thank that pilot for a smooth take-off and landing, which eased some of her anxiety a bit. It was raining and he had alerted them to the impending storms, hail and turbulence. She ate the offered snack of a poppy seed, mini baguette sandwich, filled with avocado cream, Swiss cheese, pickles, artichoke and lettuce, along with a water and a diet Coke.

The pilot made the announcements of the delayed flight connections and Jane's next flight was not affected. She was happy about that, but a bit worried that she was going to have to sprint a mile to find her flight into Amsterdam. She looked at her boarding pass and she had to check in around 10:20 a.m.

At that moment, for some damned reason, she started to cry, as the thought of her children popped into her head. *"What the hell?"* she thought. A bit later, she recovered and happened to look back at the passenger who was behind her, sitting at the window.

They introduced themselves, as she stated that she had admired his new tattoo on his left arm. He told her that it was itching, peeling and bothering him. It was a symbol of his Indian heritage. He told her his name, which was a traditional Indian name, but she had a hard time pronouncing it and therefore she also had immediately forgotten it. He told her that he lived and worked in Mississippi for many years, spoke many languages, including Spanish and English and that he was returning home from visiting his parents in Italy. She told him some things about herself, including that she had several tattoos. They wished each other luck with their ongoing adventures.

He was young, cute, nice and personable and she needed to talk to someone. He made that happen, taking her mind off of her troubles. She made a conscious effort to listen intently to him, as he told his stories of his travels and of his family. She forced herself to think before she responded and before she asked any questions. *"Thank you, sweetie, for distracting me throughout the flight,"* she thought.

Soon that flight was over and it was on to the next one. At that time, she had to literally run to catch it. She found the right concourse and gate, but she had to go through security again, had to take off her shoes, get the dreaded *'pat down'* and take out her computer again. She had to put herself back together, then sprint to the next flight. She made it in time, with another stop from a security agent, who asked her all kinds of questions about herself and about her luggage.

He granted her passage through the remaining doors and she darted down the long hallway to the gate and ramp. As she turned into the jet way, there was a crowd of people moving slowing into the plane. It was then, that she finally had time to stop, relax, take a deep breath and come back to reality. She was aware of her anxiety, but she also knew that her anxiety would have gotten worse, if she had missed that flight.

Jane asked a gentleman passenger to help her put her suitcase in the overhead compartment, which he did willingly. She thanked him, then she plopped down into her window seat. That same man sat next to her and for the next eight hours, Benjamin and Jane had great conversations for most of their ride, in between napping, of course.

They talked about their jobs, their kids, his pet and her previous pets, his trip to Italy for work, about his friend who was on the flight as well, but who was the lucky dog because he had an entire row to himself. They talked about her trip to Austria after dropping off her family, which seemed to fascinate him that she was able to do that alone for a while.

They talked about Joseph and his wonderful hospitality, sightseeing and the plenty of food that was offered and available in all of the countries that they had visited. They talked about all of the help from all of the strangers that they had encountered along the way.

Shortly after take-off, which was wonderfully smooth, after the announcements of the bad weather and so on, they were served their obligatory snacks of pretzels and peanuts, plus water and a pop. For lunch, Jane had pasta, salad, water, white wine and some crackers. She napped a bit, struggling with her pillow, then she rolled up a blanket and her red jacket and put that in the bend of her neck, too, in order to try to get comfortable.

From time to time, she would place her jacket to her nose and breathe in the smells of Joseph's laundry detergent. For some reason, that aroma gave her comfort and made her smile.

She used the bathroom at least two times, but was still uncomfortable with her bloated belly. They continued to talk about details of Ben's work which had to do with preparing livestock for table-consumption. Although to most people it possibly would have been boring, but Jane was amazed at how interesting that conversation was for her.

She needed a sugar boost, so she found her second smashed doughnut in her computer bag and whaled on that, wondering and convincing herself that a smashed doughnut had half the calories of a plumped up doughnut. *"I'm sure of it,"* she thought, jokingly.

She was going through her belongings when she decided to offer her extra Euros to Benjamin, mentioning that they would be good souvenirs for his kids, since he had forgotten to buy them something on his last trip. He reluctantly, but appreciatively accepted, after she had kept one of each for herself. She felt better for feeling as if she had done an odd, but little, good deed.

The flight got a bit bumpy, the seat belt sign came on. She shared some of her photos with him from her computer, then he got out his computer and did some work on it. She fidgeted in her seat as she tried to get comfortable. She continued to check on the time, then eventually the service staff came back around with another snack of pizza, ice cream and another beverage. *"Really? More food?"* she thought.

Benjamin mentioned that soon the flight was going to be over, stating that he wished that that airline would change the food choices on that particular flight from Amsterdam to Minneapolis.

He had taken that flight again and again for work and it was the same boring food, over and over. She told him, *"Sorry about that one."*

And yes, the flight eventually came to an end. She watched below, as the pastures, the farms, the trees, the cars, the houses and the many lakes went by. She wondered if she should stay in Minneapolis for a day or so, since she had never been there before. She quickly changed her mind, since it would cost her a hefty fee to alter her flight plans. She felt as if she needed to get home, although she was not sure if she should truly call it home any more.

What was home, to her, anyway? She wanted to convince herself that home was in Pascal's arms, for the time being. She was still concerned about going back home to Dayton or as to what she was going to find there. How was she going to be received by her friends and family? Was she going to find a job and pay her bills? Would she feel welcomed or needed? Should she stay?

In the meantime, she had a wonderful friend in Pascal, but she felt as if she knew that it would not last. Why was she still thinking that way? Joseph had told her that his thoughts on that was that she was preparing herself for an inevitable end with Pascal, because that was all that she knew. She agreed with that. She was going to try to sabotage her relationship with him, for fear it would end in another way or for fear that it would just end. She thought he could be right about that point. Either way, she knew that it would not last.

Pascal was a dear friend so far and Jane did prefer that they did not end on bad terms. She would need a good friend, from time to time and she wanted to keep all of the friends that she had. Joseph had told her that perhaps she was better off without a man in her life, at least for a while, since she feared being cheated on and she feared being lied to so much. Joseph told her to keep away from men for now, get clear-headed, concentrate on herself and her career, find a job and concentrate on her health, etc. He told her to save her money and do what he believed that she was meant to do: Travel and write. That was very good advice.

Jane was getting mellow, again, as she thought about Joseph and how it would be so easy to fall in love with a man like him and get hurt by him as well. He was charming, witty, gorgeous, adorable, driven, athletic, worldly, a true provider, but he was also just a man.

Did Jane need any man in her life? *"No,"* she thought. But it would be nice to have a strong, athletic man around, to open up stubborn jars and pop bottles.

It would be nice to have one to hug and to kiss on and to cuddle with and to talk to... It would be nice to have a man around who would invite her to a bar or a restaurant, meet his friends and with whom to watch the OSU games or Bengals games. A *football player* would be okay.

A *tall man* would be nice, to be able to reach the items on the top shelves at the grocery store or to reach the items at the top of her cabinets, instead of having her climb on a chair or climb the counter. He would be nice to have around to assist her in the kitchen, instead of having her use a spatula to coax an item forward from out of the cabinet and letting it drop into her awaiting hands.

A *cowboy* would be nice to saunter around with, to go horseback riding with (even though she had never done that before), go country line-dancing with, who would call her *"Ma'am,"* and who would respect his momma. She would love a cowboy in her life as she was sure he would wear a huge cowboy hat, have a deep singing voice and he would wear super tight jeans. *Yummy!*

A *humorous man* would be nice to have around, to laugh with and laugh at, but who would never make her the brunt of his jokes. A *worldy man* would be nice to know, to get a different, albeit, strange perspective on life and how simple men can live in it.

A *mechanic* would be nice and handy. Jason Statham would be nice. He makes a fine mechanic. Gerard Butler would definitely be acceptable, especially to listen to his accent any day of the week. *"He could have crumbs in my bed all day long, if he wanted,"* Jane giggled about that one. A *computer geek* would be great...an *accountant* would be good, too. *Sigh.*

Jane had always wanted to write about how men are just quite simple creatures. She would interview them in bars, at home improvement stores, at football games, at warehouses, etc., and her narrative would tell the truth. The narrative would be called *"Men Only Need Four Things In Life (Sex, Sports, Sleep and Satiation or Sustenance)."* When she shared that idea with Joseph, he laughed and agreed. Thinking about that made her laugh, too. She thought, *"I am gonna write that one some day. Or it could be called 'Cock Tales.'"*

Pascal had said, from time to time that *"Life does not have to be that hard"* and he was sort of right, for the most part. Jane would forcefully reassure him that he could not be talking about all people, everywhere and around the entire globe, for *"We could never know what it would be like to live in the body of a person with disabilities, unless we were disabled,"* she would tell him. Or for that matter, *"We could never know what it would be like to be so poverty-stricken, that we would never know where our next meal was coming from unless we were that poor."* Pascal had always disagreed with her and she would have to halt their conversations, right then and there, for she could feel her blood pressure rising, whenever he would say that. But, her blood pressure would never rise so high for her head to pop off.

Although he was not always specifically talking about her, she agreed that some women (and some men) make their life and their experiences and their situations, harder or more complicated than they had to be and harder than they were. Jane was not going to admit that to him out loud, but that was just who she was, too. She felt most times that she made her own life harder with all of her natural worrying. She knew that that was something that she truly could not help. She wondered if her worrying was regarding that Nature versus Nurture argument. She was convinced that it was a little of both.

But in addition, she felt that some men (and some women) did make their family members go through a hell-like existence, with their passive aggressive behavior or with their simplistic nature and perhaps their quickness to judge. They made it difficult for their families with their selfishness and with their laziness and their lack of seeing what needed to be done to make a household run smoothly. Jane felt that some men could be too dismissive, with their nonchalance about everything, citing in their opinion, the lack of importance of something that some women viewed as very important. Oh, say, like the health needs of their children, among other things.

But, again, for now, Jane did not need a man to complete her life. *"I like myself,"* Jane thought, for the most part, and she would not change too much of herself for now. Jane would cite to herself, *"I am a work of art in progress"* and her life was like one long, on-going *situation comedy.*

Jane wondered from time to time, if she was the director, the producer, the playwright, the star, the co-star, the comedy relief or just a stand-in...in her own life.

Finally, the flight was over. She thanked Benjamin for all of the good conversations and said goodbye as she was off to her next destination. Benjamin had told her about *Customs and Immigration* and had helped her fill out a declaration form to present to them, none of which she knew anything about. He told her to keep her cell phone turned off and put away and to be prepared to wait. He was right and very helpful with all of that information. So that was what she did. She stood in line and waited and waited, as well as all of the other travelers, hoping to get through that next situation as quickly as possible in Minneapolis.

During that time, a security guard charged at a man who was on his cell phone. He yelled, *"Listen up and pay attention and get off the damn phone."* *"That was exciting,"* she thought. Jane was directed to the check-in booth, where very briefly, she spoke with the plump clerk who asked her why she was away and why she was returning. When Jane told her that she had gone to Germany to drop off her daughter and grandkids. The clerk sarcastically asked, *"And you just left them there?"* Jane giggled and thought, *"Great, another comedienne!"* *"Yes,"* Jane told her, as they smiled. The clerk stamped Jane's form and she was off running…again…to the next flight.

She was directed to take the tram per the clerk at the information booth. She did just that and met a woman who worked at the airport. Betty was the name on her name tag. They got on the tram to ride to the next concourse. She was just a bit taller than Jane, she was in casual clothing and she was pushing a large cart of boxes with her for work. She was cute and had long brown hair.

They talked about the city and Betty told Jane about the mosquitoes, about the *'Land of a Thousand Lakes'* and about the Mall of America. Betty told her that there was plenty to see and plenty of things to do, in and around Minneapolis. She seemed very proud to be a native and Jane told her that she would be back someday, along with some girlfriends and go shopping. But she also told Betty that she was more interested in the lakes and in the amusement rides in the mall, more so than buying things.

At that moment, Betty smiled and the tram stopped. Jane thanked her for talking to her, she stepped off the tram and assessed the area for she was feeling rushed again. Jane did not know whether or not her next flight was on time. After huffing it to the next gate, Jane saw that she had some time to relax, so she used the restroom, brushed and flossed, touched up her makeup and then went back to the gate area.

She sat down on the floor next to the *'people mover'* and began to text Ed about picking her up at around 5:00 p.m. She added a bit more information about her whereabouts, her state of being, etc., and only hoped that he would get the message.

She texted Sawyer, as well, who immediately replied that he was mighty happy to hear that she was on American soil. *"Me, too!"* she replied. He promised to call her later.

Jane texted some of her friends, who had wished her a genuine safe trip, who worried about her and who were encouraging, especially in their many emails to her regarding her adventures. *"I am truly blessed for all of their support and love, their understanding and patience,"* she thought. She only hoped that they knew how much she loved them.

Once on the flight, she sat next to a man who clearly needed quiet time and she happily gave that to him. She prayed again for safe travel. She watched outside, *"Oohh-ing and Ahh-ing"* as she saw the many rivers, lakes, ponds and properties that made up the ground below. Some of the landscape looked much like a patchwork quilt.

She watched in awe, as the many clouds floated by. She noticed their many shapes and sizes, noting how some looked like animals, including a Springer Spaniel and a sea turtle. The latter shape automatically made her think of a former beau. She had treated him to a tattoo of a sea turtle on his arm. *"Dammit!"* she thought. *"Why does that lying and cheating man somehow make it back into my conscious thoughts? You lost the privilege of my precious time and of my concerns for you, the moment you decided to cheat on me. Go away."* Jane smirked as she knew that tattoo would be a constant reminder of her.

She thought of his son and wondered how he was doing. She could not remember how old he was, but she guessed that he should be around 17 years of age by then. She had loved his son and she missed him very much. She even believed that she had loved his son more than she had loved him.

She continued to ask herself that if ever there was a chance (or curse) to run into that ex-beau (and she did not mean with her car), would she want to slap him or would she just walk away? Would she want to hug him and ask him how he was or how his son was, or would she have the courage to say to him a simple *"F*ck you!"* and then walk away?

Due to the one time that she happened to see him, with the woman that he cheated on her with (his former co-worker), it was quite evident that she looked just like his ex-wife. Because of that, Jane knew that he had a *type* and that Jane was never it. She was never going to be it, to be the pear-shaped woman with the big boobs and big nose, wide hips and long black hair. Nor would she want to be. *Hmmm…*

She did not have an answer for herself right at that moment, but she guessed later that she would want to impulsively hug him. Jane hoped that would never happen. With someone like Jane, it would be immediately evident on her face, of what she was thinking or feeling. When Jane was happy, it was obvious. It was always easy for her to turn red when she was embarrassed. It was always easy for her to look discouraged or confused, when she was that way. It was always quick for her to look upset, when she was upset. She added all of that to the list of things that she did not like about herself. She definitely would never be able to play poker.

On that flight, the passengers got another snack of water, orange juice and pop, pretzels and peanuts. No wonder Jane was still constipated. She ate anyway and then she vegged, with her jacket rolled into a ball and resting in the bend of her neck. It still smelled just as sweet, but she was saddened because she knew that the aroma would quickly and permanently fade.

It was so beautiful and crisp outside her small airplane window and at that moment, the thoughts of that same quote from the movie *"Contact"* had popped into her head. It was about not being a poet and not being able to describe that beauty that lay before her. The sky was just that and more. It was *Absolutely beautiful.*

She was sort of happy to be going home, but sad that she had to leave all that beauty. She thought that she could possibly find the means to continue to travel in America and see just as much wonder. Somewhere in her head, she felt that she would eventually have to prepare herself for a life of single-hood, again. That thought did not give her comfort, but somehow she knew that her time with Pascal was not going to last. She just did not know why she knew. She just did not know how long it would last. She convinced herself to just make the most of it, but she knew that she was lying to herself, if she came to agree with that.

She thought that if she could travel for a time alone in Europe, then she could travel alone in the States. Jane thought that she would somehow make the strides to purchase a camper and travel. Since she had belly trouble, she would be more than happy to take her toilet with her! She felt a smile appear on her face and she laughed to herself, at that thought.

The thoughts of her children and their loved ones came to her mind again. She reassured herself that they were going to be okay. "They are grown, they are capable and able people and they are loving and kind and successful," she thought. *"They are patient, hard-working, beautiful, thoughtful, creative, and I could not be any more proud of them, than I am, at this moment."*

Jane did not know how, but she knew that she was going to be okay, too. A sense of peace came over her for a moment and she smiled again, wondering if anyone was watching her beam with tranquility and contentment.

Finally, Jane's flight landed on Ohio soil. Once back at home in the safety of Dayton's airport, she called Ed to let him know she was waiting. He had not been watching the time and told her he would be there shortly. She found a vacant bench outside, sat and waited. She closed her eyes and listened to the sounds surrounding her.

She could hear the airplanes taking off and landing. She heard cars coming and going, dropping off and picking up passengers and their conversations, as they hugged. She could hear happiness, anxiety, sadness and elation. She could hear the sounds of dragging luggage wheels and the low hum of conversations between skycaps and passengers. She could smell cigarette smoke, perfumes and colognes of waiting patrons and also, fresh cut grass and gasoline.

She opened her eyes and saw her brother driving up in her car. He helped her with the luggage and put it in the back hatch. They got into the vehicle, put on their seat belts and took off towards his home.

Then she asked, *"How have you been?"*

He said, *"Fine."* She got a smile on her face...as she waited...

During the next several weeks and months after her arrival, Jane had experienced many exciting things. She had been truly blessed to be surrounded by friends and family who loved her and who were very encouraging, kind, considerate and patient. They were genuinely interested in what she had learned and how her trip had changed her. Overall, they just cared for her and her well being. They were her true loved ones.

Jane's life was always like an emotional whirlwind, with many ups and downs.

Once back at home, the many things that Jane had wished for...

That she had dreamed about...

That she had planned for...

That she had experienced...

and were surprised by...were:

Ed and Jane talked a lot about her trip, his work and some of the family. He had attended some weddings, parties and also went boating with his friends. Jane and Ed continued to work together on learning how to play the guitar and they had become pretty good at that. She had to admit that he was very good for one who had taught himself, and he was a very patient and good teacher. She dreamed of playing on stage someday, with or without him, and perhaps at a bar for amateur night.

She expressed to Ed her deepest appreciation, for taking her into his home and for entertaining her almost daily with great stories. She was very happy to have an empathetic brother, who not only was kind-hearted, but was fun and funny. He had a great sense of humor and good timing when it came to telling jokes and elaborating on his tales.

She was happy, indeed, for laughing at any time about any thing. *"Thank you, Ed, for your unending hospitality."* She hoped that he knew that she loved him very much. She talked about making strides to save some money so she could find a place of her own, but he was not in a rush for that.

Jane and her dad went grocery shopping together, upon his encouragement, for he knew that she cooked for both Ed and herself. They went out to eat together a lot, she attended church with him as well and they spoke almost daily, or at least around his schedule at work. She was glad to know that he was doing well and that he had told her of how proud he was of her. *"I love you, dad."*

Jane kept up with the housework, cleaning, vacuuming, sweeping and mopping and dusting, taking out the trash, ironing, doing her laundry and doing Ed's, etc. She did that mostly on a weekly schedule, just to stay sane. She also worked outdoors with taking care of the hot tub, mowing, weeding, cutting back the bushes and the overgrown trees, edging and collecting the mail at the curb. It was good to contribute in some manner and doing so made her feel helpful and alive.

Jane called Sawyer immediately after her arrival and they talked for what seemed forever one day about her adventures, her woes, her plans for the future. He and his fiance continued to travel for work, back and forth to London, New York, California, Florida and Chicago.

Jane had expressed to him that she did imagine in her dreams and hopes for him, that he would find love and kindness in his life and she was happy that he had found Maria. She told him that she was pleased and elated about all of his hard work in college and that she was proud that he was a responsible man. She reassured him that her hard work of working three jobs to get him through college, was well worth it. He exceeded her expectations. She let him know every day when she spoke to him, that she was proud of him and loved him more than she could ever express.

He and Maria planned and creatively worked on their wedding and it happened sooner than Jane could have imagined. It seemed like dream. It was in Columbus, it was beautiful and the weather was perfect for the planning. But it was windy and chilly on the day of the event. Despite that, everything was perfect, down to the last detail. Maria's parents and her family were very attentive and they were some of the nicest people that Jane had ever met. Maria was blessed to have them in her life.

Everyone was there, who was needed, and everyone had a blast. Jane let them know how happy she was for them and she wished them well. They took a delayed honeymoon and all was well with the world. They were lucky to have found each other and Jane was the lucky one to be a part of their lives. She could move on to the next chapter of her life, knowing full well that they were happy. She could not have asked for anything more. *I love you both very much.*"

All of Jane's friends were excited for her return and let her know via email, texts and phone calls. She met with some of them, from time to time, at lunches and dinners, as they tolerated her showing them more photos of Europe. With some of them, she went shopping, traveling the surface streets and the highways to the mall, many other shops and many restaurants, as they continued to share with each other about their lives, work, their kids, getting older, etc. Sometimes, they vegged together, watched movies and just sat around and talked. Jane was very blessed.

As the days passed, Jane became increasingly aware that her friends and she were destined to stay in touch. But drifting away and back again was a part of life that she had to get used to. They stayed busy with their extended families, husbands, kids, grand-kids, their other friends and their new loves. They stayed busy with play dates and work. On a day, here and there, Jane had a heightened sense of anxiety, as some plans with some of them would fall through. When she tried to make other plans, here and there, they were still busy, but she was not. She finally realized at those moments, that it was a jealousy of some sort.

She thought, *"Just get over it, be happy for them and move on,"* so she did her best to do just that. She hoped that they would think of her often and that they would try to include her when they could. Jane would feel like *"an after-thought"* and sometimes referred to herself as *"An After-Dinner Mint."* She did her best to stay busy, too.

Jane emailed Joseph and told him that she hoped to see him again some day. She felt he had no clue exactly how he had helped her, exactly how much fun she had, how much she valued his friendship and hospitality and how much she valued their very detailed conversations. *"He'd make a great catch,"* she thought and she wished him the best of luck in life. She should have stolen one of his shirts and sprayed his cologne all over it. *"Joseph…I will always cherish and love you."*

The next day after her return… Jane texted Pascal to let him know she was home and she went to see him that evening. During the next couple of months, he had told her several times that she was beautiful and sexy. He told her she was one of the nicest women that he had ever met and that it was great that she had a *"fine sense of self."*

One night, his expressions and demeanor were less animated, as she could tell that he was trying to tell her something important. He began with comparing her to a rich, creamy French pastry called millefeuille, that he had consumed on his many trips to Paris. He told her he had missed her *"This much,"* demonstrating a small measurement with his thumb and forefinger. Jane was taken aback, as if for one brief moment, he was slightly embarrassed for sharing that with her. She enjoyed watching him struggle with his words, as he intermittently made eye contact during that conversation. She thought it was quite endearing.

They spent a lot of time together just talking, going out to dinner a few times and snacking, while watching TV and movies at his home. She walked his dog a few times, sometimes cleaned his house (because, in her opinion, it desperately needed it) and she wondered aloud why he would not let her meet his kids just yet.

He never seemed to have the right answer for her, but was able to state in some manner that he had waited a long time before, to introduce them to a previous girlfriend. And when that did not work out, he told himself to wait even longer. It was not what she wanted to hear, but she thought she understood what he meant.

They also spent a lot of intimate time together, which was wonderful, along with cuddling, which was always welcomed. She continued to worry about falling in love with him. She felt that she was in deep emotional trouble and she dreaded the next step. She felt as if she knew that something unpleasant was going to happen and she always hated the fact that she was right.

Pascal was a great conversationalist, he smelled great and made her happy with lots of laughter. She was giddy over him, to say the least and she knew that he knew it. She went to his favorite bar with him to watch sports events and got reacquainted with some of his friends, who seemed to welcome her. She inquired several times again, about meeting his mother, meeting his kids, but the subject was quickly changed.

Many months later, as they were at his home late one night, Jane had some vodka and was very tipsy and relaxed in his company. She had been like that many times before. It was what happened that night that hit her like a ton of bricks and it was the moment in which she dreaded. It was the pivotal moment that changed her life forever. His comments echoed in her head for many months afterward...

Jane and Pascal were lounging on the couch and out of the blue,

Pascal told her that he truly preferred to date longer-legged women.

Her jaw dropped. *"What did I just hear?"* *"What the hell?"* she thought.

He told her that she was *"lacking six inches"* and that his previous girlfriends were tall and so was his ex-wife. He told her that he was really not looking for a girlfriend, but then he said, *"Now that you have had your second vodka shot, I can tell you that while you were away, I went out with a beautiful, tall Italian woman, who I had met at the bar. We went out to dinner and we kissed a couple of times, but there was no spark. I felt compelled to tell you, but I wasn't trying to upset you."*

"What the F*CK?"...and..."Too late, Pascal!"

Jane was unable to contain her shock and disappointment, as she jumped up from the couch. She told him that her height should have nothing to do with anything. *"How would you like it if I told you that you were lacking six inches?"* she yelled. And...as she pointed with her finger, in a circular motion, to her crotch and then to her mouth, she stated, *"As long you are satisfied with this...and this... and as long as this...and this...works, what f*cking difference should my height make?"*

She already knew that that moment, was the moment that she had come to fear. Why did she know that? Why did he have to say such hurtful things?

Jane knew that he meant to say exactly what he knew would hurt her feelings, based on what she had already confided to him and based on the fact that she was comfortable enough to let her guard down with him. She somehow knew that he would be the kind of man who was capable of using her own words and feelings of insecurity against her. *"Dammit!"*

Jane started bawling, she couldn't breathe and embarrassingly, she sort of cussed him out, stating that he was *"Not all that"* anyway. Even though she did not mean to be mean at that moment, she felt that he deserved it. She felt as if she was not completely coherent, which made her all the more mad. She even called him a *"f*cking pig."*

He cruelly continued with his insensitivity. He told her that when he had first met her and some of her friends at the outdoor bar, that he and his guy buddy were out and about on a bet and a dare. He told her that they were challenged from the other barflies at his *'clubhouse of a bar'* to go out on the town, find a girl and *"Go ugly early."* They were challenged to become friends with a girl and see who could string her along the longest.

"Oh my God!"…"What the F*ck?"

Jane had never heard that phrase *"Go ugly early"* before and she yelled at him to explain what that meant. Once he did, she was so damned upset, that she thought her head was going to pop off of her shoulders and that her ears were going to pop off of her head.

She was concerned that she was going to be so much out of control, that she would find the first skillet that she would come across and hit him in the head with it. Perhaps she would hit his dog, too, just for spite. But she did neither one of those things. Not only because she could not stand upright, walk straight or even talk completely coherently, but because she really loved his dog! It would have been wrong to bash either one of their heads in. Or at least the dog's head.

She hated herself at that moment, for she thought, *"Why can't I just be mean enough to at least slap him in the face?"* She hated the fact that she was not a mean person, but she thought that if there was a class out there or a school of some kind that would teach its students to be mean and cold-hearted, Pascal would be their Headmaster! *"What a prick!"*

Jane was raised not be a violent person. Besides, she knew deep down, that she was not going to die from his massive unwarranted insults. Because so far, she had endured many from her ex and her other beaus and she had not died.

She felt foolish for being reduced to tears that night. She told him that she had too much hope and unrealistic expectations when it came to him. She sarcastically commented that she was going to find a doctor who would volunteer to surgically remove her childish dreams. She wanted to tell him that she hated him, but she did not hate him. She sort of felt sorry for him, for he was going to miss out on being with wonderful Jane, even though, she was not feeling wonderful at that moment.

He got up for a moment and told her that he would not let her leave, for she was too inebriated to drive. Therefore, Jane felt trapped and she had always hated that feeling. She had to agree with him that she had to spend the night. She was pacing in the living room...and back to the dining room...then back to the kitchen... and back to the living room again.

He sat on the couch, looking horribly relaxed and she thought for a moment that if he would just get up again, she could kick him in the face, with her strong *American thighs* and no one would have blamed her for it.

He coaxed her upstairs and eventually into his bed, where she continued to cry, feeling helpless, downright foolish and out of control.

Before she got into bed, Jane paced for a while and yelled at him that he should not have told her about that woman. She told him that he should have done the crappy thing and texted her about it, just like her previous tattooed beau had done.

She told him that he was smart enough to have anticipated her reaction, because she knew that he knew that she loved him. And she was foolish enough to tell him at that moment. She told him that he was one of the meanest men that she had ever met, adding that he should have never told her about that bet.

After that was said, Pascal paced as he told her that he was out and about that night, just for fun and that he was never truly involved with *"that damn bet."* She yelled at the top of her lungs,

"LIAR!" He told her that he was sorry for telling her that truth, as he could see that she was very upset.

"Upset...is a f*cking understatement!" she exclaimed.

Pascal told her that he truly liked her, but really wanted to be just friends. He reemphasized that he really did not want to date anyone. He told her that he was sorry for saying that he was always looking for a European beauty and not a short American.

All of a sudden, Jane got calm and her voice got low for a moment and she tried to stay coherent as she sarcastically asked him, *"Should I turn around now, so you can continue to stab me in the back... as you have stabbed me in the front and in my heart...many times already?!"* She stood there numb and regrettably continued to cry in front of him.

She could not help but wonder why he had invited her over that night in the first place. And why he let her get tipsy that night in order to keep her there and tell her what he did. But mostly, she wondered why she let herself get that way, when somehow she knew that was the night that he would shock her and contribute to changing her life forever.

Jane eventually succumbed to him urging her to lay down as he did his best to cuddle with her into slumber. Her cries went into whimpers and he did not seem to mind.

As she lay there, her mind raced with these questions:
"How can that man...her lover and her brief best friend...be so

damned calm…at a time like this?"

"Why couldn't he love me?" "What am I doing wrong?"

"Who did I kill in a past life…to deserve all this turmoil?"

"How could he be so loving…gentle…giving…in one breath, then be cold-hearted, insensitive…and downright mean, in the next?"

"If I tried to smother him with my pillow, could I do that successfully and get away with it?…

"Or better yet…I could do that and go away for the rest of my life, never having to worry about what to wear, for I could look good in orange jumpsuits. I wouldn't have to worry about my next meal and I wouldn't have to worry about having a bed or not, for the prison would supply one. I know that I would be comfortable there, for prison is where I have been for most of my life!"…

Jane did not sleep soundly, but Pascal did. She left his home at 4:00 a.m., driving slowly and cautiously to ensure her safe arrival. Her entire body was shaking and wracked with pain. Her chest especially hurt. Once home, she collapsed in her bed and bawled herself to sleep.

She never saw Pascal again.

For the next several months, she cried every day and always at night, without fail. All she could think about was his hurtful words and his hurtful actions. She tried without luck, to get his words out of her head as she told herself that she was now the *"short, fat and ugly"* woman, that no one wanted and that no one needed. She thought that no one was going to be in love with her and she felt as if she was going to die alone. She kept her sadness hidden from Ed, but somehow he knew something was amiss, for she never again announced her leaving to go see Pascal. Besides, her face and eyes looked like she had been in a boxing match that had lasted for a millineum.

Jane felt a horrible sense of doom. She was baffled on how to move forward and how to process that additional stress and sadness. She was continuously puzzled as to why he would be so mean to her. She was more than depressed, more than devastated. It was unforgivable, what he had told her and she knew that his insult was the worst of all of them.

Jane knew she had fat on her body, but what real woman doesn't? She never knew that her *genetically chubby center* on her 125 pound apple-shaped frame was a problem for that other beau, until he pointed that out...

Jane knew that she did not have perfect skin and that she was not genetically blessed, but most women are closer to being average, but who can help that? She never knew that her lack of natural beauty was a problem for that other, other beau, until he pointed that out...

Jane knew that if she wanted to be more fit and healthier, she could do something about that, by exercising, eating right and getting better sleep, and she eventually did that.

Jane knew that if she wanted to be prettier, she could wear more makeup, keep up with her hair color and get a cute haircut, and she did just that. She could get a spray on tan if she wanted, she could have surgery and *'fix'* those things about herself that made her unattractive to others, but she felt as if she was fine and cute just the way she was…

Jane could fix those things, but with Pascal's comment, she was shocked, for that was the one thing that she could not change about herself: *Her height.* She never knew that her lack of height or being vertically challenged, as they say, was a *problem* for him or for anyone for that matter…until he pointed that out…

Mind you, she had been teased a lot, but she had never known why, because Jane was not that short. She was one notch over five feet tall…and *so what?* She could be standing next to a little person, but somehow, it would be her that her beaus would find time to pick on, she thought. She should not be picked on or teased for her height. *"No one should."* So why had that been a problem for her, all of her life?

One of her friends had told her that perhaps her height had been brought up because it was the only thing that they could find to belittle her, to make themselves feel better. *"Okay."* Jane thought she understood that, but still, *"Why?"* Her reaction to those comments about her height, must also be the one thing that they had made a mental note of, and therefore used it against her. Throughout all of her years, her reaction to jokes about her height had ranged from a disappointing glance to a full- blown cuss fest, to everyone who had made fun of her.

If anyone dared to make fun of Jane, they would point out anything...like:

Her thinning hair and the fact that her hair had been many colors. They commented about the loss of her eyebrows (that's another situation), about her slightly curved spine, about her inherited wide nose and her *"Cheerleader Legs"* and *"American Thighs"* (as she was nicknamed in high school...*Thanks, guys!* That was sarcasm).

They made fun of her small boobs (that one has been brought up before and *screw all you for mentioning that, you cold-hearted bastards!).*

They made fun of her lack of income, her impoverished childhood, her large, comical and dysfunctional family and her tattoos.

They would razz her about a previous chubby dog that she had owned or the fact that she wore the same clothes and shoes day in and day out for many years, and that she bought items at thrift stores.

They joked about the fact that she loved 80's music, Mexican food, and spinach, raspberries, strawberries and peaches in her scrambled eggs.

Or they would even make comments about the fact that she loved to dance, sing, whistle, and that Halloween was her favorite holiday...and so on.

But *Why?* Most of those things had been mentioned. But it had always came back to her height. That was the one thing that all childhood friends had mentioned and that all previous friends had mentioned. Her height was the one thing that all of her exes had targeted, in addition to all of the other insults that came out of their mouths.

But why? What was up with that? Jane thought of this and more for the next few weeks. She jotted down her thoughts, she continued to journal about her life. She tried to figure out what she could do to make her life simple and stress free. She needed to find a way to quickly erase Pascal and all the others…and all of their insults… from her head. *But how?*

To be perfectly honest, Jane did not realize that she was short. Though she somehow knew that she had a lifelong, ongoing *"false sense of self."* She was *just* Jane. Just *Plain Jane.* She mostly did not give it a second thought, and it did not register in her mind or stay in her thoughts for too long, when she was growing up.

When she was growing up, she had been bullied and picked on regarding her gift (or curse) of gab. When she was growing up, she was picked on for being small, but afterwards, she would make comments back to those bullies and quickly dismiss it.

She *was* Jane. As she continued on into her teenage years and then into high school, she tried her best to mind her own business if she could, make new friends and tried to blend in. She was just living in her own skin and she continued to be herself.

She eventually got married, had children, got divorced, moved out with the kids, they grew up and then she eventually was living on her own. She continued to be the kind-hearted, sweet and generous person that she was, that her dear parents raised her to be.

It was not until now, Jane journaled, that apparently the lifelong insults had really stayed with her and were buried deep within her mind. Now they were catching up with her. She could no longer dismiss them and she was going to make sure that she was no longer *going* to be dismissed!

Jane wanted to be the cold-hearted, mean, nasty person that everyone else was, who seemed to be happy with themselves being that way, as they took their time to pick on others and put others down. *"Why do they look happy and I don't look happy?"*

As she had gotten older, she also wondered why everyone who drank seemed to be happier. They looked happier and they were having more fun. She finally had to admit that she just did not know what she was doing…in life. And *screw all of you,* for insulting her and putting her down.

Jane continued to journal. She was at a loss on where to place Pascal's insults, in her head. She was at a loss on how to process those entire, full-circle insults, as the previous *'ex-boyfriend-charged'* insults also came to the surface of her brain. Those unresolved insults showed up daily, nightly and without fail.

All of her other insecurities and sadness, regarding her estranged family and estranged friends, and her feelings of failure regarding her house and her job, showed up. Her woes and worries about stress-eating also showed up without warning, without invitation… unwarranted, unprovoked and unwelcomed.

Jane had trouble with sleeping, eating, concentrating and making simple decisions, for the next several months. A daily task of figuring out what to wear, became astronomical and almost unbearable. She would bawl over anything and everything.

On some good days, she was able to get showered and dressed in 30 minutes or less, but those days were few and far between. She felt as if she had nowhere to go, no one to talk to and no one to console her. She felt no one would ever want to hear about what had happened to her. She hated to admit it, but she missed Pascal's strong arms around her and she hated herself for still thinking of him.

She did not want this devastation from Pascal to define her, but somehow, it was going to. She wanted her wonderful, positive trip to Europe to stay on the surface of her brain, but it did not.

Jane was a *massive freaking mess.*

Jane turned to a dear cousin for help. For a change of pace and for a while, she moved in with her cousin, Michelle and her husband, in northern Ohio, to look for work, but failed to secure a job. Michelle could see that Jane was depressed, as she tried to hide her crying from her. It was clearly evident on her face.

Jane helped around the house, walked their dog and went out to dinner with them. Jane helped with some yard work, watched the house and the dog and watered the plants, when they went away for a family vacation.

After quite a bit of time had passed, and she still could not find a job, Jane had to admit defeat. She eventually moved back in with her brother, but in actuality, her belongings remained at his home, so she truly never felt as if she had left. She truly never felt as if she had a home, anywhere on Earth.

Throughout the next few months, Jane slowly regained her self-esteem and her positive sense of self. She drank wine occasionally and she took sleep aids occasionally, to try to ensure a better night's sleep. She continued to journal, which helped her tremendously. She thanked God everyday for all of her blessings. She believed that writing down her thoughts would help get them out of her head, but she was realistic to know that her sadness was destined to stick around for a while. Her sadness stayed on her face for many months to come, with dark circles, less makeup and an evident *"I don't give a crap"* attitude.

Jane made many attempts to try to get herself back into a routine. She visited her chiropractor a lot *(Thank you, Dr. H!)*, she got a necessary mammogram, she went to the dentist and got worried about the future and health of her teeth. Her dentist told her to stop her stress, stop grinding her teeth at night. She almost peed her pants as she laughed so hard at his comment. In order to get rid of her stress, she thought, she'd have to change her DNA.

Jane got new glasses, she hiked around the neighborhood, she got a few massages, she got a new haircut and new hair color. She exercised more, sticking with a routine that she could live with and she was diligent just to stay healthy. She never lost her belly completely, but she gained muscle all over. She lost around ten pounds and she maintained her weight and she eventually felt better overall.

Jane continued to look for work, putting out tons of resumes and surfing the internet. Then when she least expected it, she got hired by a nearby school. She started work in the fall, met new friends, got reacquainted with former co-workers and had a blast working with many special kids. She learned a lot from them and was very thankful to be working and being productive again.

She needed to feel worthy as she surrounded herself with beautiful, positive and fun people. She created picture frames and developed pictures of her beautiful kids, in-laws and grandkids and displayed them around her bedroom, as a reminder of what she was truly thankful for. She continued to work on herself and rid herself of negative thoughts. It was a daily chore to try to get rid of the thoughts of feeling like a failure, and especially the thoughts of being rejected...again.

She became increasingly aware that her time on this Earth was limited and she was aware that she was still feeling doomed, from time to time. She remained hopeful, as she had made life-enhancing plans and carried them out.

Jane still found time to cry uncontrollably and forgave herself for it. She allowed herself to cry for a few minutes, then forced herself to stop. This went on and on for what seemed like an eternity.

Jane wrote in her journal that she would make daily attempts to finally forgive Pascal and all the others for their painful insults, lies and deceit. She forgave herself for believing in what they had said to her.

On one particular lonely night, Jane wrote a very long letter to Pascal, that she never intended to send. She called it *"CRYING UNDER THE INFLUENCE."* She downed many sips of wine and struggled as she wrote:

Your honesty was appealing, in the beginning. The others were never upfront, honest or even caring. Today, you are toxic, you are poison to me. Your alcohol and cigarette addictions are your weaknesses that you can't seem to combat. My addiction is YOU. I am watching you kill yourself and I wished YOU knew why. You hate yourself so much that you are willing to sacrifice yourself in front of your loved ones. You come across confident but you are compensating for fear. Somehow you know that I'd never let you down, that I'd never cheat, that I'd stand by you, no matter what. But since you've always known heartache, cheating, lying and mistrust, you are comfortable with that.

You will keep me at a distance on purpose because I represent hope, unending patience and understanding and you fear that, plus you believe that you don't deserve that. You are basically non-judgmental, or at least that was what I thought. You say what's on your mind, including that you love me (platonicly), that I'm beautiful, smart, funny and honest and that my honesty and confidence are what makes me so sexy and beautiful. (I am not confident lately). I am fixated on you because of that.

No man has ever been that honest or that direct (although I don't believe everything that you say). You were physically unselfish in the beginning. You introduced your friends to me, then took them away. You shared stories with me that I could not be a part of and that made me sad, jealous, confused and disappointed. You were very attractive to me and I had never had that and I wondered why you'd be remotely attracted to me. But now I know the truth: You were not. Today, I do not find you attractive.

I know that I am cute, but not beautiful, as I know you perceive beauty. I am kind, giving, devoted, dedicated and loyal and still I was never enough. If I had anything to offer anyone, that would be the first thing that I would do. I would give without fail, for I have always thought of myself last. You fear me, because I would never let you down. You want to surround yourself with aesthetic beauty, never looking too deeply because you would find yourself there within those discovered deep recesses of selfishness and shallowness and you are comfortable there.

Unless I get hit by a car, I will outlive you because you will be cancer-ridden and have a failing liver and when that happens, you will need someone to warm your heart, hold your hand, reassure you, as you venture into that vast unknown. I am that person now. I feel stuck on you because I sensed that you loved me. Your beauty, knowing smile, honesty and charm, devotion to your kids and friends, your animated story-telling...are all of those things that made me feel warm, safe, comfortable, wanted, desired, cherished and yearned for, in your company...in the beginning. What a fool I was...and am and continue to be.

The letter continued and none of it made much sense to her, as she wrote down her haphazard thoughts. Jane was tipsy, distraught, in love, rejected and heartbroken. She felt as if, little by little, piece by piece and with each passing day, that she was losing a part of her soul, a part of her heart. But she just could not dig herself out of her deep depression. She was in deep physical and spiritual and emotional pain…and Jane was truly lost:

Why you would not share and extend yourself to me, into the many aspects of your life, beyond our late rendezvous, was continuously upsetting and baffling. As I had told you, I have a self-diagnosed 'disease' of tolerance and hope and that was some of the reasons why I could not let go. I never let go. That says to me that I don't care enough about myself and that you don't care about me. It says to me that you never will and that my entire well-being was not important to you… or even to me.

My stature was an excuse (You lied to me about that. You had told me that you had dated a short girl in high school). I felt that you loved me, but you are just lying to yourself.

You didn't call to check on me, to see if I had made it home safely. Did you want to? Did you wonder about and worry about me, like I did you? Jokingly, you said that you wanted to marry a wealthy, terminally ill, 95-year old woman. You would service her weekly (or was it weakly?) and wait until she keeled over. What a terrible comment. So wealth is really what you are after. Wealth that you did not earn? That makes you selfish and shallow and I think, somewhat lazy-thinking. You are not entitled (to anything). Not even the air that you breathe.

My height was such an excuse. If I was wealthy, or at least better off than I am today or better off than I have been all of my life, would you reconsider me as an option? Yes. This I know now. My height, be damned. Should I want to be with a man who thinks that way? No, I should not. I have realized that I have never truly been deeply loved by any man…in all of my life.

I have discovered that I have at least two flaws, among many: I never get mad and I never hate. I get upset, sad and disappointed. But never mad or hate. Perhaps I should tell myself to get mad at you and hate you. Then perhaps I would heal faster from this scary life-changing heartache and heartbreak. I have discovered that every guy that I have been involved with has had no father in his life. What can that mean? What was it in me that had sensed this and why do I feel a need to 'save' these men? I should concentrate on saving myself, for I am the one who is lost and needs saving.

Perhaps somehow I knew that these relationships were doomed to fail, for fear of something. But what am I afraid of? Why do I need (another) family? What do you fear if you allow me to meet your family and let me into more of your life? What harm am I inflicting on myself by having hope in a hopeless situation? What am I desperate for? I may never know…

We made love and I cried again, but you didn't seem to mind. I can do that with you. I could be vulnerable, weak and embarrassed, excited and it did not bother you. The others had no room for that. Why? That's also the appeal about you.

What were you expecting to happen after we had spent so much time together? It was inevitable for me to fall. How could you not feel the same, as we had shared so much, physically and emotionally? We had seen each other cry. Did your friends not like me? Did they influence your decision because you perceived that we were not in the same league? I truly enjoyed them for the time being and I thought that I would miss them, but in reality, they were the ones who baited you into meeting me, originally. They are foolish, too. You are a fool as well.

There was a line from a movie: "Don't discount one night stands. They're very liberating." Is this where I am headed to ensure that I will be touched? How long can I go without being touched...until my heart builds a permanent wall and my soul shuts down forever? Am I doomed to frequent the Dayton bars, just to score a little more than cuddling? I hope not. I fear becoming an embittered spirit because being that kind of person would alter me forever. It would be a doomed life for me, to be embittered...just like you are! What happened to you?

How can I have faith in myself, when no one else does? It's amazing to me how one person, with their unfounded, insensitive comments, can strike me down and verbally kick me, damage my spirit and burst my bubble. And I let them. Why does that prevent me from functioning like a normal human being? I have been wondering why this is. *What has happened to me that makes me so damned sensitive?*

It is those things within me that make me who I am. It is who I am, that some people can only take in small doses or for that matter, not at all. I expected and hoped to find the decent man in you, who could be strong enough to keep me around. I wanted to find in you the strong man who would want me around forever, but you are weak, just like the others. I am weak, but only for a little while longer.

Ironically and strangely, I have been told by all of you, that I should "Relax...let nature take its course...and live and let live." F*CK All of You! I am relaxed. It is only when I get excited in a relationship and when I am hopeful, that I just don't seem relaxed. (I was obviously and evidently excited, as you should have been, too). All of you say that, then find your way into the bedroom and the arms of another. I do not get why I am good enough to f*ck, but not good enough to date or even to be taken seriously as a partner for the rest of your life.

Even most days I cannot stand my own company. I have been deeply betrayed and abandoned and have never felt more alone... today...than any other day, in my 40 plus years. I can't stop crying and punishing myself with foreign films, independent films and sappy American movies. I am trying to get a better understanding of myself, my place in life, my purpose. But so far, no breakthrough.

With all these wasted months, I am no closer to understanding me. But I have come closer to almost hating all men, for all of their betrayals, their lies, their cheating, seducing and physical harm that has been portrayed in these movies. I have watched these horrible *outcomes, within the confines of my small bedroom that I currently call home...in which I currently see no escape.*

I am in between homes. I am in between jobs. I am in between dress sizes, hair styles, families, religions and boyfriends. I feel like the 'IN BETWEEN GIRL.' Soon, I will be 50 years old and still I have made the same mistakes and watched wasted time go by. But are they mistakes or just educational steps along the way? What I need to figure out is which way I am to go next. What I need to figure out is NOT why you do the things that you do, that you lie and cheat and insult just like my other beaus and my ex...but why I have come back for MORE...and why I have taken it for so long.

Whew! She continued with her letter. She was on a roll, with what seemed like sheer poetry:

There is always someone prettier. There is always someone taller. There is always someone skinnier. What's a girl to do? There is always someone more educated, more organized, more wealthy, with a better family than mine. What's a girl to do? We all are deserving of love, peace and contentment, so why am I an asshole magnet? I want to be loved, cherished and understood, not just tolerated, made fun of, laughed at, made the target of one's joke and banged for your convenience. (Unless I initiated it, of course. Did you get that that was sarcasm?)...

Thank you for being the stronger one and leaving me in pieces. One day I will be able to put myself back together, perhaps in a year from now or a decade from now. So in the meantime, what's a girl to do? Congratulations! Since your goal was to hurt my feelings, you succeeded! I am or was obsessed from your addicting smile, your abundant charm, your smell, your taste and touch. I was possessive and in an unending state of confusion, for I had given you all that I am, with my heart, mind, body and soul. What's a girl to do?

I will find my strength from within, after facing many sleepless nights, tear-stained pillowcases, empty boxes of tissues and the sounds of my own wailing echoing in my own ears. You should be forced to stand in the middle of a room, surrounded by heartbroken and wailing women and if you were compassionate, you would never be insensitive again. Will you be there for your daughter, when she will inevitably have to go through the same thing with her loves?

I KNOW with all of what is left of my heart, that ultimately, I will be fine and one day LOVE OF MYSELF will find me…before my broken heart's last beat.

Despite crying through her draft, Jane felt a bit better from her long-winded prose. She was still in her street clothes, but when she was done, she curled up in bed and she cried herself to sleep.

As she drifted off, she made the life-altering decision to never let another into her heart and soul for the rest of her life. She decided to never let another person ever touch her again, emotionally or physically or otherwise. *"Hugs be damned."* She also knew that she would have to work on that process daily. Jane was a *'knee-jerk hugger,'* whereas she reciprocated others' initiated hugs, without thought, without hesitation. So therefore, she would have to think before she reacted to all situations that she would be in, from that day forward. This was something that she never mastered as a child or even as an adult.

Jane half-heartedly took the advice of Bonnie Hunt, in the movie *"Return To Me,"* when she was giving dating advice to Minnie Driver. Jane decided not to shave her legs, until she found peace from within. *"Don't shave your legs. It's your only link to reality,"* Bonnie told Minnie. Even though *peace of one's self,* was not what Miss Hunt was exactly advising Miss Driver. In actuality, it was about staying focused on her first date with an exciting, handsome man. And, handsome, indeed, was what he was...

Jane decided not to try to groom herself for one more moment, one more part of her body, that she would always groom, for the sake of dating, for the sake of feeling prettier, for the moment. It was not necessary, she convinced herself and it was not important to her any longer, or at least for the time being.

Jane knew that if she met a man tomorrow or met a man down the line, who threw her into another whirlwind of giddiness and fairy tale fantasy, she could regain her composure by quickly thinking about her itchy, hairy, stubbly German-heritage legs. That thought, then in turn, would bring her back to reality.

She wanted to ensure that she was never going to get hurt again. She wanted to ensure that her physical self was not her main focus, but her focus would be internal harmony. Jane knew that was a silly and strange decision, but if she was going to do one less thing, that was *'typical'* for her to do, then why not that? She knew that decision meant not wearing dresses, shorts or skirts, for a while, but so be it.

She knew that that decision would eventually subside, like most damning thoughts about herself. She knew that it was part of her strange healing process that she had to go through again. She knew, or at least hoped, that it was not going to last for much longer. The one thing that made her slightly giggle, was the thought of making the decision to wear her dresses, etc., if she wanted, and to see the disgusted looks on the faces of anyone near her, when they saw her massively hairy legs.

For some damn reason, that gave her a bit of a smirk of hope on her face, for she knew that when she was feeling humorous again, it meant that she was going to be fine. Humor was a part of her healing process.

Jane also made the decision to wear less makeup, for she currently did not care and she did not feel pretty. She did wear some because she did not want to scare the children at work. Without any makeup, Jane felt that she looked ill. She looked weathered and worn, since her skin was not perfect, since her face did not have an even tone and since lately, she was getting a bit oily in her T-zone. *"Menopause sucks,"* she thought, but she also knew that her skin tone all over was being altered from within because of her ongoing stress. It was because of her lack of sleep, lack of eating well and the lack of her needed allotment of water and vitamins, that she looked hopelessly fatigued.

Pascal popped into Jane's head every day, for some time, as she continued to try not think of him. She thought of how happy she had been and how happy that she thought he could be with her. Then she was hurt again, when he did not text or call or email her, on her birthday. Her birthday came and went without fanfare. She should not have expected anything like that from him. *"His memory was diminishing from his alcohol consumption,"* she thought. She continued to worry about him from afar, feeling as if she knew something was going to happen to him and that he would try to contact her.

She knew that she was fooling herself, for he did not care about her, he did not love her. She did her best to remind herself of that, whenever he showed up in her thoughts. She knew that it was important for her to be rid of the thoughts of him by the holidays, but she failed globally at that. She focused on breathing instead, as she made an effort to hold back tears, throughout those weeks and months. Most times she failed at that, too.

She felt alone during the holidays, as she did not get to see her kids. They were away and busy and she understood that. She had to admit that she got jealous or envious, as she listened to the plans and busy-ness of her co-workers. They made plans to travel, spend time with their kids and families and husbands. They made plans and went shopping, decorated and baked, wrapped and visited, and went out to dinner with friends and went to parties and would ring in the new year…with many loved ones. And she had none.

As the holidays came and went, she tried to convince herself that *"It was just another day."* But she was lying to herself again. She bought things for her dad and her brother, and had mailed things to her kids and their families, but it was just not the same. Wrapping the gifts for her family was not as fun as it used to be. She could not afford gifts for her friends. She had not bought a tree in years, she did not decorate and she could not bear to listen to holiday music. Most nights, the house stayed silent.

Her brother was gone most nights, as he was with his friends or he was at work. She tried to read, but couldn't concentrate. She tried to watch movies, but couldn't concentrate. She tried to do more exercises, but she could not muster up the energy, so she did... nothing.

The holidays were not the same as real time spent together, with whom she loved. It was not the same as being with someone to love her back and it was not the same as a real hug. She wanted and missed a real *"I LOVE YOU"* kiss from the man that she thought had loved her unconditionally.

She felt all alone, for all of her family did not speak to her, except her dad, which on most days, was enough. He was upset indeed, as the rift continued. She was upset along with him and for him. He confided in her, about what else was going on in the family and she did not mind. She told him that their lives were no longer a part of her own. She just did not know how to help him. She missed them, but she knew deep down that they did not miss her. She was just going to have to be okay with that. There was no choice.

Throughout the next several months and in between, after her return, Jane's life felt quite chaotic. She felt frenzied in her head and she was upset with herself that her woes and stresses about Pascal continued for so long. She desperately needed a mental reprieve.

Jane attended a Halloween party. She attended lots of Friday night high school football games. Most days, she wanted to want to get out and be social. She avoided some birthday parties, some graduation parties and all other holiday gatherings, if she had been invited. She went to a couple of funerals and went to a movie now and then. She attended Toni's son's wedding in Columbus and it was beautiful. She cried.

She visited with her dad and had many more lunches and dinners with him. They talked about life and death, as he let her know that he was *"preparing to go the rest of the way alone."* She was content that he was happy with attending church and had made lots of friends there and at work. She prayed for him daily. She told him that she loved him on a regular basis and she continued to thank him for all of his help. Her words could not express her gratitude… but she tried.

She knew that he was sad from time to time, when the anniversary of her mother's death came and went and when her birthday came and went. Her dad was sad when their wedding anniversary came and went, but he made it through, and she was thankful that he remained positive. Jane dreaded his passing, whenever that were to occur and she tried not to think about it…most days.

When it was not the holidays, she kept up with reading the adventures of others on Facebook, she read online national and local news, she listened to her radio station and sang along to a lot of music, which was very helpful.

She would blast the radio, when Ed was away and dance around the house, literally. She would sing aloud to *"Live Like You're Dying," "Brighter Than The Sun," "You Don't Know You Are Beautiful," "Dark Side," "One Thing," "Home," "Domino," "Raise Your Glass"* (The song that she thought was written about her) and *"Hey, Mama,"* among many others.

During some weekends, Jane attended some festivals by herself, ate good food, drove for miles and miles (which she loved to do) and visited far away friends and distant relatives and spent the night with them. She ate out occasionally, dog-sat and house sat, apartment sat and cleaned for extra income and did her best to stay in touch with most of her friends.

For Jane, it was nice to *'get away'* for a few hours while watching movies, and to be consumed by the adventures and woes of others. She hid her face at some of the scary parts, she cried a lot at the sad parts, and she bawled a lot at the losses. It was somewhat therapeutic.

Her house went into foreclosure and there was nothing that she could do about that. The one thing she did do, was add that to the long, growing list of stresses in which she suffered. She cried many more nights, but she knew deep down that she was not going to suffer much longer.

Soon after her arrival from Europe, Jane's daughter, Megan, finally emailed her and told her that all was fine, that the girls would be learning German, that she had met many new friends, was going back to school and was having a good time, traveling with her family to other parts of Germany. *"At last!"* she thought. That was one less thing she had to continuously worry about, on whether or not they were fine.

They continued to email, mail packages to each other, for birthdays and holidays and talk on the phone, as she was able to talk to her granddaughters and her daughter, on a regular basis. She could not express how much she loved them, but she felt confident that they knew it.

She knew deep down that she had raised a wonderful daughter and therefore, she was a great wife and a wonderful, giving mother and friend. Her daughter would tell her about the goings on of her attentive and wonderful husband and of what challenges that he faced at work. Megan told Jane about the friends that he had made and of the progress that he was making in the military. She prayed for all of them daily and she wished for them a safe return, whenever that was going to be.

"One of my life's goals is complete," Jane thought, proudly. In her opinion, as a responsible parent, she was to make her children as independent of her as possible and she did that successfully. She could not have asked for anything else from her life. *"Thank You for*

allowing me to get at least one thing right in my life! I love you all very much." As she continued to write about her life, Jane wanted to know why she was still so sad and why for so long. Her kids were happy and healthy. What more did she want or need?

On one somewhat sunny day, she was contacted by Toni, who let her know that she had some bad news. Jane had been getting dressed in the bathroom, when Toni told her to sit down. She went to her bedroom and sat at her desk, bracing for impact. Toni had been reading the obituaries and was shocked by one in particular.

Pascal had died and she was not sure how Jane would receive the news. Jane did not receive it well. At first, Jane's breathing started to slow, as she tried to catch it, then her heart started to race. Toni read the article to Jane and then Jane bawled like a baby.

Toni did not have more information for her. Jane hung up the phone and just sat for a minute, then as the news sunk in, she started screaming. She rocked back and forth in her chair, trying to muffle the sounds that surprised her. She ran to the bathroom and threw up her breakfast.

Jane was glad that Ed was at work that morning, for she knelt on the bathroom floor and wailed for what seemed like an eternity. A bit later, she got up, turned off the light in the bathroom, which made the window-less room very dark. She curled up in a ball on the floor, knowing full well that the floor was not completely clean, that it had dust and hair on it and she did not care. *OCD, be damned.* She cried herself to sleep. She lay there for several hours on the cold, cream-colored ceramic tile.

Once she awoke and felt calm, she got up, turned on the light, regained some composure, then she realized that she did not have any phone numbers or last names of any of Pascal's friends. She did not know how to contact his ex-wife. She did not know what to do, but to contact the funeral home and inquire of how she could get in touch with his family. She called a bit later and the funeral home staff could not help her.

Trying to behave normally, she went to work and then she stayed indoors at home after work and moped around the house. She kept her sorrows to herself. She cried herself to sleep for the next several nights. She had a lot of crazy, baffling and horrible dreams, which she knew were typical of her, when she was under stress. Jane was quite tired of it.

She had many terrible nightmares when her mother had died and she was hoping for a reprieve, during that added stressful and dreadful time. Jane wanted her life to continue in an upward, positive path, but alas, the fates had other things in mind for her.

Jane's nightmares were quite disturbing, including ones where Pascal was punching her in her face. In her dreams, he would punch her in the car, in his living room, in her home and at the bar. Since as long as she could remember, all of Jane's dreams and nightmares have been detailed, graphic and quite colorful and she remembered all of them.

During one particular dream, Jane and Pascal were having a confrontation at his bar, on the outside patio, where she was waiting for her friends to arrive. She was there to see a band and Pascal was always there, so he approached her and asked her if she was there to see him.

She told him that she was not, but that she was meeting friends, etc. and that, *"It is not always about you!"* He got mad at her tone, leaned in closer to her and stated in a low voice that she was not welcome there. He told her that he was there with friends and all of them wanted Jane to leave. She told him that she was not leaving. She stated, *"It's a free country,"* and she was free to do whatever she pleased.

Pascal told her that it was best that she left, for he was there on a date with a tall, beautiful, European, athletic soccer player. He did not want his date to be uncomfortable with Jane there. Jane stated that she was not going to bother either of them, and that his friend need not know who she was, that she would remain invisible.

Pascal repeated that Jane needed to leave and that he did not want her to ruin his dinner by her presence. To add insult to injury, Pascal stated, *"You are stubborn and you are like a Chihuahua, who only thinks that she is a Giraffe!"*

In her dream, that comment was infuriating to Jane, so she regretfully commented that she was not there to ruin anything because, *"You are capable of ruining things yourself! I never want to interfere with anyone who thinks that they need alcohol to have a good time, you stupid F*cking, drunk alcoholic!"*

Without hesitation, Pascal punched her in the face, sending her reeling backwards over a chair, where she hit the back of her head on the wrought iron patio fence, then slumped to the ground. Jane was temporarily knocked unconscious. Her left cheek bone was broken. Moments later, she struggled to get up, she was dizzy and began to throw up, then collapsed back down to the ground, where she laid there in a daze.

As Jane woke up from her nightmare, she jotted down what she remembered. She remembered that she was put in handcuffs by the police.

Jane thought about that dream and decided to try to analyze it: Jane feared being hit. She had been called names, was talked down to and was hit by her threatening ex. Since that abuse during her marriage, Jane realized to some extent that she feared men who resembled him. Pascal was tall but not big, but his (original) charming demeanor had won her over, so she did not fear his tallness at all.

In the dream, Pascal's friends *'backed him up'* and she had always wondered if they were a part of why he did not want to see her anymore. Even though Jane knew deep down that she would never call Pascal names (to his face), her frustration over his desire and need for his alcohol was very upsetting. She knew that he had a problem from the beginning, but quickly dismissed it, for she was happy and content in his presence, despite it.

As Jane wrote down her thoughts, she knew deep down that her dream was not completely about Pascal, but more of what she feared or was discouraged about in her life. It was more about her disappointment with him and her previous disappointments and heartaches that she had never resolved. It was more about her disappointment in not having a lot of friends who *'had her back,'* and that she felt unwelcomed, in many situations.

In the dream, she was waiting for her friends that never came. She wrote down that it was the *'not having her back,'* comment that was offered up in the dream, when she fell backwards and when she hit the back of her head. She was not a psychoanalyst, but it was a good thing for her to try to get to the bottom of her nightmares.

Jane knew that most of what the dream was about, was because of her insecurities, her perceived downfalls and failures in her relationships. It was about her quirkiness and odd behavior that everyone told her that she had had, since she was a child.

It was also about her coming to terms, again, with another insult aimed at her physique, which was something that she could not change. *"This is just who I am,"* she would tell herself…as she jotted down her thoughts.

In that dream, Pascal's insult of being a small annoying dog was an insult geared to thoroughly hurt her feelings. It was an insult that Jane knew she had aimed at herself. Jane didn't want to be thought of as *the dog,* but she longed to be thought of as a sleek and slender, beautiful creature.

Pascal had never said those specific things to her. By then, Jane felt that if she had stuck around for more time with him, it would have been only a matter of time before he would get more creative with his comments, his insults and find more ways of hurting her. She not only felt it, she believed it right down to the very core of her mind, and down to the very core of her heart and soul.

She found that most of her dreams were messages of some kind and on some days she got those messages, loud and clear. That dream was loud, but it was not completely clear. Jane could only focus on Pascal's horrific act and her pain. She believed that that act of punching her, was a way to belittle her, to get her to shut up…and a permanent way of getting rid of her, and to make her disappear (or be invisible). She did not want to admit to herself about her insecurities and failures just yet.

Some of her other dreams included her running a lot in the woods and being pursued by some faceless creature. In one dream, she was naked and trapped in a cabin in the mountains, in the snow, with the warm glowing embers in the fireplace, dwindling away. There was a large clock on the mantel and it was slowing down with each passing moment. Jane would wake from those dreams, crying and sweating and feeling as if she had been calling out to Pascal. When she awoke from most of her graphic nightmares, she almost always had terrible headaches. She knew that time was running out.

Jane tried to be productive and focused at work during the day. On some days, she was not even sure how she had gotten to work. She would admit to herself that she was numb and *driving like a zombie.* At work, she was easily distracted and she kept silent about her sadness, even though it was evident on her face. *"Did anyone notice my dark circles?"* she wondered.

Despite her deep, deep sadness, Jane was always happy and helpful when the kids arrived at school. Those kids made her life a bit better with each passing day. There was always something that would happen that would make her smile and give her some hope. For Jane, all kids represented some form of hope.

Jane was heartbroken all over again and she was not sure how she was going to dig herself out of that emotional situation. She did not want to fall back into another long state of '*blueness*,' so she convinced herself to attend the funeral, against her better judgment. It was strange that she was concerned about her looks at that time, but she got over that unimportant and insignificant thought right away.

Several days later, she did attend the memorial service and she was basically okay while there, hoping against all hope that she would not embarrass herself. The service was brief, but to the point. Afterwards, she looked at the many posted photos, smiled and cried a bit. She spoke with many of his friends who remembered her, as they talked about how Pascal had died.

One of his best friends sat with her at the wake and told her that Pascal had been engaged to be married. It had turned out that the woman that he had cheated on Jane with, was his fiance. They had been driving home from the bar as they always did, late one night. He was drunk and crashed his car into a tree. They had careened down an embankment on a winding road and that was that. She was also killed.

His friend asked Jane if he could bluntly talk to her. He told her that he had learned how to be the kind of guy that could be direct, taking cues from Pascal, whom he had come to love and admire.

She told him that he could be blunt with her, but she asked him to refrain from hurting her, if possible. She asked him if he was going to be mean, and he told her that he was not going to try to be.

As they sat together in the corner of the small chapel, he told her that he and Pascal had always wanted to tell her that they was sorry for being jerks. Especially since the night that they had met each other at the bar that summer. She could feel her eyebrows furrow, as she got a puzzled look on her face, as he continued.

He told her that they were being stupid and were *'targeting'* girls that night. They could not turn down a dare from the boys at their bar. They just jumped into their car to see the band that was playing at the downtown outdoor bar, where she and her friends happened to be.

When they saw Jane and her friends, they drifted their way, for they had known some of them. They talked to them and listened in on their conversations for fun. Jane held her tongue as he told his side of the story.

Pascal had picked Jane out, stating much later to his friend, that she *"looked like she had a hint of desperation,"* as well as a hint of curiosity. Pascal told him that Jane looked like she was a fun spirit, that she had an animated face, a grand sense of humor and that she had one of the prettiest smiles that he had ever seen.

Pascal told his friend that he really liked Jane as a dear friend, but Pascal also knew that he was going to have to end their relationship, for he sensed that she was falling in love with him. He told Jane that Pascal talked of her often, with admiration and with warmth in his heart, and a slight sparkle in his eyes. But Pascal was not sure why he had continued to remain Jane's friend, way after the bet was over.

Jane could feel her blood begin to boil, but maintained her composure as much as possible. She wondered why that jerk would share that much with her, especially during a funeral, of all places. But, she had to admit to herself, that she wanted to know more. She thought that some of the things that his friend was trying to say were meant to be kind and sweet, although she wanted to doubt every word. The rest of what he told her was unforgivable. She felt some sort of obligation to sit and continue to listen, even though she wanted to punch him in the face.

He said that Pascal had been seeing the girlfriend, his fiance, for some time. Jane knew that it was the woman that he spoke of upon her return, whom he had stated that there was no spark between them. It did not give her comfort in knowing that Pascal had lied, but she knew he did. Jane did her best not to see that woman in the photos, but when she got a glimpse of a picture of the two of them, her curiosity had come to an end.

She was beautiful and most certainly tall. Jane did not expect anything different and it did not make her happy that they had died. As a matter of fact what it did, was make her numb. Jane had to admit that she wanted Pascal to find happiness. Jane needed Pascal to find happiness, even though she had wanted it to be with her.

His friend stated that Pascal seemed happy, then took a moment to introduce her to Pascal's children. She was nervous and excited, for some reason, but did her best to not let them know that she was in a deep sorrow. She had been crying, like everyone else there, so she felt as if she would not give herself away.

They were beautiful, as she had imagined. She expressed her condolences for their loss. His son walked away, never uttering a word. She did not know him, but she had seen pictures of the kids when they were little and he was as handsome as his dad. She also felt bad for him, for she could see the distraught look on his face. She took a moment to pray for their swift recovery.

His daughter sat next to her, told her that Jane's name sounded familiar and asked how she had known her father. What was she to do? His daughter was an adult, his oldest, but she was also a grieving child. So Jane lied and told her that they had met through other friends, not that they had met at a bar.

His daughter told Jane that he had spoken of her and she had wondered why they had never met. Jane told her that he was cautious and protective of his children and that their relationship was of a deep friendship.

Jane stated that she was sorry that she never had time to keep in touch more with him, but somehow, Jane felt as if his daughter knew better. She hugged Jane goodbye and thanked her for attending the service. Jane was baffled that she cried more when his child let go of her.

Soon the wake was over. Exhausted and slightly inconsolable, Jane got into her car and drove around the corner, parked under a shady tree at the curb, slumped down in the driver's seat and bawled for an hour. She slowly drove home, as to ensure her safe return.

In the many months that followed, she took one day at a time because that was all that she could do. And so…life went on…and on. But she felt as if she was never going to recover from all the build up of sadness, stress, sorrow, and pain.

It was hard for her to come to an immediate peace from within, as her feelings kept surfacing then hiding and resurfacing again at the most inopportune times. There was nothing like going grocery shopping and bawling in the produce section. She discovered that it was very difficult to run on her treadmill while crying and trying to sing along to the tunes on her mini music player, which including *"Easy"* by Rascal Flatts…and *"Bad Love"* by Eric Clapton…and Jimmy Buffett's *"Someone That I Used To Love."* But Jane had managed, somehow.

There was nothing like trying to eat and feeling as if her food was quickly going to come back up. She would try to put on makeup, especially mascara, looking at her haggard reflection and constantly wiping away uncontrollable tears. There was nothing like feeling as if she was completely alone…again.

As Jane cried herself to sleep most nights, she continued to be in a love with a man who never loved her. She loved a man who was no longer around, whom she could not hate, yell at, give her letter to… or hit in the head with a skillet.

During the evenings and on most weekends, no one called to check on Jane, except her dad occasionally. She convinced him that she was just not feeling well. She never told her co-workers, her brother or her dad about what happened to Pascal. She was not sure why. She would go home from work, put on some lounging clothes, stay out of Ed's way and try to read and journal. She did not eat much and she had lost a lot more weight. But mostly, she would curl up in bed and try to sleep.

She felt with time, that she was going to be okay, but she was not so sure. She stayed dizzy and lightheaded. Her mind was unfocused and hazy. She was very worried about…herself.

She went to see a new doctor and the doctor told Jane that she had a heart murmur. Jane had some pain and light-headedness, but she never thought that she would get that kind of bad news. Jane had an Echocardiogram. Days later, the doctor told her the negative results. Jane had figuratively built a wall in and around her heart. From that point on, Jane knew that her death was nearer, but somehow she was not afraid of it.

Jane had another dream. As a matter of fact, Jane was not convinced that it was a dream. Was she sleep walking? Or was she making strides to make that delusion a reality? Was she so pain-stricken, confused and heartbroken that she was not completely living in reality? She tried to stay focused on the fact that she was very distraught. She thought it was a Sunday.

Jane had found her brother's gun in the bureau in his room. She knew that she could keep it hidden from him and use it, when the time was right for her. She kept it under her mattress and for some reason, knowing it was there, was reassuring to her. She did not know how to use a gun, but she guessed that she could figure it out quickly.

Feeling downright hopeless and desperately tired of crying, Jane picked a cool night. She found a large blue tarp in the garage and when her brother was not home, she wrote one message on a small sheet of paper and taped it on her bathroom mirror.

The note said, *"I am the camel. He was the straw."*

Without any further explanation to anyone and without one bit of hesitation, Jane got into her car and drove south towards Cincinnati. The traffic was light and the wind was whipping at her car from the west. She drove in silence. She was calm, she felt peaceful and she felt no longer afraid of her life or even of her own death.

Jane had no clue where she was driving to and she had no clue on what was driving her. She finally made a choice to stop in the city of Monroe, so she could find the public park that she had frequented and hiked in, many years earlier. It was a place where she had felt secure and where she had felt alive and happy, some time ago.

She parked her car away from the light poles, in the corner of the parking lot, nearest to one of the ball diamonds. She turned off the engine and climbed into the back portion of the hatch. She stripped off all her clothes, down to her naked and frail, aging body. She folded her clothes and placed them on the back seat.

She wrapped herself in the tarp and could feel the cold plastic beneath her. She could feel the cold top portion of the tarp, as she enclosed herself within it, as it slowly rested on her toes, her thighs, her belly, her small erect nipples and on her face.

She lay still, with the gun in her hand and resting at her right side. She listened to the crinkling sounds of the plastic, until it settled. She listened to her own breathing, listened to the crickets in the surrounding grass and listened to her heart pounding. *"Soon,"* she thought, *"the beating will be over."*

For some reason, Jane was no longer scared, but wondered when she was going to make her final move. She felt all alone and did not seem to mind it, that time. She took in a long, deep breath and brought the gun up to her belly and let it rest there...for a moment. It was cold. Then she brought the gun up to her temple and just when she was about to pull the trigger, Jane's phone rang. It was in her jeans pocket. *"Damn!"*

"It is late at night so who would be calling me?" she wondered. Jane's OCD kicked in and she could not stand to listen to a ringing phone. She had to at least look to see who was calling her. She quickly unwrapped herself, found her jeans, pulled the phone out of its pocket and saw that it was Megan calling from Germany. She tried not to answer it, but she knew she had to...

"Hello?"...

"Hello, Grandma!" Jane started crying as she answered the call

from her

5-year old granddaughter. She could hear Megan's voice in the background, as she coached her child, to help her say, *"Thank you for our gifts from Ohio."* Their conversation continued for a moment, as her granddaughter went on and on about the gifts that she had received, including the cool magnifying glasses, the colored glass rocks, the dress-up clothes, the deck of math flash cards and four toy microphones.

Jane had sent a package to them a while back and she had forgotten about it. Megan got on the phone and was giggling about her daughter's enthusiasm. Megan said, *"Hold on."* Then she put her 3-year old on the phone next, and Jane's youngest granddaughter went on and on about the dresses. Jane was bawling. Megan got back on the phone and asked, *"Whatcha doing?"*

Jane started laughing hysterically, as she was shivering uncontrollably, then she replied, *"Nothing. What are you doing?"*

Megan said, *"You popped into my head and I felt compelled to call you. What's that noise in the background?"* Megan asked. Quickly, Jane told her that it was the sound of sizzling and sauteing mushrooms, onions and green peppers, that she was preparing to put in her scrambled eggs. Why did Jane say that?

Her daughter said, *"I thought you hated that combination, because it had made you sick before."* So, Jane told her that she was going to try that concoction again, to see if she could stand the taste and the smell, and that she was planning on forgiving those vegetables for making her sick many years ago. She told her that she was just going to give them a second chance.

Megan giggled again. Jane loved her children's laughter. After her daughter talked a bit longer, she rushed off the phone, telling her mother that she loved her and would call her again soon. Jane told Megan the same. *"I love you"* and Jane hung up the phone.

Jane started laughing hysterically, then a moment later, she calmed down and started to cry. As Jane lay there, naked and cold, feeling quite stupid and selfish, she closed her eyes and forgave herself...for tempting with fate. She forced herself to think about Sawyer and Megan and how distraught they would be with her horrible selfish choice. She thought about her grandkids, who would never come to understand why their grandmother chose to permanently leave them. She knew deep down that she wanted to see them grow, fall in love and get married.

She thought about Pascal and wondered what life would have been like, if she had never met him. She forgave Pascal right then and there. She cried herself to sleep.

Jane woke up...sat up...and looked around at her surroundings. She was in the confines of her own bedroom. She was sweating and cold and for some reason her right hand was hurting. She looked down at her hand and it was clenched in a tight fist. She clasped her hands together and placed them on her heart and she said a prayer.

She prayed for a quick recovery from her loss, sorrow and heartache. She prayed that she would never get to that point of wanting to kill herself, and she prayed for her unresolved feelings of anguish and hurt to go away. Somewhere in her heart, mind, body and soul, she forgave herself...for everything.

She finally admitted to herself that she had thought and hoped that Pascal was *'The One.'* She knew that she was fooling herself, for there was no *One* for her, in her lifetime. She finally came to accept that. He never could have been *The One,* for he was a helpless addict, he was ultimately cruel, he was too selfish and shallow of a human being, to be worthy of Jane. And so were all the others.

After much time had passed, she prayed and planned for more adventures to come. She made strides to have a healthier heart. She was eventually able to do that and more.

Jane had had a dream occur to her one weekend night, while she was just at the peak of sleep: She was in a forest, feeling lost and helpless, where her surroundings were dank and dark and somewhat menacing. She saw a dim light at the top of a hill at the horizon.

As she walked towards that light, she could feel as if her mind was working overtime with many thoughts and many feelings. She felt as if her true soul mate was already taken by some other woman and he was unhappy, but he also felt trapped and felt out of control. *"Perhaps he was injured and could not speak,"* she thought. *"Perhaps he had already died."* In her dream, Jane was content on knowing that she never needed to search for that man, for he did not exist, for he was already gone.

Months earlier at work, someone had asked her what she was looking for in a man. She told them that she had a few requirements: *That he was employed, had teeth and was breathing.* She had laughed about that comment then and she laughed about it still. Jane knew that she was joking, but she also knew that her life was going to end, without that Hollywood ending. She knew that it was going to end without fanfare. She knew that it was going to end like the obvious, real and expected endings of the foreign films that she had borrowed from the library and had come to understand and embrace.

During that dream, for some reason, she felt as if she was okay with never needing to search. In that dream, as she ascended that hill, she could see something that she felt resembled her future. She thought about Pascal. At the top of the hill, she looked down to her side and found her old suitcase. She picked it up, and with one forceful swoop, she chucked it out into the foggy oblivion that surrounded her. She lay on the prickly pine needles that blanketed the ground and cried herself to sleep. She prayed for peace for herself and even for Pascal and his damaged soul.

When she woke up from that dream, somehow Jane knew that those childhood, childish, fairy tale endings were not meant to be for her. She knew that it was up to her to find something that she was passionate about. She would work on that and never feel as if she was working hard again.

She found solace in that thought, of just being productive, responsible, indispensable, good and kind-hearted, happy at working and surrounding herself with positive friends. She found peace in knowing that she could be happy with things *"as they are"* and knowing just how to let it be, let nature take its course, as she knew she could, without being told that she should. She had to find a way to forge on, for the sake of her children and her grandchildren.

She was not sure how she knew, but she knew that she was going to be fine...for the rest of her life... however long that may be. Jane relished in the thought that she was right.

In her prayers to God, she would say, *"Thank You for my many wonderful days, for my many wonderful experiences, for my two wonderful children, my in-laws and grandchildren and for my many true wonderful friends...and allowing me to live my life to the fullest...on my terms...and with my own many resources...and with no regrets. Amen."*

Everything is Forgiven. The End.

From the Author

A heartfelt Thank You goes out to my children and their
families, my granddaughters, my dad, my many family members
and my true friends, for helping me get through another day,
another year, another moment...of writing.

My test has been Time.

Your test has been challenging, to get me through these
hard times, the bad times and the good times. All of you
have stepped up to that challenge, of encouraging me,
believing in me and loving me through it all.

Saying Thank You just doesn't seem to be enough.

This journey of writing and journaling my thoughts and experiences
has been therapeutic. Keeping with a schedule of sorts has been
difficult, but it was obviously do-able. Your sincere love and care
for me means more than I can ever express.

Cheers.

With journal in hand, here's to many more stories to experience,
many more trips to take, many more journeys and paths to follow...

May our paths always cross.

www.ingramcontent.com/pod-product-compliance
Lightning Source LLC
Chambersburg PA
CBHW032233010726
47494CB00002B/470